TWELVE

Time Interventions - Book One

James Sherwood

"There is no future ... just the past steadily accumulating"
Haruki Murakami

Twelve

For Gloria

TWELVE

James Sherwood is hereby identified as the author of this work in accordance with Section 77 of the Copyright, Designs and Patents Act 1988.
Text copyright © James Sherwood 2015.
Cover design and illustration by John Moss copyright © 2015.

This book is sold subject to the conditions that it shall not, by way of trade or otherwise, be lent, resold, copied, reproduced, hired out, either in printed or electronic form, or otherwise circulated without the author's or publisher's prior consent.

Printed in 11pt Garamond and published by Amazon

Also available in Kindle and other eBook formats.

Author's Note

This novel is a fiction set against real historical events. However, the characters and locations that are included bear no relation to actual inhabitants or the addresses I have given. Though some parts are based on these events, they are the product of the author's imagination and are used fictionally. Any resemblance to actual persons, living or dead is entirely coincidental.

Email: jamessherwoodauthor@gmail.com
Manchester, England

ISBN: 978-1505886894
All rights reserved.

About the Author
James Sherwood

Since his early days as a boy in the Black Country of the West Midlands, James Sherwood has had two great loves. Art was first, so that by 1994 he had spent thirty years teaching Art & Design at Grammar Schools in Manchester and as a lecturer and one-time consultant in colleges around the north-west region of England.
Then, following early retirement, the next twenty years saw him working in web design and computer graphics at the small graphic design company which he had founded in the City of Salford.
But it was inevitable that sooner or later he would turn his attention to his second love – writing.
This, his first published novel, was inspired by time spent with his wife Gloria in the Balkans, Italy and Central Spain, where much of the narrative is set, as well as his own adopted home in Manchester, where the story's chief protagonist is based.

Twelve

Chapter 1: Autopsy

The body on the mortuary wash table had a rib missing.

'Are you sure you haven't simply miscounted?' said the chief pathologist.

'Give me some credit, Marsden,' replied Fosse. 'I tell you, there are only eleven on the right. Lift the rib cage a little and I'll try again.'

Marsden forced the ribs further apart so that Fosse could probe deeper with his fingers. 'There's no mistake,' he insisted. 'All twelve are present on the left, but there's definitely one missing on the right. I can't locate a floating rib.'

'It'll be there somewhere, but we can't hope to see anything in this confused mess,' the pathologist continued. 'Bone spicules everywhere. Maybe if I give more suction and drain off the interstitial fluid, we'll be able to see what's going on in there.'

Post-mortem procedures were well advanced. An incision ran from the shoulders down to the pubic bone and the sternum had been opened with surgical shears, so that the upper body and abdominal cavities were almost completely exposed.

The cadaver appeared to be a man of Asian or Middle Eastern descent. He had died as a result of a road traffic collision near Blackrod, and sustained critical injuries, including serious chest trauma with multiple broken ribs, a ruptured spleen and a punctured lung, as well as open compound fractures to both legs. There were extreme injuries to the head, and widespread catastrophic damage to internal organs.

Eventually fluids and bloods were drained and Fosse could better see inside the chest cavity. His response was unequivocal. 'No, it's simply not there.'

Marsden took over. He continued feeling around inside the chest until he was satisfied. He confirmed Fosse's conclusion. 'Yes, I agree. One of the ribs is absent. What do you make of it, professor? Has it been removed?'

'Well, there's no sign of an entry point or operation scar,' said Fosse. 'If it has been, I can't for the life of me imagine how it was done.'

'Most baffling!' said Marsden. 'Perhaps we'd better wait for the accident report and have another look at the hospital's x-rays. Something very odd is going on here.'

*

Sometime later that day, the two men waited for a hospital registrar to arrive with the file they had requested.

'The victim survived on life support for six hours after the accident, having already received conventional emergency procedures,' he began. 'Initial x-rays confirm pretty much what you found: multiple organ failures, broken bones and head injuries. We were equally bewildered to find him missing a rib.'

He handed the iPad to Fosse, who examined the screen briefly, flipped through two or three images and passed it to Marsden.

'Well that clinches it. There isn't one! ' he said. 'So do we have any identification for this fellow?'

'Not yet. He had no papers on him, not even a wallet or credit cards. Nothing to identify him at all,'

Twelve

replied the registrar.

'This is very curious,' said Fosse.

'There are other incongruities too, Professor. As you know, he had suffered massive intra-cranial haematoma and required substantial blood transfusions. However, initial cross-matching really baffled us. He appeared to have no known blood group. At least, not one that we could identify. It was neither A, B nor O types.'

'So you weren't able to cross-match at all?' asked Fosse.

'Yes, eventually, we could. Despite being unidentifiable, it cross-matched with A, O and B types. Whatever it is, it's perfectly compatible with all three.'

'How is that possible?' said Fosse. He looked quizzically at the pathologist.

'Don't look at me – this is entirely outside my experience,' said Marsden. 'Whoever, or whatever this fellow was, he's proving something of an enigma. This is by no means what I would call normal.'

'But you said there were other incongruities,' Fosse continued.

'Indeed, there were, Professor,' he replied. 'Though the subject remained unconscious throughout and we worked hard to resolve the secondary damage caused by brain swelling and the virtual collapse of the left hemisphere, readings for neural activity were off the scale. You'll see what I mean when you read the report.'

Fosse briefly scanned a few more pages and returned the tablet to the registrar.

'I see,' said Fosse. 'Would it be possible for me to have a hard copy, and perhaps printouts of the x-rays?'

'Certainly, Professor. I'll get some made and sent over to you at the university.'

*

Emeritus Professor of Forensic Pathology at the Victoria

University of Manchester, Maximilian Fosse had retired from active surgical work several years earlier. Nowadays, apart from occasional lectures, he spent most of his time researching for a forthcoming paper on contemporary forensic techniques, and had asked to participate in the post-mortem that morning as one of a series of case studies. Truth to tell, he was happy just to be back in theatre again, even a mortuary. It was good to get involved. He had found retirement tedious, and practical forensics was a branch of medicine that he loved and in which he had excelled. It was this excellence that had earned him the exalted professorship. He no longer had an active academic role, but in view of his long distinguished career, and as a professional courtesy, the university had retained a desk for him in a small back room. As he studied the report in detail, more confusing facts began to emerge.

He was intrigued.

Initially, the victim had been admitted to the Accident and Emergency Department of Central Lancashire Infirmary, where he never recovered consciousness and was still unidentified. The post-mortem examination had proved anything but routine, but from Fosse's point of view, it was a forensic scientist's dream case. He was excited and eagerly looked forward to getting stuck back in. However, his pleasure at the prospect was interrupted by a knock at the door. A plain-clothes police officer came into the office.

'Professor Fosse?' he introduced himself. 'Detective Sergeant Charles Seymour.'

'Ah, do come in, officer,' answered Fosse. 'I was told to expect you.'

Judging by his inflection, the police officer was a native Mancunian, and by his tone a man bored with his work, without apparent enthusiasm or expression. His badly creased suit and generally dishevelled appearance suggested that he had slept in it overnight. Fosse's

Twelve

impression was that this tired figure looked neither healthy nor happy with his life.

'So how may I help you, detective sergeant?' said Fosse.

'Just a routine visit. I need to tie up a few loose ends regarding this accident, Prof. If you could fill me in on what you've got so far, I'm sure we can wrap this up fairly quickly.'

'I'll tell you what I can,' replied Fosse, 'but I only have the results of the interim post-mortem. The full report isn't available yet and we still have no apparent identity for the victim. Have you managed to make any progress on that front?'

'Nothing to write home about,' the detective replied. 'I will be interviewing hospital staff later this afternoon and maybe then we'll know something.'

'So nothing was found in the vehicle to identify him, then?'

'Not much. Little or no pocket litter – just small loose change. Looks like it was a hire car, so he should have presented a driving license when he made the rental. They usually retain a photocopy, so we should be able to check his details with the DVLA. Otherwise there was nothing on him to give the slightest indication of who he is or where he's from.'

'What about his clothing?'

'Unusual. Expensive, but all the labels were removed. He had no phone either. It's a big mystery.'

'So how did the accident happen?'

'Well, there were six vehicles involved in the pile up. There was dense fog and black ice on the carriageway. It's not untypical at this time of year. The victim's car was crushed almost beyond recognition when a heavy goods vehicle jack-knifed into the back and pushed his car into the one in front. That impacted upon the next vehicle, and so on, creating a virtual domino effect. It's a miracle anybody survived in the carnage that followed, but he was the only fatality. Poor sod didn't really stand a chance.'

'So where's the vehicle now?'

'Police compound. It's already been through a superficial external examination, but it was so badly mangled that the driver had to be cut the out of the wreckage. When I left, they hadn't managed to get into the boot. Maybe it will tell us something when they get it open.'

'Was drink involved?'

'Doesn't look like it. Everybody tested negative at the scene. As I understand, the autopsy showed the victim was also alcohol free. Just bad road conditions. It was an absolutely filthy night and it's a notorious accident black spot.'

'I see,' said Fosse. 'So where do you go from here?'

'We still have a few options. I'll check against the police national database to see if anything's known and I might also run a missing person piece in tomorrow's newspapers. Somebody out there must know him – friends, family, colleagues - everybody leaves some kind of trail behind. We're not even sure if he's British. He's obviously Asian, so we've put in a routine request to the UK Border and Immigration Service for recent arrivals from abroad, just on the off chance he's known to them.'

'I assume you'll keep me informed?'

'If you wish, Prof, but I don't want this dragged out any longer than necessary. I'm hoping to wrap things up by tomorrow.'

'I'd like to know the outcome to the investigation in any case. We could always arrange another meeting, if that would serve any purpose,' said Fosse.

'If you think it would be useful. I'll let you know. Okay?'

*

Three days later, when Fosse had digested the finer details

Twelve

of all the paperwork, he invited Seymour to join him at the University.

'The facts of the case are quite straightforward, detective sergeant,' he began. 'As you know, death occurred about six hours after admission to the infirmary. But, despite the best efforts of the emergency crash team, all surgical procedures proved ineffective. The official cause of death was recorded as massive organ and heart failure, which is fairly routine in such serious accident cases. After that things get interesting.'

'How so?'

'First, there's the unexplained missing rib. We have no idea why or how it has been removed. Or if, in fact, it *has* been removed. There is no trace of a skin entry point or scarring, which is very unusual. It might just be an anatomical abnormality, of course. That would be the simplest explanation. Variations in rib numbers do occur naturally, although they are very rare. Split ribs, so-called bifurcated ribs, are not unknown either, but they're usually distributed symmetrically, in matching pairs. A single missing rib is virtually unknown.'

'Is it possible he might have been born one rib short?'

'I have considered the possibility of a congenital birth defect, but there is no compelling evidence to support that. For the time being, I'm proceeding with the likelihood that it was a surgical option and my working hypothesis is that the rib *has* been removed. I haven't the faintest idea how. But it would have been a very sophisticated procedure and without an entry scar I'm at a complete loss to know how it was done.'

'Maybe I'm a little slow, Prof, but humour me,' said Seymour. 'What purpose could be served by removing a single rib?'

'That's a very good question,' Fosse replied. 'On the one hand, the rib could have been diseased, malformed or broken beyond repair, requiring its removal. On the other, the twelfth floating rib is one of the few bones that can be removed without significant impairment to physiological function. It could have been used to harvest bone marrow or stem cells. But both hypotheses are highly speculative. And it still doesn't explain the lack of scarring.

'Then, we come to the problem of the unidentified blood group. It compares with nothing we've ever previously seen in human haematology. Unusually, cross-matched bloods from all three groups were assimilated into his system with no apparent detriment. They certainly prolonged his life, albeit temporarily, despite the eventual outcome. But he didn't die from incompatible blood cross-matching.

'Thirdly, we come to this mystery man's brain function. Monitored brain patterns throughout emergency treatment showed intense activity, despite his comatose state. He exhibited highly elevated bioelectrical activity, even though he had suffered catastrophic brain damage. It was so badly compromised that he should have died instantly – but he didn't – he was very much alive. Had he survived, normally we would have expected him to be in a vegetative state. In fact, significant regenerative processes were observed while he was unconscious. His brain seemed to be attempting to repair itself against all the odds, even though survival was always an unlikely outcome.'

'This is not just another run of the mill accident case, is it?'

'Far from it,' Fosse concluded. 'However, a great deal more investigation is needed before we can draw any definitive conclusions. It would be premature to speculate. But, I have to admit – this man is a mystery.'

'I understand your caution, Professor,' replied Seymour. 'But I do need some answers, fairly quickly; otherwise my boss will be on my back.'

'Look,' said Fosse. 'I'm just about to sign out for the day. We could continue our conversation further over

Twelve

a drink if you like.'

'Can't be today,' said Seymour. 'I am expected home. Maybe tomorrow.'

'There's a nice little bar just around the corner from here. They keep a fine bottle of single malt under the counter for me. I could meet you there at around eight tomorrow.'

*

Seymour met Fosse next evening at the Crazy Horse Wine Bar, a few hundred yards behind the main university building.

'So what can I get you?' asked Fosse when they had settled in a corner booth.

'Just a sparkling water thanks,' replied Seymour. 'Still on duty I'm afraid.'

'Of course,' said Fosse. 'I should have realised. But you don't mind if I partake?'

'No, go right ahead – I'm easy.'

'Please call me Max. I'm not very keen on Prof and Professor always sounds very formal outside the university.'

'Okay, but call me Charlie.'

'So what have you found out, Charlie?'

'Well, not much. There's been no response from the newspaper bulletin. Otherwise, limited results ... when I say 'limited', I may be overstating it a little. What we actually have is a sighting.'

'A sighting? Of what?'

'Our John Doe had a visitor while in the Intensive Care Unit.'

'Does that mean you've located his family?'

'I wish,' continued Seymour. 'Turns out an unknown female visited his bedside, briefly. The duty nurse described her as tall and athletic. She wore dark glasses and a red sports top with a hood, blue jeans and baseball shoes. But clothes don't really help without a physical description. The nurse couldn't see her face, but said she thought she saw blonde hair beneath the hood. Her impression was very sketchy. Fairly useless, I'd say.'

'So do we know who the woman was?'

'Visits to ITU are very restricted – usually close relatives only. She claimed to be the victim's sister and that was taken at face value. But, she spent only a few minutes at his bedside, before bending over and whispering something to him. Then she kissed him on the forehead and left abruptly.'

'Did no-one get her name?'

'They didn't get the chance. She left before anybody could question her. We examined security footage of the main entrance which gave us times for her arrival and departure, but she seemed to know where cameras were and made a point of avoiding them. The total time she spent in the hospital was just seven and a half minutes. She was at the bedside for no more than two minutes. Hardly what you'd expect of a close relative, never mind a sister whose brother is at death's door, is it?'

'I wouldn't have said so,' replied Fosse. 'You say she was blonde – not Asian?'

'That's what the nurse insists she saw. Could've been a wig, of course, but this is definitely turning into an odd case.'

'As Alice was heard to say *"curiouser and curiouser"*.'

'You can say that again. So what's next on your agenda?' asked Seymour.

'Well, now that the post-mortem itself has been completed and the cause of death officially determined, it gets the legal process out of the way. That means I can begin the detailed clinical autopsy. That's my specialism. The body should be moved to the University Medical School in a day or two, unless somebody comes forward to claim it. The university has agreed to retain me on the case as it fits nicely into some research I'm doing. I plan to

Twelve

work closely with the Head of the Pathology Department, Doctor Grant. I have to say, this investigation takes my research way beyond what I'd hoped or intended. It's too unique an opportunity to pass up.'

'I envy you, Max. It's usually just routine stuff that lands on my desk.'

The two men talked on for several hours. Fosse, in total and self-satisfied enjoyment of his favourite liquor, while Seymour sipped his water reluctantly in unspoken envy.

Chapter 2: Manchester Central

Over family dinner that evening, Seymour recounted the events of the day. It was unusual for him to bring cases home, but this one was different.

'So why are you involved?' asked his wife, Sarah. 'Isn't it a medical matter?'

'Well, it is mostly. Forensics is dealing with things at a primary level, but as we still haven't been able to identify the dead man, there's stuff that still needs clarification. That makes it a police matter. It's landed on my desk and is taking a good deal longer than I expected.'

'What caused the accident?' she asked.

'It looks like it was just speeding on icy roads. It's a headache for the insurance companies to sort out. So far, there are no criminal charges pending, but I have to complete the accident report and I'm not making much progress.'

'So . . .' she continued, '... how did you cope with being with this Professor in a B - A - R?' She had spelled it out so that their young daughter would not understand. Neither parent noticed, but Daisy's face showed that she fully comprehended.

Sarah could not begin to understand the temptation it had been for Seymour watching Fosse drink whisky. She would never know of the times he would have sold his daughter for just one small drink. Thirst and guilt were his constant torments. They had become permanent millstones around his neck. However, he passed it off lightly.

'Not a problem.' He hoped the lie would go unnoticed. 'Wasn't tempted.' He lied again. 'Settled for mineral water.' He quickly changed the subject. 'Interesting man though, this Professor Fosse,' he said. 'Apparently he's a brilliant academic and leading forensic surgeon. I quite liked him in an old fuddy-duddy kind of way. It's a curious case - this accident victim had one rib missing, and

Twelve

nobody knows why.'

'Like Adam,' said Daisy.

'Quite right,' said Sarah. 'The Bible says God made Eve out of one of Adam's ribs.'

'So did God take this man's rib, daddy?' Daisy continued.

'Who can say?' replied Seymour, slowly sipping his drink, pondering upon his daughter's innocent comment and on how inadequate was tap water as a beverage.

*

In the darkness of their bedroom, later that night, Sarah eventually broke the silence.

'Did you really not have a drink?' she asked.

'I've already told you.'

'So you weren't even tempted?' She was persistent.

'Of course I was tempted. I always will be, as you very well know, Sarah,' he replied. 'This isn't ever going to go away. But I made you a promise.'

'I know, but I do worry about you. A bar is not a great place for you to be frequenting, so long after… well, you know what I'm saying.'

'I know full well what's at stake,' he replied irascibly. 'But just leave it, okay? You just have to trust me.'

The events of more than a year earlier still dogged their relationship. Drunk on duty, Seymour had compromised evidence in a major criminal trial. The disciplinary enquiry had forced him to take leave of absence to attend rehabilitation for his addiction.

Sarah stood by him throughout that testing period, but they had barely survived it. She had made the future of their marriage conditional upon his remaining alcohol-free. Seymour thanked God it was all in the past. But the memory of the bad times still haunted him and sleep seldom came quickly nowadays.

They resumed their separate silences in the darkness.

*

Early the following morning, Fosse and Seymour met up at the Medical School, and waited patiently to be collected from its grand Victorian foyer. They had arranged to meet with Doctor Amelia Grant, who would act as lead pathologist, as it was her department that would facilitate the detailed biological investigation.

Seymour had missed out on university. The institution was well outside his comfort zone, and the unexpected casualness of twenty-first century education took him by surprise. He had anticipated a flurry of black gowns and mortarboards, a latter day *'Goodbye Mr Chips'* culture, but his assumptions were ill-founded. It was increasingly difficult to distinguish lecturers from students and there was a tangible air of expectancy and promise about the place. This ethos was foreign to the cynical police culture with which he was familiar.

Just then, the approaching *click-click* of stiletto heels on the marble tesserae floor drew their attention and made both heads turn. A young woman came up and addressed Fosse. She was perhaps in her late-twenties, sported flaming red shoulder-length hair and had the palest opalescent skin. Her fitted black suit, the crisp white shirt clipped neatly at the collar by a cameo brooch and her shiny cuff links were considered and stylish.

Seymour was mesmerised, his thoughts strayed far from police matters.

'Is it Professor Fosse?' she enquired.

'It is,' Fosse replied.

They shook hands curtly and she introduced herself as Katherine Chaplin, Doctor Grant's personal assistant.

'This is my colleague, Detective Sergeant Charles

Twelve

Seymour,' said Fosse.

She smiled and nodded at Seymour. 'If you would kindly like to follow me, gentlemen,' she requested politely. 'I'll take you along.'

She led them down a wide curving stone staircase to a subterranean level. As they descended, Seymour commented on the fine quality of the building. He had scant appreciation of interior design and he was not remotely interested in architecture, but it was a pretext to engage her in conversation. His comment went unanswered. She showed both of them into a large office whose air hung heavy with a sickly aroma of disinfectant and formaldehyde.

'Doctor Grant will be with you shortly,' she said. 'Please take a seat. Can I get either of you a drink? Tea or coffee?'

'Tea would be lovely, thank you,' said Fosse gracefully.

Seymour requested a glass of water and his eyes followed her intently as she left the room.

*

Senior Lecturer and Head of Department, Doctor Amelia Grant swept into the room, her white laboratory coat trailing behind in the slipstream. Fosse introduced her to Seymour and they sat down around her desk. It was a spacious inlaid walnut affair, judging by what could be seen of it beneath the profusion of papers scattered across its surface. Seymour felt like an errant schoolboy, slightly intimidated as he faced her across the enormous desktop. Compared to his own modest workstation, it was extravagant and bordered on the ostentatious. But deep down, he would have loved one half as grand.

He was lost in this contemplation for several moments, paying little heed to the conversation going on around him. Eventually, he regained a degree of attention, reached over and took a sip of water.

'We have already done some preliminary work and I should have a full report in a couple of days,' Doctor Grant began.

'So what have you found?' asked Fosse as he returned his teacup carefully to the coaster on the edge of the desk.

'Our initial work reveals that the man was a virtually perfect specimen. He had immaculate teeth for example, with no decay, discolouring or evidence of remedial dental work. We could neither find evidence of previous illness nor disease. All his muscular tissue was healthy, well-formed and free of atrophy or stress. Joints exhibited very little evidence of wear, with no sign of rheumatic or arthritic degeneration. The hands showed no sign of his ever having done heavy or manual work and there was nothing under the fingernails of any significance. Apart from the tattoo of a chess piece knight on the left forearm, I'd say he's as immaculate as the day his mother gave birth to him.'

'Yes, I noted the tattoo,' said Seymour.

'We don't see that as especially relevant to our immediate investigation,' Doctor Grant went on. 'Of course, we are continuing the in-depth study of the genetic aspects of the case. The brain is already being studied in microscopic detail, as are the cerebral and neurophysiological data collected before death occurred, but it will be a few days before we have the DNA results.'

'Without wishing to point out the elephant in the room, doctor,' Fosse interjected. 'What have you concluded concerning the missing rib?'

'Ah … the rib.' She drew in a long breath and considered her words.

'Up to now his flawless condition could be explained away as a healthy lifestyle and strong inherited characteristics. However, the rib, or lack of it, is a different matter. We are now fairly certain that it was surgically

Twelve

removed.'

'But how do you account for the absence of an entry wound or post-operative scarring?' asked Fosse.

'I wish I had an answer, Professor,' she replied. 'Improbable as it seemed at the outset, when we examined the vestigial connection where the rib should have attached to the spinal column, it was clear that there had originally been a rib in place.'

'So how on earth was it removed?'

'I can only speculate, but we think it involved some sort of laser incision. The costal cartilage reveals clear signs of discolouration, almost certainly due to intense scorching or burning. But where, and more importantly, how this was done, is completely beyond our understanding.'

*

It was a few hours later when Seymour telephoned Fosse's office.

'Hello Charlie,' replied Fosse. 'Anything new?'

'We've found some paperwork and documents in the car,' replied Seymour.

'That sounds a bit more promising. What kind of documents?'

'Loads. They were in a travel bag in the boot and most of the mangled bodywork had to be cut away before it could be reached. There were five passports of different nationalities, and several credit cards, as well as the car hire contract and other stuff.'

'Five passports?'

'Yep. And on the face of it, they all appear to be genuine. Either that or they're excellent forgeries, but we are having them checked out. The British and American passports were both in the name of Patrick Cameron. There were also Saudi and Pakistani visas. They'd been stamped on entry to both of those countries. It's all looking a bit dodgy. Surprisingly, there was also some CIA identification; we are consulting the American Embassy on that one.'

'But they can't all be genuine, can they?'

'I wouldn't have thought so, Prof. Nevertheless, judging by the entry stamps, this Cameron bloke managed to get through several foreign passport controls with them. Fakes or not, they're very convincing. Cameron apparently rented the vehicle at Manchester Airport and I've already spoken to them by phone. They have CCTV in the reception and parking areas, so we might pick something up from that. I am also contacting his credit card company to get an address as well as bank details. Of course, he may not have given his real address in the first place. I fear it's just become a lot bigger than just a local traffic accident. It will probably involve the Security Services sooner or later.'

*

Two days later, they met up at the Crazy Horse again. 'Now look, Prof,' Seymour began. 'I need to talk to you seriously for a moment ... and it's a tricky one. I have no wish to cause offence, but there is a very important point I am obliged to make.'

'Sounds ominous,' replied Fosse. 'And please call me Max.'

'Okay Max. I just need to make it clear that any of our conversations concerning this case must be kept strictly between ourselves. It shouldn't really have gone outside my office in the first place. Christ knows what would happen if it were known that I'd discussed it with a civilian. It has to remain just between us two, at least for the time being. There are potential security issues involved.'

'Of course,' said Fosse. 'I realise that this is a police matter, and I completely understand what you are saying, but as far as the university is concerned, I am the specialist

Twelve

in post-mortem matters. Whoever this Patrick Cameron turns out to be, for the time being his body is under university jurisdiction. That means I'm part of this, whether you like it or not.'

'I know. However, the point needed making, Prof. I'm just saying that the fine line between information sharing and confidentiality is a blurred one, and I may already have crossed it.'

'Okay. I've taken your point on board. Meantime, what are you drinking?'

'Just the sparkling water,' replied Seymour.

Fosse went over to the bar and returned with the drinks.

'Tell me to mind my own business, Charlie, and you don't have to answer this at all if you think I'm prying, but how long have you been on the wagon?'

'It's that obvious, is it?'

'No, not really. It's just that now you are actually *off* duty, sparkling water would appear to be an odd choice. You can't really prefer that fizzy water stuff to a real drink, and you don't particularly strike me as a teetotaller either. It doesn't take rocket science to realise that you're a recovering alcoholic.'

'Yes, I am, but I have it under control.'

'If you say so. I'm sorry to have mentioned it.'

'That's all right. Of course, it will always be a problem; that's the nature of the beast, but with a little help I've managed okay. I haven't had a drink in almost a year.'

'Are you attending Alcoholics Anonymous?'

'I've been to a few meetings, occasionally, when I've felt the need. But it's a lot of hassle and I couldn't be bothered with keeping a diary and all that kind of stuff. I suppose I'm a bit of a loner by nature and I prefer to do it myself if I can. It took a long time to admit to the problem, and not before I'd almost screwed up my marriage.'

'You want to talk about it?'

'It's a long story.'

'I'm not going anywhere for an hour or so.'

'Well, where to begin? I was half cut most of the time, at home and at work. The wife threatened to leave if I didn't get help. It came to a head when I screwed up evidence in a major drugs trial. An internal police tribunal investigated serious irregularities and found me guilty of misconduct. I was immediately suspended and reduced in rank. I was lucky. It could have meant instant dismissal, but my previous good record weighed in my favour. So I was given three months leave of absence and ordered to go into rehabilitation. That's why I'm very wary of any threat of suspension now. If I fall off the wagon again it won't just be the job I lose - it would be my marriage too. You could say I'm living on sufferance. I'm trying very hard to keep on the straight and narrow and I intend to beat the habit. That, in a nutshell, Prof, is why I'm drinking sparkling water and why this needs to be kept strictly between ourselves.'

'Well if I can do anything,' said Fosse. 'I'd be happy to be on the other end of the phone. Anytime, day or night.'

'I'm sure your wife wouldn't be happy with that.'

'I don't have a wife,' he replied. 'So that won't be a problem.'

Seymour stared into his glass of water contemplatively. 'It's a topic I try to avoid even thinking about. I don't know why I'm telling you all this anyway. We only met a couple of days ago.'

Fosse leaned forward and placed a hand on the policeman's shoulder. 'Sometimes it's better to get things out into the open, and virtual strangers often make the best listeners.'

'You're a good person, Prof,' Seymour concluded. 'Now, can we please change the subject?'

'Of course. So tell me what you can regarding the

Twelve

mysterious Patrick Cameron.'

'First, the credit card company has supplied a statement of the latest activity on the card. He last made a hotel booking in the Lake District and he must have been on the way there when the accident happened. The home address given for him is quite real, but the house has been empty as long as anybody can remember. We're currently trying to obtain a warrant to enter the premises. But, as the security issues regarding the passports are still being kept under wraps, no criminal activity can be disclosed, and the magistrates are dragging their feet as a result. It could take some time.'

'Have the security services contacted you then?'

'Not yet. Until somebody tells me otherwise, it's still my case. As things stand, if no-one comes forward to claim the body the case will be shelved as unsolved, or end up on my desk as a low priority. The only crime so far is the possible document forgeries, but that'll be out of my hands. It's not the kind of work I get these days.'

'Do you work alone then? Isn't there usually a detective inspector supervising such cases?' enquired Fosse.

'Normally there would be,' said Seymour. 'But I'm regarded as a liability by other DCs, and I don't get on with my station boss. He wanted me chucked out or moved elsewhere after the tribunal. Drink and demotion have done me no favours either and more ambitious coppers don't want me as a partner. So, I'm left largely to my own devices. It suits me fine. I prefer working alone anyway. Apart from that one blot on my copybook, I've always been a good copper.'

'Well you can rest assured that I'll give all the support I can, Charlie,' said Fosse.

'I appreciate that, Max.'

'You actually called me Max.' said Fosse. 'I must be getting through to you at last.'

'Fair point.'

'So how did Cameron get the ID anyway?' said Fosse, after a few minutes of stony silence. 'I noted that you didn't say that Patrick Cameron was his name, merely that it was the name he had used.'

'It turns out that according to the name and date of birth given on the driving license he was born in Inverness in October 1978. But that's the problem. Patrick Cameron died at just six months of age - recorded as a cot death. So we know the ID he's using is bogus and the identity theft has remained unchallenged until now. The British passport is genuine – completely legitimate, even though it was issued based on an assumed false identity. So we still don't know who Cameron is, or if he was native-born British or an immigrant. The potential security risk is still on the cards until we know otherwise.

'There's more, and here's where it gets very interesting. UK Border Control at Manchester Airport recorded his entry flight originating in Saudi Arabia and the exit stamp was from Jeddah. So my bosses are already talking to the security services about possible anti-terrorist implications.'

'Indeed, that is worrying,' said Fosse. 'He obviously went to great lengths to set up this identity.'

'Yes, I should say so, and very successfully too. Probably been using it for some time. The current passport was issued eight years ago, and it's the third issue using this name, so he had been passing himself off as Patrick Cameron for at least twenty-six years, maybe longer! Christ knows what other aliases he had?'

'I suppose a Middle East connection is not altogether unexpected,' said Fosse. 'Given his colour. I'd have said his family came from that part of the world or somewhere in Asia. Of course, there are significant numbers of Asians living in Scotland, so we shouldn't attach too much relevance to his Scottish registration. Cameron's parents might indeed have been first generation immigrants living somewhere around Inverness.'

Twelve

'Still not much to go on.' said Seymour. 'But I can't help wondering what the purpose of all the subterfuge was. And who the hell is Patrick Cameron - really?'

Chapter 3: Grange

The next morning, Seymour was called into the office of his station boss, Superintendent Joseph Golding, known by everyone at the station as 'Holy Joe'. He had been a Methodist lay preacher before joining the Police Force, but seemed nowadays to have somewhat lapsed and was universally regarded as a nasty piece of work. Two other plain clothes officers stood behind him. Seymour had not seen either of them before.

'Can I introduce Chief Superintendent Worsley of Special Branch and Doctor Fred Jameson,' said Golding. 'The security services have come on board this Cameron case since the discovery of the multiple passports and CIA documentation in his car.'

Worsley stepped forward.

'Without going into too much detail, detective sergeant,' he began. 'Potential security issues have been flagged up, since it emerged that Cameron travelled from the Middle East, almost certainly under an assumed identity. The CIA identification, which he was carrying, has also raised serious concerns with the Americans. They are sending over someone from the Company to liaise with us. It's possible Cameron may have been radicalised in Asia or the Middle East.'

Then he turned his attention to Jameson. 'Doctor Jameson has been assigned to the case as consultant forensic psychologist and criminal profiler. He currently lectures in the Department of Muslim & Islamic Studies at Exeter University and has worked extensively with the FBI in California. He also advises several UK police departments on anti-terrorism and radicalisation issues, and is a member of the Offender Research Profiling Unit, which the Home Office has recently set up. He will be examining potential threats which the Cameron case has highlighted.'

'But as Cameron's dead - where's the threat?' asked

Twelve

Seymour.

'It's unlikely he was alone,' said Jameson. 'They often work in small cells of two or three people.'

'Therefore, for the time being,' Worsley continued, 'Superintendent Golding has agreed that you should continue with the investigation of the case. It might amount to nothing and we could be over-reacting, but we are erring on the side of caution. If you unearth anything significant, it should be passed to Special Branch who will take over the investigation. Other Security Services may become involved later. For now, it needs to be kept very low key. The last thing we want is the tabloids getting hold of the story and whipping up a public furore with unsubstantiated rumours.

'I suggest that, initially, you might begin by checking out Cameron's intended destination,' Worsley continued. 'There may be some leads there. We have established that he was travelling to Grange-over-Sands in the Southern Lakeland of Cumbria. We know that he made a hotel booking at a guest house for the day of the accident. Find out why he was going up there.'

*

The Kirkstone Hotel was a very small family guest house, set high on the hill overlooking the town of Grange-over-Sands. It was a three-storey building of grey Lakeland stone, and was located close to the town's few amenities. Its greatest asset was the panoramic views of Morecambe Bay on the seaward side. On a clear day, you could see all the way to Blackpool Tower and the long beaches of the Fylde Coast. Inland, the southern Lakeland Fells formed a dramatic backdrop, which accounted for the region's reputation as a popular tourist destination. Grange was a well-known summer beauty spot and had abundant small guest houses; reserved, quiet, and much favoured by mature visitors for these qualities. However, in the short rainy days of November, it was out of season and virtually deserted. Seymour wondered why a man would fly from the Middle East in order to drive to an inconspicuous little township in the Southern Lakes at this time of year.

The hotel proprietors, Albert and Muriel Gardner, were polite and hospitable. Seymour identified himself and explained the purpose of his visit.

'Mister Cameron never turned up,' Gardner volunteered. 'But his credit card payment had already been validated and we can't offer refunds at such short notice. He seemed a nice enough man, though. Very well spoken over the telephone. Very public school, if you know what I mean.'

'So it was just you who spoke to him?' asked Seymour.

'My wife took the initial call, but handed it over to me. I usually process all the telephone transactions,' Gardner replied.

'Did he come over as Middle Eastern or Arabic?'

'I wouldn't have said so.' He turned to his wife. 'What do you think, Muriel?'

'No,' she agreed. 'He didn't sound foreign; I should say he had been born in England. He had a really nice accent. You know, quite posh ... educated. Certainly not an Arab gentleman.'

'And not Scottish either?'

'No, definitely not Scottish.'

His instincts had been confirmed. Cameron was home grown.

*

Seymour decided to stay overnight as the day was rapidly drawing in and the guest house had vacancies. That evening he took a leisurely stroll around the town. As he walked down the main street towards the seafront, he pulled up the overcoat collar around his ears as the damp

Twelve

chill blew in from Morecambe Bay. Eventually he arrived at the promenade; its well-tended borders and clipped hedges extended along the coast for almost a mile. Besides himself, only a dog walker and an elderly man carrying an umbrella braved the late autumnal evening. At the end of the promenade, he sat down on the wall to watch the Irish Sea rolling in across the sands. There was a brisk onshore wind and it had begun to drizzle with a fine damping mist. Presently, the elderly man came over and engaged Seymour in conversation.

'It's the fastest tidal race in Britain,' he boasted with unwarranted pride. 'Very treacherous too. Somebody dies every year trying to walk across the sands to Morecambe. The tide's too quick for 'em, you see. The tide – it's very fast.'

'You don't say,' said Seymour, disinterested.

'Indeed I do. It's said to come in so quick that a man couldn't outrun it.'

'I wouldn't like to chance it myself.'

'Very wise,' the old man concluded. 'There is an official guide across the sands at low tide, you know. That doesn't stop some fools still trying to go solo. One died out there just a couple of days ago. Educated man too by all accounts. Just disregarded all the warning signs.'

With that, he turned away and extended his umbrella. 'Well I must be going. Enjoy your stay. Good night.' He walked off back towards the town. Seymour followed a few hundred yards behind and returned to the hotel.

*

The breakfast room was virtually empty that morning. Just Seymour and one other man, who sat a few tables behind. Their substantial morning meal took place in the muted atmosphere that prevails over British breakfast.

'Would you like anything more, Mister Seymour?'

asked Muriel, breaking the silence. 'Another slice of toast perhaps, or a pot of tea?'

'More tea would be most welcome, Mrs Gardner,' he replied. 'And I wouldn't mind seeing a newspaper if you have one.'

'It's only the local paper, I'm afraid. We're a bit off the beaten track and the nationals don't get here till later in the morning.'

'I'm sure it will be fine.'

On reflection, Seymour thought the local newspaper might offer some clue as to what Cameron had planned to do in Grange. He scanned the headlines but nothing significant presented itself. Mostly local events - births, marriages and deaths. Small stuff. Nothing out of the ordinary; nothing of any real interest. He sat reading as Muriel returned to clear his table.

'Excuse me, Mister Seymour,' she said apologetically, brushing breadcrumbs from the tablecloth. 'May I disturb you?'

'Go right ahead, don't mind me,' said Seymour. 'I'll just sit here for a while, if I won't be in the way.'

'Of course you won't, Mister Seymour,' she said. 'We're not very busy anyway. There's only one other guest, Mister Pascoe, over there.'

She gestured to the other figure seated behind him. The man was, perhaps in his late forties or early fifties, slim built, and sporting a neatly trimmed moustache. He wore spectacles and was dressed in what looked to be an expensive Saville Row suit, judging by the hand stitching around the collar. Pascoe looked up and acknowledged Seymour with a nod, before continuing his breakfast. Seymour responded in like manner.

'The season's finished and there's not a lot for me to do,' Muriel continued. 'So please don't rush yourself. Take all the time you need.'

Seymour continued perusing the newspaper. Later, Muriel came back.

Twelve

'Did you find anything interesting, Mister Seymour?' she enquired. 'I suppose you read about the death on the sands the day before yesterday?'

'No,' replied Seymour, 'I missed that.'

'Middle page,' she said. 'So common these days it doesn't even merit a front page mention.'

'I was talking to a man on the promenade, only last evening. He told me about the treacherous sands across the bay and mentioned a recent death.'

'Another drowning. Very sad, and it keeps happening. You'll no doubt have heard about all those cockle pickers who died in the rising tide a few years back. It was all over the news.'

'Yes, I vaguely remember that. That was near here was it?'

'Just a few hundred yards up the coast, towards Morecambe.'

Seymour finished reading the newspaper and decided to take a leisurely stroll back into the village, for unlike the previous evening, the rain had ceased. The high winds had abated, the tidal race diminished to a calm swell and it was a gloriously sunny morning, chilled only by the more-or-less permanent gentle sea breeze that came off the estuary. Out of season the town had very little of interest, though he paused outside the newsagents to read the rain-sodden handbill announcing the drowning. He thought little more of it and walked on.

Presently, he came to the railway station. The small mid-Victorian building had formerly been its ticket office, but now it was unmanned. An elderly woman was sweeping up fallen leaves from the platform. Seymour went over to speak to her.

'Excuse me, love, but can you tell me where trains go to from here?' he asked.

'They go to Barrow-in-Furness in that direction.' She pointed westward. Then she turned to the east. 'Lancaster and Carlisle is that way.'

'So if I wanted to get to Manchester what would be the best way?'

'Well I'd catch the train to Carlisle and change there, if I were you.'

'I see, so is there no direct connection then?'

'Not since the branch line closed in the 1960s,' she replied. 'But trains go direct to Manchester from Windermere. You can take the bus there from just outside.'

Seymour thanked her. She went back to her sweeping while he walked over to read the train timetable. One was due any minute. As he was reading, Pascoe walked onto the platform. They acknowledged each other with another nod before he joined him at the timetable.

'Morning,' said Seymour. 'Better weather this morning, after last night's rain.'

'It certainly is,' replied Pascoe politely. Then, more directly: 'Weren't you at the Kirkstone Hotel earlier?'

'Yes. We shared the breakfast room together.'

'I thought you looked familiar.'

From close up, Pascoe was every bit as elegant as Seymour had first thought. He was immaculately dressed, and carried a soft leather briefcase with the gold blocked initials 'A D P' neatly stamped into the flap. Otherwise, he had no luggage. Seymour thought it a little incongruous that a man of such self-evident style and class would choose the Kirkstone Hotel. The establishment was clean and welcoming, adequate for a single night stopover, and no doubt fully deserving its three star rating, but he imagined that Pascoe would have been more at home in the Savoy, the Ritz or some other five star hotel.

Both men continued perusing the timetable for a while before the distant whistle of an oncoming train made Pascoe look round.

'Sounds like mine,' he said. 'Are you getting on?'

'No. I've got stuff to do in town,' replied Seymour. It wasn't exactly true, but as he didn't reckon on seeing

Twelve

Pascoe again, it hardly mattered.

The locomotive pulled up immediately opposite where they were standing. Of the half dozen passengers on board no-one alighted.

'Enjoy the rest of your stay,' said Pascoe. 'Good day.' With that, he stepped aboard the last of the three carriages. The engine let out another shrill whistle and rattled away noisily from the platform. Seymour stood watching as it disappeared around the headland and on its way eastward out of Grange.

*

'So did you manage to turn up anything new in the Lakes?' asked Fosse when they met up in the wine bar later that day.

'Nothing significant, Prof. I'm still no wiser as to why Cameron was heading there. Nice trip and it got me out of the office, but a complete waste of time.'

'Pity,' said Fosse. 'It looked like a good lead. And it's Max.'

'Sorry – Max. At least I've established that Cameron was educated, probably in an English university. The hotel staff described his telephone voice as very well spoken and educated.'

'So the trip was rather fruitless,' said Fosse.

'All part of the job. That's the way police work goes.'

'I can only imagine. Look old chum, I'm afraid I have to go. I'm meeting Amelia Grant in half an hour. Sorry to cut things short, but I'm keen to hear the latest results of the forensics.'

*

Seymour was mulling things over and sipping his glass of water, when a female voice addressed him from behind.

'Is that what passes for a drink in wine bars these days?' it said.

Seymour stood up and turned about. It was Katherine Chaplin. He stared at her momentarily, betraying no hint of recognition.

'It's Katie,' she prompted him. 'Katherine Chaplin.'

'Sorry?'

'From the university. You can't have forgotten me already?'

'Oh, sorry,' he responded with slight embarrassment. 'Of course. Forgive me. My mind was elsewhere. How are you?' (My God, he thought, she really is gorgeous!)

'I'm very well,' she replied. 'Didn't know you frequented this place.'

'I don't. I was introduced to it quite recently by Professor Fosse. You remember him from our meeting the other day?'

'Of course. The celebrated forensic surgeon.'

'So they tell me,' he replied. 'We're collaborating on the accident investigation. But I expect you know that.' They were still standing facing each other rather formally. 'But where are my manners?' he said awkwardly. 'Please sit down and let me get you a drink.'

She sat down, asked for a cocktail and Seymour went over to the bar. He returned with the drink and sat down opposite her.

'Do you live around here?' he enquired. (Shit! He thought. Pitifully inane small talk).

'Just a short walk. I have a flat in the old Redhill Mill. It's a little bit on the expensive side, but I love it there. Besides, a girl has to have a few luxuries.'

Seymour's eyes wandered to her mouth. He watched her lips moving without registering a single word she was saying. Fabulous lips. Thankfully, thoughts are silent. He regained some composure and coloured slightly,

Twelve

fearing that he had gawked a little too long and too intently.

'So why exactly are you drinking water?' she asked.

'Habit,' he said. 'And I'm still technically on duty.' It seemed a reasonable answer.

They talked for more than an hour before she made an excuse to leave. It was getting late she said. Seymour was disappointed. It had been a long time since he had taken pleasure in the company of another woman, and time had flown by so quickly. 'I must get an early night,' she said. 'I have to take the minutes at Doctor Grant's breakfast conference early tomorrow morning.'

'I'll walk with you,' said Seymour. 'It's not much out of my way, and the exercise will do me good.'

They strolled along the dark streets, engrossed in small talk, until they arrived at the cobbled alleyway that was the entrance to the old mill complex. They reached the door; she thanked him and said how much she had enjoyed his company.

'Likewise,' he said. 'We should do this again sometime.' (What was he thinking? Stupid thing to say.)

While they stood talking, the motion-sensitive security light above the entrance repeatedly switched on and off at the slightest movement, and both suddenly burst into spontaneous laughter. 'Sorry about that,' said Katherine, beckoning him to follow her into the vestibule. 'We can't stand out here flashing on and off like a beacon all night! Look. Why not come up for a coffee? Just for half an hour.'

'Best not,' said Seymour. 'I really should be getting back home.'

'Will your wife be expecting you?' she asked.

'Who says I'm married?'

'It stands out like a sore thumb. You have the look of a married man. Even without a wedding ring, I can tell.'

'And what exactly can you tell?'

'Married men are so easy to spot. You all have that

look of being reserved - a sort of safe tamed look. Single men are much more predatory. Married men look owned. So does your wife own you?' She taunted provocatively.

'I wouldn't say that. But I've been away for a couple of days, that's all, and she'll be expecting me home. I don't want to be late.'

'Maybe some other time then?' she persisted. Then she added cruelly, '. . . or would your wife object?'

He struggled for words. 'We've been going through a bad patch lately.' (Why on earth did I say that? he thought).

'Not a problem,' she exclaimed curtly. 'See you.'

And with that she let him out and slammed the door noisily behind him.

Chapter 4: Vauxhall Cross

The house was woken early next morning by loud persistent knocking at the front door. Seymour drew on a robe over his shorts and went downstairs, as his wife stood watching and listening from the landing. He was confronted by two dark-suited men standing on the door step.

'Detective Sergeant Charles Seymour?' said one.

'Yes, I'm Seymour,' he responded. 'Who's asking?'

'I'm DI Jack Marsden and this is my colleague DS Brian Woodruff.'

Marsden presented an SIS warrant card. Seymour looked over the man's shoulder at the large black limousine waiting in the roadway, its engine still running. Security Service - MI6, he thought. He hesitated and his dubious expression was self-evident.

Marsden explained that it was related to the investigation of Patrick Cameron's death and that he needed to accompany them. 'Everything is quite in order,' he assured Seymour.

'Do I have any choice?'

'Afraid not. But you can check with your station chief, if you feel the need,' said Marsden. 'You should pack a bag for several days.'

'Where are we going?'

'London.'

The two men waited in the downstairs hallway as he explained things to Sarah. She hastily threw a few things into an overnight bag while he showered, shaved, dressed, grabbed a hasty sip of hot coffee and a slice of buttered toast.

'Where are they taking you, Charlie?' she asked.

'London, they say. It's not altogether unexpected. I thought Security would become involved sooner or later.'

'You haven't been doing anything you shouldn't, have you? Are you under arrest?'

'No, don't worry. It's routine, to do with the Blackrod accident enquiry. I should only be a few days. I'll call you when I get there.'

She thrust a vacuum flask into his hands. 'For the journey,' she said. 'Please take care.'

'Thanks love,' he said, kissing her on both cheeks, in an exceptional show of affection. 'And please, please don't worry,' he reassured her, as he walked over to get into the back of the waiting car.

The limousine drove away at speed as Sarah stood on the front porch, still in her dressing gown, watching it disappear from view. She wondered how long her husband would be away this time.

*

The meeting to which Seymour had been summoned took place on the third floor of the large imposing building at Vauxhall Cross overlooking the River Thames. He was shown into a board room and offered a seat. Sitting opposite, across a desk, were four figures – three men and a woman. By the manner of his summons, he assumed that they were all high ranking security service personnel. A central figure, seated in a high chair addressed him.

'Can I offer you a coffee, detective sergeant?'

Seymour shook his head and mumbled a polite 'No thank you, sir.'

'Then I should make the introductions,' the man continued. 'My name is Colonel Sir James Andover. I am executive head of Her Majesty's Intelligence Service. We are convened here under the formal direction of the Joint Intelligence Committee.'

Andover introduced the woman sitting next to him as Caroline Massey, Head of MI6 Global Anti-Terrorism Team. The two others remained anonymous, but Seymour had an inkling of their rank and of the exact nature of the enquiry. It was important enough to involve all three

Twelve

branches of the security services. It looked pretty serious.

'Before I get to the point, detective,' Andover continued. 'I have a duty to point out that what transpires here falls under the strictest terms of the Official Secrets Act. Your presence makes you subject to that Act and all of its restrictions. Later you will be required to sign your acceptance of these conditions.'

He opened a file on the desk before him. 'Have you been informed of the purpose of this meeting?'

'Not entirely sir,' Seymour replied. 'But I assume it's related to the Patrick Cameron case.'

'Quite so. We believe you may have already made inroads into the investigation. But first, I'd like to spend a few moments going through your personal file.

'Your record shows that in 1991 you served in Kuwait as part of Operation Desert Storm in the first Gulf War and held the rank of Lieutenant in the Royal Fusiliers. You took part in Operation Granby at Wadi al Batin in January of that year, and were mentioned in dispatches for your outstanding work in that campaign, were you not?'

'That's correct, sir.'

He sat back in his chair and Caroline Massey spoke next. 'You also served for a time in Northern Ireland,' she began. 'Later, in 1996, you were awarded the Queen's Police medal for your work in the Manchester bombing.'

'Yes, ma'am. But it was a team effort.'

'Your modesty does you credit, detective, but it's misplaced here.'

She closed the file and pushed it aside.

'Now we come to the man known as Patrick Cameron. I believe you have already looked into the circumstances surrounding his death.'

'I have been doing so for several days, ma'am, but I've come up with very little.'

'We understand, DS Seymour,' she continued, 'That you have recently traced the man's intended route to the Lake District. To Grange-over-Sands I believe. What can you tell us of what you discovered there?'

'It has proved to be a virtual dead end, ma'am,' he replied. 'I was unable to find out why he was on the way there when the accident occurred. The hotel management reckon he sounded British. He was a cultured man according to the manager, but he only spoke to him on the telephone. He described him as having a refined accent. That's about it.'

'Were you aware that one of our leading scientists died in Grange-over-Sands on the day after Cameron was due to arrive there?' said Massey. 'He drowned in the Morecambe Bay estuary, overtaken by the incoming tide. This was one of the issues raised by Doctor Jameson in his initial report, which we have just received.'

'I did see a local newspaper report about a drowning and the hotel staff mentioned it,' Seymour continued. 'But I had no reason to connect it to Cameron's visit.'

'It could be pure coincidence but we are keeping an open mind. However, it does fit Jameson's projected profile and your information confirms what we already thought, that the man calling himself Patrick Cameron was probably a British national. But what interests us more is where he set out from.'

'I understand he flew in from Saudi Arabia,' said Seymour.

'That's correct. He passed through Jeddah after beginning his flight on November 3rd at Allama Iqbal Airport in Lahore. He arrived in Jeddah early on the fourth. He spent two days in Saudi before continuing his journey to Manchester and arrived at the Airport on the seventh. He made a one way booking, so he was planning to stay. We have people currently in Jeddah looking into the two unaccounted days,' she concluded.

'So you think there really is a potential security risk, then?' said Seymour.

'We believe so. We have acquired evidence of his

Twelve

entry into Somalia and possibly Djibouti or Eritrea in the 1990s and he may have insurgency links in that area. We'd like to know what he was doing there. As you will be aware, the region has become notoriously unstable in recent years and there may be a threat to our national security. Al-Shabab and other groups are very active throughout northern and central Somalia. We believe Cameron may have been radicalised and was training in terrorist techniques somewhere in the Middle East or East Africa.'

'Sorry, I don't understand,' said Seymour. 'You say he was active in East Africa in the 1990s. With respect, ma'am, he could've been no more than a young boy, or at most a teenager back then. How's that possible?'

'It is just one of several puzzling factors of which we are aware. Child soldiers are not exactly uncommon in these sorts of conflict, either, but that's the least of our worries. There are more important things at stake. That's where you come in. We need a specialist detective and you would appear to be eminently qualified. Your superior officer, Superintendent Golding, has recommended you as highly suitable for the task.'

'I'll do my best, ma'am,' he replied respectfully. (Holy Joe, he thought ... never! It was completely out of character that he'd recommend Seymour for any job.) Following the outcome of the tribunal, the wanker had made his view abundantly clear and there was no love lost between them; he was the last person to recommend Seymour for anything. On the other hand, it was one way to get rid of him, at least for a time. That's what this was all about – he was certain of it.

'Well if there's nothing more for the moment,' said Andover in conclusion. 'I think we can wrap up this meeting.' He rose to leave. 'Oh yes, detective,' he said, looking back over his shoulder as he reached the door. 'We have booked you into a small hotel in Euston Road for the time being. It's nothing fancy but I trust you'll find it adequate for your purposes. Miss Massey will be your case officer and will no doubt wish to speak to you further tomorrow. Good day.'

*

Agents Marsden and Woodruff arrived early next morning to accompany Seymour back to Vauxhall Cross. On this occasion he found himself alone in the room with Caroline Massey. It was his first opportunity to get the measure of his new controller. He suspected that she was the main protagonist in yesterday's meeting, even though she had been the subordinate member of the panel. She held a penetrating eye contact. This, combined with her sharp voice and exaggerated explosive consonants, commanded complete attention. He realised that it would be folly to underestimate her, and prudent to proceed cautiously.

"We have made an extensive vetting of your personal record and it has been agreed that you are to be seconded temporarily to our unit, DS Seymour,' she informed him in a matter of fact way. The statement brooked no argument - it was not up for discussion.

'Beg pardon?' Seymour was somewhat dismayed.

'You have been recruited to our service, detective sergeant,' she continued, 'and are to regard yourself as a member of the security services for the time being. Whether this will be a permanent, occasional, or one-time appointment has not yet been determined. There will be a small but commensurate increase in your pay grade and rank while you are working with us.'

He contemplated the new status that had been thrust upon him, while she moved swiftly on.

'Now to the business in hand. Sources in Asia have today suggested that Cameron's journey began somewhere in the Himalaya region, possibly in Nepal or Bhutan; that's a massive territory. We think he travelled overland to Ludhiana in the Punjab and from there to Lahore. Then

Twelve

the trail goes cold for a couple of days and we have no idea what he was doing during that time. What we do know is that he flew on to Saudi Arabia. So this investigation has widened to include Central Asia, East Africa and possibly the Middle East.'

'That's quite a journey,' commented Seymour.

'Indeed it is. And, a matter for some concern,' she added. 'Doctor Jameson has already flagged this up as the profile of a man who may have been radicalised - Asian descent, second generation British born, probably marginalised in wider society, etcetera. But he's untypically older and apparently better educated than your average jihadist - a leader or intellectual, perhaps, not a blind faith follower. Therefore, we are alarmed by reports that the day before he left the Punjab there had been an attempted car bombing in Lahore. Fortunately, a quick thinking passer-by raised the alarm and a potential catastrophe was averted. We believe he was a local man. At any rate, he seems to have single-handedly foiled the plot and prevented a potential massacre. Several hundred children could have died or been seriously injured.'

'So do you think Cameron was involved in this attempted bombing?'

'We have only circumstantial evidence,' she replied. 'He did make extended stopovers in both Lahore and Jeddah, but that could be coincidental.'

'I'm not a great believer in coincidences.'

'Quite so. However, for the present you should concentrate your enquiries on the home front. We'd like you to return to the Lakes. We think Cameron may have been meeting somebody.'

'Why? Do you have evidence for that?'

'Perhaps this might answer your question.' She switched on the television monitor at the back of the room and began to run security camera footage of the car rental office at Manchester Airport. It clearly showed Patrick Cameron, accompanied by a second person. Seymour immediately recognised him as the same man with whom he had shared the breakfast room two days earlier at the Kirkstone Hotel, and later at the station in Grange.

Massey observed Seymour's recognition. 'You recall seeing this other man?' she said.

'Yes, he was at the Kirkstone Hotel in Grange. Went by the name of Pascoe,' Seymour replied. 'So when did they part company? Cameron was alone in the car wreck.'

'This second recording of the secure parking area shows they went their separate ways. Cameron drove off in the hire car and we believe this Pascoe man walked towards the train station. We also have earlier footage of him greeting Cameron in the Arrivals Hall of the airport. Therefore, the meeting was plainly pre-arranged. Pascoe evidently travelled separately to the Lake District. That in itself is suspicious – why not travel together? Of course, he may have taken a bus, but a train seems more likely. If he checked into the same hotel as Cameron, some sort of joint operation was on the cards. They had something planned.'

'So this wasn't a coincidence?'

'Plainly not,' said Massey. Then she reopened Seymour's file. 'I'd like to talk a little more about your time in the army.'

Seymour wondered what her new purpose was, and felt ill at ease.

'You did active service in Kuwait, so I assume you are familiar with weapons?'

'Well, I wouldn't say I was familiar, ma'am. I carried the standard self-loading rifle in the Gulf, as well as a handgun, and a semi-automatic in Belfast. But I haven't fired one in over twenty years.'

'But you have fired weapons?'

'Yes ma'am.'

She paused. 'Have you ever killed a man?'

'During the Gulf War, yes ma'am. Not since leaving

Twelve

the forces.' He hesitated. 'If you don't mind my asking, am I expected to use firearms?'

'It's regulation for all security personnel. Think of it more as precautionary. You will be issued with a Walther P99 and expected to carry it at all times. You should be ready to use it, if and when it becomes necessary.'

'I am very much out of practice and it's a weapon I'm not familiar with.'

'That will be dealt with in the fullness of time. I will arrange for you to do some retraining. I assume you're agreeable?'

'I suppose so, ma'am.' His response was anything but agreeable, but Massey carried on regardless.

'Okay, so that's settled. As for your continuing involvement in this investigation, you will need to go back to the Lake District. Look deeper – ask around. Confirm this Pascoe man's full name if you can, so that we can establish a credible identity for him, as well as the address he gave when he checked in. So far we know precious little about him.'

She noted his uncertainty. 'Is there a problem?'

'Not as such, ma'am. But ... excuse me for bringing it up, wouldn't one of your regular security specialists be better suited to this investigation? After all, I'm just a simple copper,' he said. 'I'm not experienced in security work.'

'That's makes you ideal for the role,' she continued. 'And, you came highly recommended. We need a detective who knows how to take care of himself and your army and police records speak for themselves.'

'If you say so, ma'am.'

'The fact is,' she continued, '... our agents are becoming sloppy; too many public schoolboys and Oxbridge chinless wonders. We can't seem to get the right people these days. New blood and a fresh eye are needed. We felt the case required the skills of a harder man - somebody a bit tougher - more street wise, if you will. You struck us as the right man for the job, and as you were already involved in the investigation, you were a logical choice. Of course, ostensibly, you will continue to carry out your normal duties as a detective, but you will in fact be working for us, covertly. Your station chief will be informed that you are collaborating with us in the investigation, but not that you have been recruited to the security service.'

'I understand, ma'am.' Despite his inferred consent, Seymour felt he'd been railroaded into an uncomfortable position for which he was neither prepared nor qualified.

'Your greatest value to us, detective sergeant, is that you are still an unknown and won't attract any undue attention. That's your strength. Your military training might also come in useful. You are, as you put it, just an ordinary copper from the sticks. No offence intended.'

'None taken, ma'am' he replied. 'But exactly what part does my military training play in all this? Should I expect trouble?'

'I cannot say,' she concluded. 'But if Cameron and Pascoe had been radicalised and were plotting something, things may get a little dirty. We could be facing any one of a half dozen insurgent factions. Al-Qaeda, Chechen, Al-Shabab, or extreme groups we haven't even heard of. Many people out there just don't like us. Expect the worst – in my experience, sooner or later it inevitably materialises.

'Here is my telephone number.' She handed him her business card. 'It's a secure line and it will put you through immediately. Report directly to me and no one else. If you need anything, you may call me, day or night. A credit card account will be set up in your name for contingencies and miscellaneous expenses. Don't go wild, and get receipts. That's all for now.'

Chapter 5: Lahore

It had been two weeks earlier, just before eight-thirty in the morning, when a garishly painted delivery van pulled into the parking lot adjacent to the Garhi Shahu Police Station in the centre of Lahore. The pale October sun rose early, as the southern hemisphere gradually turned to springtime, and even at this hour, the city air was sultry and oppressive.

The high-sided vehicle attracted little attention. It was one of several trucks and vans stationed against the fence behind the main assembly hall of the girl's convent school. It was customary for deliverymen to park up there as they waited for local traders to open the innumerable small shops and business premises that were packed tightly together along the Allama Iqbal Road, just off the square.

Few people were moving about. Only a solitary armed officer stood guard at the main entrance to the police station opposite. Occasionally, a few others arrived for duty.

Presently, the van driver jumped down from the vehicle, raising a cloud of dust as his sandals hit the dry earth. He turned to slam the door behind him. He was a young man, just out of his teens by the look of it, deep-eyed, lean and decidedly under-nourished. It was a common physique among the poorer working classes of Lahore. He wore the traditional loose-fitting form of dress, the shalwar kameez, favoured by men and boys throughout Pakistan, along with the customary waistcoat. In this respect, he appeared unexceptional. Had there been passers-by, none would have paid his arrival any particular attention.

He walked round to open the back door of the van and took out a covered basket, which contained a selection of freshly baked flat breads. When he emerged from behind the vehicle, he waved to acknowledge the police officer across the square, as was his habit. The officer raised a hand to return the greeting. Then the deliveryman made his way slowly towards the school entrance.

It was his regular bread delivery round, he was early, it was hot, and there was no need to hurry. As he reached the school gate, the security guard recognised him and passed him through the barrier without a challenge.

The Fatiqa Girls' Catholic Convent School was the most prestigious in the city. Its pupils were from the wealthiest elite families in Lahore and included the daughters of several high-ranking foreign diplomats as well as those of local politicians and bureaucrats. It was a distinguished institution, supervised by the local Board of Education. Mixed education was virtually unknown in the Punjab, and this establishment catered strictly for girls. Such schools were predominantly Christian and most of their staff were European nuns. Their distinctive white habits were a common sight as they went about their business in many cities like Lahore.

Inside the school building, the long corridors echoed with both Urdu and English voices, in roughly equal measure. Though staff were all bilingual, English was the first language of most, and many spoke it in a strong Irish brogue.

Only a handful of pupils had arrived as it was still early. It would be another quarter hour before classes began, by which time the rooms and corridors would be busy with the hubbub of chattering girls.

The deliveryman slowly made his way down the cool corridors to the refectory kitchen. Once there, he placed the breadbasket on a trestle table and waited as he always did. Kitchen staff had not yet arrived and normally he would require a receipt before leaving.

He stood for a while by the window, vacantly staring across the square at the police station. Then, looking around to check that he was alone, he took out a mobile phone from under the basket cover and hastily stuffed it down the loincloth beneath his robe.

Twelve

Eventually the head cook arrived. He furnished the customary receipt, despite the fact that, on this occasion, had he known, the deliveryman had no need of it. The deception had to be maintained. Receipt in hand, he walked back to the gate at an even slower pace than when he had arrived, frequently looking at his watch and excusing himself as he brushed past groups of young female pupils in the corridor.

The school bell rang just as he made it to the gate. The guard wished him good day before he made his way back to the vehicle. Once there, he opened its back door again.

The van interior was packed to the roof with barrels and steel drums. Each filled with explosives and concoctions of ball bearings, nails and broken glass. He looked around, made a final check, primed the fuse mechanism and activated an electronic detonator. Everything was in order and he was ready. Finally, he blessed the prophet in Arabic with an 'alayhi-salam,' closed the door and walked away quickly.

When he had turned the corner into Allama Iqbal Road he waited five minutes, took out the phone from beneath his garment and looked at his watch a final time. He was satisfied that the school's main assembly would have begun by now. The hall would be packed with the whole congregation of teachers and students about to enact their morning devotions in corporate worship. It had been timed exactly for maximum impact - planned for the van to explode its deadly contents immediately against the outer wall of the assembly hall.

He was about to punch the detonation code into the phone, when a man suddenly rushed at him from behind and forced him bodily to the ground. He wrestled to pin the would-be bomber down at the shoulders with his knees, restraining one of the man's hands behind his head and scooping up the phone with his other.

Throughout the scuffle the assailant shouted

loudly, drawing the attention of the officer from his post at the police station door, as well as stunned pedestrians and cyclists who came over to witness the engagement. Within moments a large crowd had formed around the two men struggling in the dust.

'Police! Police! Get the police,' the man screamed. 'This man is a car bomber!'

Chapter 6: Genetics

When he returned from London, Seymour telephoned Fosse from his station desk.

'Hello, old man,' said Fosse. 'You been away?'

'Just for a couple of days in London. I'll fill you in on what I'm at liberty to say, if we can meet up later.'

'Sounds cryptic,' replied Fosse. 'I have some news too.'

'Good. I look forward to catching up, so I'll see you in the usual place at eight, okay?'

'I'll have the sparkling water waiting for you,' Fosse joked.

'Piss off, Prof!' ended Seymour good-humouredly.

Fosse laughed aloud and rang off.

*

No sooner had he replaced the receiver than a colleague came over to his desk.

'Holy Joe wants to see you,' he said. 'Looks bad.'

Seymour got up from his desk, walked over to the office door and knocked. When he was bid to enter, he went in and stood before the desk.

'Remain standing, sergeant,' instructed Golding, '... and, bring me up to speed with the stuff that's been going down in London.'

'Can't say,' Seymour hesitated. 'But thanks for the recommendation.'

'Can't say?' Golding repeated with a sneer. 'You having me on, sergeant? Just cut the crap, and don't give me any of your flannel either. I'm not asking, I'm telling you to report everything. And it's 'sir' when you address me.'

'I really am not allowed. Official Secrets Act. Sir!'

'Never mind Official Secrets!' Golding blustered. 'You're not with your new London cronies now and you'd do well to remember that I'm your ranking officer. This is an order. I want to know exactly what you were doing down in London.'

Seymour stood intractably silent, his head bowed, avoiding eye contact with his inquisitor. Moments passed before Golding, increasingly annoyed, issued an ultimatum.

'Right. One last chance. Full written report on my desk by first thing tomorrow or a great deal of shit will come down on your head. Do you understand, sergeant?'

'Fully, boss. But I can't do that.'

Golding fumed in frustration and his face reddened by the second. Seymour reiterated in a vain attempt to diffuse the situation. 'I have been instructed, at the highest level, that the matter must remain between myself and the security services. My hands are tied.'

At a loss for an appropriate response, Golding clutched the most convenient straw that came to mind and remarked snidely. 'You still drinking at work or something?'

'No, I'm not! And you can fuck off, you supercilious wanker!' replied Seymour.

'I'll have your badge for this, Seymour!'

'Do whatever you have to, but I'm just doing my job as I was instructed.'

'Your job is to obey my bloody orders,' Golding snapped. 'In view of your intransigence I'm going to issue you with a written warning – a copy will go on record and the insubordination will be reported on up the line.'

'Well, you must do what you think is right – sir,' Seymour replied sarcastically.

Golding, who had fiddled nervously with a plastic ruler throughout the whole confrontation, stood up abruptly, causing his chair to fall over behind him with a loud crash. At the same instant he smashed the ruler down on the desk with such force that it shattered into pieces and shards flew across the room, clattering on the glass partition wall like shrapnel.

Twelve

'Stupid bastard!' said Seymour.

'Get out! Get out!' Golding shouted repeatedly. 'We'll see who's a stupid bastard. This isn't the end of it, Seymour. You're well and truly done for now!'

Seymour made a swift exit. As the door closed behind him, he was met by the astonished stares of everyone in the outer office. Shocked by the noise of the clash that had taken place, every eye followed him as he left the station and exited the building.

*

That evening Seymour faced a dilemma. How much of all that had transpired in London would he be able to confide in Fosse? Golding could go fuck himself, he thought. He was damned if he'd tell him anything, just as a matter of principle. However, Fosse was a different matter altogether.

'I will tell you what I can, Prof,' he began. 'But it might be less than you're used to. The case is now covered by the Official Secrets Act. I did warn you this might happen when the security services got involved.'

'I completely understand,' replied Fosse. His tone was indignant. 'But everything we've discussed up to now has had serious security implications, so it's a bit late to get up on your high horse or to be pernickety over details. And, it's Max!'

Seymour felt lightly reprimanded. It was the closest Fosse had ever come to losing his temper and its rarity made it even more acute. This had not been a good day. It was the second time he'd been taken to task in twenty-four hours. Golding's rant was water off a duck's back, of course – he could take it or leave it. But in the short time he had known Fosse, Seymour had grown to respect him as a knowledgeable colleague and a burgeoning friendship had already developed between them. Therefore, the admonition made him wince.

'Anyway,' Fosse continued. 'I, for one, feel free to discuss the case openly. As for yourself, you must judge the extent of your own permitted revelations. Having said that, I'd like to put this little *contretemps* behind us and move on, if that's okay with you.'

'Yeh, let's. It's just been a very bad day, Max. Sorry. So what've you got?'

'Well, the results of my clinical diagnostic work in haematology are very revealing. Apart from intracranial haematoma around the brain, you'll remember that Cameron had suffered many other extensive injuries and required a number of transfusions. And, although we couldn't identify his blood group as such, it readily cross-matched with all other blood groups.'

'I already know this. So where is it leading?' said Seymour.

'Well, conventionally, we have to check for any dangerous incompatibilities before transfusions take place,' replied Fosse. 'It can be fatal if you get the wrong blood match. Usually, either one of A, B or O types cross-match perfectly for everybody. That would be our normal expectation. However, in Cameron's case, not just one, but all three blood types were compatible with his own. It's as if his blood was an exact synthesis of all three.'

'So how is that significant?'

'We are coming round to a working hypothesis that Cameron's blood has been engineered,' Fosse replied. 'It appears to be an artificial concoction of some kind.'

'Can that actually be done?'

'We didn't think so. Or not so far as Amelia Grant or I knew. We could find nothing in any scientific papers either. On the other hand, who knows what the back room boffins are developing? We live in interesting times, old chum, and this is effectively a new blood group. That is, it's new to us at the university. As I say, there's no other logical explanation. It has to have been engineered!

'Also, the background to Cameron's racial

Twelve

characteristic is unprecedented. I began to look into scientific papers relating to the use of genetic data to investigate the geographical structure of populations and genetic diversity.'

'Sorry, you're losing me now.'

'The procedure can be used to trace human migratory patterns. We can track a person's ancestry as far back as prehistoric times.' Seymour, looked bewildered. 'Okay. I'll try to simplify it then,' Fosse continued. 'By using a form of radioactive isotope, we are able to determine where an individual's ancestors originated – where in the world their forebears or the genetic line came from. Naturally, given his dark skin colour, we would have said that Cameron was of Asian descent. Everybody assumed that. But it isn't! He is, unequivocally, European. There is no Asian pathway in his genetic line whatsoever.'

'Let me understand this,' said Seymour. 'Are you saying he's white?'

'Incredible as it may seem, that's exactly where the results are pointing!'

'So how do you explain the skin colour?'

'I have no solution to that conundrum, Charlie. I wouldn't know where to begin. It could be a mutation - possibly. But we checked and re-checked. He was definitely a Caucasian man, and his family originated in northern Europe, possibly around Belgium or Germany. In other words, he was Anglo-Saxon.'

'Does anyone else know about your findings?' asked Seymour.

'No. This material is only known to me, Amelia Grant, and now to you, of course. We've been instructed to delay any wider distribution of all further findings, and ordered to send the results to some office in Milbank.'

Seymour looked perturbed. 'Milbank? That's MI5. It seems all three security services are keen to be involved and I don't know what's going on. Can you delay sending it off?'

'I suppose so,' said Fosse. 'But it's tricky.'

'I know. Truth is, I think MI6 and now MI5 are involved in ways they're not letting on,' concluded Seymour. 'I believe that they knew some, if not all of this, before you did.'

'Do you think they have a hidden agenda?'

'It's possible. I'm not sure yet. Let's just say I'm suspicious. I think I've just been recruited to MI6 as a throwaway.'

'Throwaway?'

'Well, they explained that I may only be seconded for this one specific intelligence operation – a sort of temporary arrangement. What they call a *floater*. That's fair enough. But by their own definition - throwaways are regarded as expendable assets.'

'I see. That doesn't sound good.'

'Tell me about it. But, let's not worry about me for the time being – it's just a hunch. Is that everything you have come up with?'

'No, it's not. The brain pattern data was interesting too. Our recordings of Cameron's neural function and the MRI scans of his cranial cavity were unprecedented. Areas of the brain that are unique to conscious thought were active while he was still in a deep coma. They shouldn't have been of course. It's not possible to be *conscious* and *unconscious* at the same time. However, that seems to be exactly what was taking place. They suggest that he was using a highly focalised level of mental activity while still comatose. Both sensory and motor functions were actively processing something.'

'This sounds more and more like science fiction.'

'It does, doesn't it?' Fosse replied. 'Taking all these incongruities together we can only conclude that this man was extensively enhanced or modified in some way.'

'You could be describing some kind of alien or superman,' said Seymour with more than a little incredulity.

Twelve

'Well, I don't want to speculate,' said Fosse. 'Let's just say that this man possessed many unique and unusual physical characteristics that were previously unknown in human beings. He may not have been a super man, but he was certainly a special man.'

'So who or what is behind these so-called modifications?'

'I cannot imagine,' replied Fosse. 'But given the special interest the security services are showing in the case, you and I may be getting into what the old map-makers called *terra incognito*, my friend.'

'You may be right, Max. This is certainly unknown territory for me,' said Seymour. 'So is that everything?'

'It's all I have so far,' replied Fosse. 'What about you?'

'There is one little nugget of information I picked up at MI6. They told me about this boffin who had drowned in Morecambe Bay the day before I arrived. He was a doctor of some kind and they were particularly interested in him.'

'Did you manage to get a name?'

''Fraid not. I did read about it briefly in a newspaper at the hotel, but didn't pay much attention at the time. Vauxhall think it might be relevant. They believe Cameron may have been implicated in his death in some way. They're sending me back up to the Lakes tomorrow to look into it.'

'I can't see how Cameron could possibly have been involved. He died before arriving at the Lake District.'

'I know. I pointed that out, but they remained very, very interested.'

'There's something fishy about this whole affair,' said Fosse. 'More to it than meets the eye, I think.'

'You may be right,' said Seymour, ' and I don't mind admitting that I'm entirely out of my depth.'

'For what it's worth, so am I,' concluded Fosse.

Chapter 7: Kendal

On his return to the Lakes, Seymour drove directly to Windermere. The town lay about twelve miles from Grange-over-Sands and boasted a small railway station at its northern end. The timetable confirmed the direct link to Manchester, just as the old woman at Grange station had said. It was possible that it was how Pascoe had travelled to Cumbria. Immediately next door to the station was the Lake Star Taxi Company, which seemed a promising place to start investigation. Seymour went in and spoke to the man who was operating a switchboard behind the counter.

From the booking ledger he confirmed that on the day in question, a man had taken one of their taxis to Grange, though he could not recall much of him.

'We get people in and out all day long, officer,' he said. 'I don't really take much notice. I think he may have had a moustache and specs, but that's all I remember. So long as he paid, what he was doing or where he was going was his business, not ours.'

Seymour thanked the man and left.

*

The journey back to Grange shadowed the lakeside south through Bowness and continued on to Newby Bridge, before entering the narrow lanes of the Cartmel Peninsula, just as Pascoe's taxi ride would have done. He was greeted warmly when he arrived back at the Kirkstone Hotel.

'Detective Seymour,' said the manager. 'We didn't expect you back here so soon, but you're most welcome.'

'This is not exactly a social call, Mister Gardner. Still on official business.'

'Oh, I see,' said Gardner. 'Anything wrong? I mean, I trust your previous visit was satisfactory.' He became unnecessarily agitated.

Twelve

'Nothing you should worry about, Mister Gardner. It's about that other guest that was staying when I was last here. Name of Pascoe.'

'Oh yes. Mister Pascoe. Nice quiet gentleman.'

'How long did he stay here?'

'Just the one night, if memory serves me right, but I will check in the book.'

He went away, returned with a bound manual, and flicked through the pages. 'Yes, here it is. Mister Arthur Pascoe. He stayed for just the one night.'

'Presumably he registered with an address?'

'Yes, he did,' said Gardner. 'I'll write it down for you. I believe it's somewhere in Manchester.'

'Thanks, that's very helpful,' Seymour replied. The address that Gardner produced was the same as that Patrick Cameron had used for the car rental.

'Could I see the room he stayed in?'

'Of course. Nobody's been in there since he checked out. We're not busy now the summer season's over – it's always a bit slack at this time of year. But I must warn you, the room hasn't been cleaned yet.' He was profusely apologetic. 'We're usually fairly empty from autumn through to spring, you see. And, people don't want to be on the second floor, so cleaning it has not been a priority. There's no lift either, and rooms on the top floor are much smaller. It's due for some redecoration, so you'll have to overlook the state of it. I'll give it a quick wipe over before you go in, if you like.'

'No, no. Better it remains exactly as Mister Pascoe left it, if you don't mind.'

'Well, if you're sure.'

Gardner led him up the two flights of stairs and opened up the room with a latchkey that he kept on a chain attached to his belt. 'Shall I leave you to it, detective?' he asked. 'Or would you like me to hang around a while? It's just that I have a few chores to see to downstairs, but they can wait if you need me here.'

'No, you get on with your work,' said Seymour. 'I'll call if I need you.'

After Gardner had gone back downstairs Seymour stood in the doorway slowly surveying the interior. He could hardly believe his luck – the room had not been disturbed. It's confined space had a sloping attic ceiling and an even more cramped adjoining bathroom. Plain to see why it was cheaper and less popular with visitors. It was sparse with minimal furnishings. Covers were thrown back and the dishevelled bed sheets lay unchanged. Seymour could not help shuddering at the unsavouriness of the room. He was thankful that his own stay at the Kirkstone had been in a cleaner room and in a better state of decoration.

Basic tea making facilities and an antiquated electric reading lamp stood on the bedside table. A partially empty teacup beside the lamp had already begun to develop signs of a fungal growth. It had remained unwashed since Pascoe vacated the room.

'Perfect,' Seymour muttered under his breath.

He pulled on a pair of rubber gloves and took a plastic sample bag from his pocket. Then, he carefully emptied the residual tea dregs down the sink and transferred the teacup into the bag.

As he worked his way methodically round, he came to the bathroom. A towel still lay strewn across the tub, where it had been left. A tarnished mirror over the sink was spattered with the residue of Pascoe's ablutions and the washbasin still had a few traces of dried-on toothpaste. To his absolute delight, Seymour saw a single human hair behind the tap on the washbasin. He took out a small envelope, scooped it up with the flap and returned it, sealed, to his breast pocket. At last, maybe, he was beginning to get somewhere.

*

Twelve

When he had completed his room search, Seymour went back downstairs and spoke to the manager once again.

'A couple more questions, Mister Gardner. A few things I'd like to clear up. It's what you said about the Pascoe's room. You said that most people didn't like being up there; that it was small, in need of refurbishment and a long way to struggle with heavy suitcases. Not most people's first choice, I believe you said.'

'That's right,' said Gardner. 'But the rates are cheaper. Some of our guests are on a tight budget and the top floor suits their pocket.'

'But from the little I saw of him and what you told me, Pascoe didn't look particularly impoverished. So why would he choose the cheapest and arguably the least comfortable room in the house?'

'Mister Pascoe specifically requested the top floor. Said he was a very light sleeper. He wanted some peace and quiet away from street traffic and rowdy residents, so he said it suited him perfectly. I did think it a little odd at the time.'

'Exactly. This is hardly a busy street and there isn't a great deal of traffic noise. Especially at this time of year. As you've already said, the hotel was virtually empty that night. Apart from Pascoe and myself there weren't any other residents were there?'

'No, there weren't. Just the two of you. I offered him a better room on the first floor, but he declined it. We try to give our guests what they ask for, but we do get some quite odd requests from time to time, so we thought little more of it.'

'Did he go out at any time?'

'Not to my knowledge. So far as I am aware he remained in his room during the whole of his stay and didn't come back down till breakfast, when I believe you saw him for yourself.'

'I did,' agreed Seymour. 'Very briefly.'

'So is there anything else, detective?' he asked.

'There is, Mister Gardner. I've taken a teacup from the room. I hope that's all right. I'll return it when we have concluded our investigation.'

'No problem. We're not short of tea things. Keep it.'

'One final thing then. Do you happen to have a copy of the local newspaper for that morning? There was an article that I saw over breakfast that I'd like to go over again.'

'Unfortunately all our old newspapers go for recycling. They were collected yesterday.'

'I see. Would it have been printed in Grange? And would they keep back copies?'

'No, not in Grange,' said Gardner. 'The offices and print works are somewhere in Kendal. I can find out for you, if you like.'

'That would be most helpful.'

*

Furnished with the address of the publishing company and a tourist map of the town centre Seymour set out to drive over to Kendal. Traffic was already building up for the Saturday market by the time he'd reached the outskirts. Kendal, he discovered, was the market town for the whole of South Lakeland. It was busy, and he soon became frustrated by the congestion and long tailbacks, so decided to park in the suburbs and walk back into town. Eventually, he made his way to the offices of the *Westmorland Weekly Herald*, just off the High Street. As he entered, the jingle of a small bell above the door announced his arrival. A young man looked up from his work and came over to the counter.

'Yes sir,' he said cheerfully. 'How may I help you today?'

'I believe you keep back copies of your recent newspaper publications.'

Twelve

'We do, sir. Every edition since 1847,' he replied. 'They're all available online.'

'Would it be possible to look at last week's edition?'

'Certainly, sir,' he replied. 'If you'd like to come round the counter I can access the edition on my computer for you.'

Seymour sat at the young man's terminal and browsed its contents until he found the page he was looking for. Scrolling down to the article, he read the headline:

"CELEBRATED GENETIC SCIENTIST DIES ON ESTUARY SANDS"

Its first paragraph read:

"Cumbria Police announced that the body of Doctor Wesley Alan Cruikshank was discovered early yesterday morning in Morecambe Bay. His is the third tragic death in the estuary this year, yet another unwitting victim of the shifting sands and unparalleled tidal race out on the sands. Fleetwood lifeboat and the coast guard were called out, but Doctor Cruikshank was found to be dead when they reached him. A major Nobel Prize nominated scientist, Doctor Cruikshank was a keen and experienced mountaineer and fell walker, but this was believed to be his first foray into coastal walking. Police said that he had underestimated the risk of being caught out on the sands during the region's notoriously fast incoming tides, especially at this time of year. Close colleagues speak of his pioneering genetic research into Alzheimer's and dementia. His recent research into gene and cell manipulation had begun to show positive benefits in the treatment of these debilitating conditions and early test results had proved successful in halting their progress and in some cases to reverse the effects altogether in laboratory mice. Initial testing on human subjects was planned for later this year. Experts in the field believe that his premature death has probably put back the

development of effective vaccines in the treatment and prevention of Alzheimer's by ten years, and that his passing is a major setback to research in genetic science. We would like to take this opportunity to express our deep regret and send heartfelt condolences to his family and loved ones for their loss."

At last Seymour grasped the significance of the death of an eminent scientist in Cumbria, how that might arouse the interest of MI6 and why Patrick Cameron's planned journey there would attract their attention. Fosse had already suggested the possibility of genetic engineering in the Cameron post-mortem and Cruikshank was working on cell manipulation. Coincidence? He was still staring at the screen when the young newspaper clerk returned.

'Did you find what you were looking for, sir?'

'Yes thanks,' Seymour replied. 'Can I get a printout of this article?'

'Of course,' he replied. 'I'll get you a hard copy in just a jiffy.'

Once the printer had discharged the sheet, Seymour folded it and placed it in his coat pocket, before thanking the young man and leaving to walk back to his car.

As he drove back to Manchester, his mind raced with unfolding possibilities. It looked increasingly likely that the security services had already made a link between Patrick Cameron and Doctor Cruikshank. They just hadn't bothered to tell him about it. Genetic engineering was a potentially contentious issue - he knew that. But why would they conceal a connection? The secrecy troubled him. He would need to be more cautious in future when dealing with his new masters in London.

*

It was sometime later that Seymour sat waiting for Fosse to arrive at the Crazy Horse Wine Bar. He had hardly sat

Twelve

down when Katherine Chaplin came over to him.

'Hello mister married policeman,' she taunted impishly. 'Still on duty I see. May I join you?'

'Of course,' Seymour replied. 'Let me get you a drink first.'

He returned from the bar, sat down and watched her sip the drink a while, fascinated by the bright crimson lipstick smear forming around the rim of her glass.

'Is something wrong?' she asked. 'You look pretty wretched.'

'It's been a very long day, Katie,' he began. 'But your company is a great pick-me-up.'

'I thought you might not speak to me after our last meeting.'

'Why's that?' he asked.

'Well, I was a little naughty, and I virtually slung you out.'

'I didn't give it another thought.' He lied.

'You haven't been around for a few days. Have you been avoiding me?' she said.

'No. Just away two days on business in the Lake District,' he replied.

'I absolutely adore the Lakes. You must take me there one day.'

'Must I?'

'Yes, you just must. Absolutely!'

*

An hour later, Katherine asked him if he would see her home once more.

'Much as I'd like to,' said Seymour, 'I'm meeting with Professor Fosse here shortly, and he's due anytime.'

'You could easily take me home and be back in two minutes.'

'I really don't want to miss him, Katie. It's important.'

'So text him. I'm sure he'll wait if you're not back in time.'

Seymour was still considering the prospect when she prodded him in the ribs impatiently. 'Go on,' she said. 'Don't be an old stick-in-the-mud!'

'Okay, you win. But I can't stay. Just to your place and then straight back here.'

'Very well, but you are a spoiled sport,' she chided.

When they stepped outside it was pouring with rain, so they dashed quickly, dodging the puddles, back to her apartment block. She let herself in and dragged him in after her by the sleeve.

'I've told you I can't stay, Katie,' he said.

'Well you can't stand out getting drenched in the rain. And you don't have to rush off immediately. Your date will wait.'

'It's not a date, but I do have to go. Now.'

He turned towards the door to leave. But before his hand reached the handle, she thrust herself in front of it, both arms stretched out to block his exit. She looked at him defiantly. 'You can kiss me if you like,' she said.

'Katherine, what are you doing? Why are you doing this?' He was momentarily shocked, but his response was more a rebuke than a question.

'You know why. Don't pretend you don't know that I'm very attracted to you,' she admitted. 'And I know you want me. I've seen the way you look at me.'

'That's irrelevant, he replied. 'I can't get involved.'

'Just kiss me!' she said.

He stared at her incredulously. But she persisted.

'You have to kiss me before I'll let you pass.' She stared him out brazenly.

'No, I can't.'

'But you want to ... so just do it.'

Patience completely exhausted, suddenly, despite Seymour's rejection, she pounced at him with such speed that he had no time to react. In an instant she threw both

Twelve

arms tightly around his neck and embraced him in a lingering full-mouthed kiss. He should have seen it coming and stepped back immediately. But he didn't. This shouldn't be happening, but she was right. It was something he had thought about ever since their first meeting.

Unable to catch his breath under the pressure and intensity of her advance, he forcibly pulled himself free, brushed her aside and left as quickly as he was able. As he walked away he heard her call out his name. But he dared not look back, and quickened his pace.

Chapter 8: Forensics

Fosse was already standing at the bar when Seymour got back to the Crazy Horse.

'Been waiting long?' said Seymour.

'Not long,' Fosse replied. 'You look a bit shaken, Charlie. Something untoward happened?'

'Nothing important.' Least said the better, he thought.

They sat down in a corner booth and Seymour recounted everything that had transpired in Grange and Kendal. He handed the news item printout to Fosse.

'My god!' Fosse exclaimed. 'It's Wes Cruikshank!' He was visibly shocked.

'Did you know him?' asked Seymour.

'Indeed I did. We were at Westminster at the same time, and both read Medicine at Cambridge. After graduation we worked together at Porton Down. I think he went on to lecture at Harvard after that, and we lost touch with each other. I'm flabbergasted!'

'So you knew him well?'

'It was a long time ago, but yes, I did. We were colleagues. He went on to produce a large body of groundbreaking research and his work was widely published in scientific papers all over the world. What a bloody tragedy! Wes Cruikshank – who'd have thought it?'

'What were you working on at Porton Down?'

'I'm embarrassed to say for a time we did research together into chemical and biological weapons for the MOD. I hated it and got out as soon as I could.'

'That's a big change from forensic pathology isn't it?'

'Not so much as you might think. I did some serious post-graduate retraining afterwards. It's a long story, perhaps for another time.' He paused reflectively. 'So Cameron may well have been connected to Cruikshank's death after all.'

Twelve

'Well, both of them may have had connections to biological research,' said Seymour. 'I don't know how, yet, but my suspicions are that MI6 are involved in all this. I'm also beginning to wonder whether Cameron was one of Cruikshank's biological enhancement subjects! Genetic engineering just keeps cropping up. And the more I think about it, the deeper they seem implicated. I keep asking myself whether I've been set up. Why would they choose me for the investigation when they already have plenty of operatives who could do the job? Their reasons were plausible enough I suppose ... but I just don't think they were telling me everything. If my suspicions are correct, then the less I tell them, the better. I'll have to report something back, though. Just not everything.'

'So now you are officially working for MI6?'

'I was about to tell you Max,' he continued. 'Yep, it's official. And, I'm no longer a detective sergeant.'

'They've reinstated your detective inspector rank?'

'They have. It may only be for the time being, but it's to be kept under wraps. To all intents and purposes I'm still just a copper, so this information stays between us. Like everything else, okay?'

'Of course. You've already made that clear. But I suppose your wife will have to know, won't she?'

'I haven't given that much thought, what with one thing and another. It's just that if I do tell her she's bound to ask questions that I won't be at liberty to answer. It's complicated. Probably better if she doesn't know.'

'Well, if you think so. I'm sure you know best.' Fosse was dubious.

'I've also been issued with a side arm,' Seymour continued.

'A gun? Where are you keeping it?'

'Still in my overnight bag,' said Seymour. 'It's a standard issue firearm. I have to carry one, officially anyway. Except, I don't intend to. It's a bit out of my comfort zone.'

'It does all seem a bit cloak and dagger,' said Fosse.

Then Seymour handed the plastic bag containing the teacup to Fosse. 'I found this, and I have something else that might prove useful.' Next, he took the envelope containing Pascoe's strand of hair from his pocket. 'It's in there.'

'So what am I looking at exactly?' asked Fosse as he peered into an apparently empty envelope.

'Look a little more carefully, Max. There's a hair. It belongs to a second man named Arthur Pascoe. I think he was a partner of Patrick Cameron. They were booked into the same hotel in any case. I met him during my first visit. Then in London, they showed me some security footage of him with Cameron at Manchester Airport. Run an analysis on both the hair sample and the teacup if you can and see what you come up with.'

'You want this done privately?'

'Strictly between ourselves, as usual.'

'Okay, if you're sure.'

'I am. I want to know who this Pascoe guy is, quite apart from MI6's interest, as well as how involved he is in the Cameron case, if at all.'

'I'll do what I can,' said Fosse. 'But it won't be easy. Best I do it at the university where it's a bit quieter and less busy. Nobody will be suspicious if I'm seen working late; I often do. So tell me about this Pascoe man.'

'It's the name I was given for him at the hotel, but god knows who he really is. His briefcase had the initials 'A D P' on it but that's not much to go on. So how long do you reckon it will take?'

'I'll go back and do it immediately after I leave here. I should have something by morning, hopefully.'

'One more thing,' said Seymour. 'I might have an address for Pascoe; it's the one he gave the hotel. It's local - the same one that we found for Cameron.'

'D'you plan on going round there?'

'I thought I'd stake it out, just to see who turns up.

Twelve

You never know, the neighbours might know something. I'll also search the police database to see if anything is known of Mister Arthur D Pascoe.'

'I suppose you now have access to the MI6 files as well?' said Fosse.

'I do, and there's also the DVLA. If he's ever applied for a driving license, they'll have it on record.'

*

As he made his way home, Seymour was preoccupied with the events in the Lake District and of Katherine Chaplin. He could not get out of his mind what happened in the vestibule of her apartment block. He knew that there was no future in it, but the memory persisted. The taste of her lips and the fragrance of her perfume would not leave him. Neither would the way she had pressed herself against him. It had been with such unexpected force that he could still feel her physical imprint on his chest.

The house was in complete darkness, it was past midnight and everyone was asleep. He opened the door quietly and let himself in, undressed in the blackness of the landing and slipped into bed quietly beside his wife. She stirred and turned over to face him.

'You're late tonight,' she murmured. 'Busy day?'

'You could say that. It's proving a tough one to crack, love,' he whispered. 'I'll tell you about it in the morning. Now try and get some sleep.'

With that, he planted a gentle kiss on her exposed shoulder, rolled away and soon fell asleep.

*

Seymour received an urgent order to attend the South Division police headquarters next day. It looked important, but in light of the exceptional things that had surrounded his professional life lately, he was neither particularly surprised nor worried by the summons.

The building was a dominating glass and steel edifice, towering over the surrounding suburban skyline. It contrasted sharply with the tired Edwardian red brick building in which he worked. This was the first time he had been privileged to enter the building and he was singularly unimpressed by its boxy modernity.

From the reception desk, he was escorted up to the outer office of the Deputy Chief Constable on one of the upper floors. Presently an officer called him in.

The Deputy Chief Constable was accompanied by a Chief Inspector.

'Please come in detective Sergeant,' said the Deputy Chief. 'Take a seat.'

Seymour sat down and waited to be addressed.

'I have asked you to come here, detective,' the Chief continued, '... because it has come to my attention that you've been subjected to a degree of intimidation in pursuit of your present – how shall we say – *sensitive* enquiries.'

'May I ask how this came to your notice, sir?' asked Seymour.

'That's of no consequence. Very little takes place in a division that I don't eventually hear about. However, your station chief has written a strongly worded complaint concerning alleged insubordination and your gross disrespect for his rank.'

'Sir,' said Seymour in acknowledgement.

'He accuses you of calling him, and I quote, a ... ahem... a *'wanker'*, a *'stupid bastard'* and telling him to *'fuck off'*. Have you anything to say about that?'

'Yes I do,' replied Seymour. 'With respect, he was behaving like a stupid bastard, sir. He tried to intimidate me. I was instructed not to discuss the case with anybody, and in my opinion, the investigation was really none of his business. I felt he needed warning off in the strongest possible terms,'

Twelve

'I see. His memo confirms that the confrontation occurred when you refused to report what had taken place at Vauxhall Cross. Did you make your position under the Official Secrets Act absolutely clear to him?'

'Yes sir, I did. He knew full well how OS works.'

'Then you acted quite properly and the officer concerned was entirely out of order. As a result of his intrusion, Control has urgently requested his removal. This unfortunate episode was also witnessed by your fellow officers, which is regrettable. The potential damage he might have done could have seriously set back our relationship with the security services, which are always tricky. To this end, Superintendent Golding has been transferred to another district within the city, and Chief Inspector Forman has been brought in from the Mercian Constabulary. He is assigned to your division and will act as the new chief station officer for the time being.'

'I understand,' replied Seymour.

'Good, that's done with. So do you have any questions?'

'Just one, sir. May I ask who my line manager is? Chief Inspector Forman or Vauxhall Cross? Who do I report to?'

'You will work directly with London, and be answerable to them. I also understand, via the Chief Constable, that your MI6 controller has insisted on the reinstatement of your previous rank, which has now been approved.

'CI Forman is apprised of the nature of your secondment but he will not be involved in your investigations in any way. As far as your work is concerned, his role will be in a purely enabling capacity. For any of your immediate requirements, you should request them of him. Otherwise you will deal directly with London and be free to act independently. Therefore, as you have been told, you should consider yourself an MI6 operative, effective immediately. This is to be known only to myself and Chief Inspector Forman.'

'Do I get a choice, sir?'

'It's a little late for reconsidering things, detective. Of course you are free to decline the offer of secondment, but think very carefully. In view of your recent history, you are likely to remain a detective sergeant for a very long time, possibly for the remainder of your career. Alternatively, you can accept advancement to this more advantageous position and enjoy greater career opportunities as well as a considerable raise in your pay grade. You may also find it useful in laying the ghost of last year's unfortunate professional problems. Least said of that, the better. Meantime, MI6 has requested that, as far as your colleagues are concerned, you will appear to carry out your normal functions as a detective sergeant. Do you have any other questions?'

'No sir. I think that covers everything.'

'Just one more thing then – try not to call your superior officers stupid bastards or wankers in future. They don't like it.'

'I'll do my best.'

*

When Seymour arrived back at the station office, a small group of detectives gathered around, eager for news concerning the removal of Holy Joe from the station. He informed them that Chief Inspector Forman would be taking charge of the station immediately and that was 'all he could say' about the matter. As to why Golding had been removed, he was 'not at liberty to divulge', but most of his colleagues already knew the reason. News of the confrontation had spread like wildfire around every division of the local constabulary and Seymour's reputation had improved dramatically as a result. Analogies had been made to a David and Goliath encounter and Seymour had become station hero of the hour.

Twelve

Following Seymour's scant explanation, the group dispersed to their desks, but periodically one detective or another would peer through the glass partition into the office, to confirm that Golding really no longer occupied his chair.

*

Within the hour, Katherine Chaplin walked into the station office and strode purposefully up to Seymour's desk. Every eye followed her with intense and lustful interest.

'Hello detective,' she said sheepishly.

'Hello, Katie,' He looked up from his work.

'Still talking to me?' she said in a half whisper.

'Depends on whether you intend to behave yourself,' he said with equal portions of censure and playfulness.

She remained standing, uncertain for a few moments, until the faintest hint of a smile on Seymour's face broke the tension and she breathed a sigh of relief.

'So to what do I owe the pleasure, Miss Chaplin?' he said at length.

'I've brought over this envelope from Professor Fosse,' she replied. 'He's been working on something all night. He was still at it when I arrived for work this morning. It looks important ... and secret.'

She handed him the large sealed Manila envelope. Seymour tore it open immediately and glanced briefly at its contents. It was the result of Fosse's DNA test on Pascoe's hair strand, as he had anticipated.

A briefly scrawled note was attached.

"Seymour,
Here are the results you asked for. I need to talk you through them, but I think you'll be fascinated.
Phone me. Max."

'Is everything okay?' asked Katherine, when he had finished reading it.

'Yes, it's fine. Just business,' he replied.

'No,' she went on. 'I mean us. You and me. Are we okay?'

'Katie,' he said in exasperation. 'What am I going to do with you?'

She tilted her head slightly, looked him full in the eyes and spoke in a low voice. 'I could answer that, detective, but I'm afraid you'd run away home again.

Chapter 9: Databases

Max Fosse's house was set in a leafy avenue of the city's southern suburbs. A desirable residential area, much sought after by young professionals and nurses, the latter owing to its proximity to the hospital. The location enabled Fosse to make the leisurely walk into the hospital or the university each morning.

His was a large detached residence of the inter-war period, in a typical English vernacular style and vestigial remains of Art Deco sunburst motifs still remained on the leaded windows and on the door of the porch. The front garden was overgrown and unkempt. It was plain to see that Fosse was no gardener.

Seymour rapped loudly on the large knocker, a hall light illuminated and Fosse appeared in the doorway. 'Come in, Charlie,' he greeted. 'Welcome to my humble abode.'

Fosse disappeared into the kitchen to make drinks, after he had shown Seymour into the living room. It was effectively a private library. Shelves overflowed with books and folders or were strewn with a profusion of essays, notes and other papers. Between the bookcases, walls hung with old photos and sepia lithographs of classical subjects. On a side table, a chess game was in-progress and beside it were several Sudoku puzzle books. It was the den of an inveterate academic.

How different his own familiar world was, thought Seymour. He had never fully understood such a love of books, or the accompanying thirst for knowledge that seemed to frequent their collectors. He had no passion for such dry and dusty pursuits. School days had been distinctly unpleasant, and an abiding detestation had remained with him into adulthood. Reading was not so much a pleasure as a practical utility, but Fosse's evident love of literature reminded him very much of his own father's.

Fosse returned with two mugs of tea and invited Seymour to sit down next to him on the old leather Chesterfield sofa; it was the only unoccupied space in the room. He observed Seymour's preoccupation with his book collection.

'Read much, Charlie?' he asked.

'Not a lot, Prof - sorry, Max. Not since school days, but I do have a few books my father left me,' he replied.

'Was he a keen reader?'

'Not really, but he was a cabinet-maker by trade and had a decent collection of books on furniture. I used to help around the workshop when I was a kid. When he died, he left everything to me. I keep them mostly for sentimental reasons, but they've long been consigned to the loft. Sad, really.'

'Well books aren't everybody's cup of tea, I suppose. Each to his own.'

They spent a few moments silently sipping the dark Assam tea infusion.

'I see you're a chess player,' said Seymour at length. 'Who are you playing?'

'Just myself,' Fosse joked. 'That way I always win! Well, I suppose, it would be more accurate to say that I always lose.'

Fosse chuckled. Seymour turned to a more serious topic.

'So talk me through these latest results, Max. Your note sounded cryptic.'

'Well it is, really. The DNA is of a European male.' Fosse began. 'The hair sample and the teacup produced almost identical results to those which we found in Cameron.'

'So,' said Seymour, 'Is that unusual?'

'Yes, very. The results would appear to suggest that Pascoe and Cameron are genetically very closely related. I'd go so far as to say they had to be brothers.'

Twelve

'But Cameron has brown skin and Pascoe is definitely white.'

'I know. But, as I have already suggested, it looks like some very advanced genetic engineering was carried out on Cameron. The same may also be true of Pascoe. I suspect that this has involved some form of cloning procedure. It's the only sense I can make of it. And there's more. Pascoe shares Cameron's faultless state of health. Their DNA are almost carbon copies of each other's.

'I also took a trace of residual saliva from the rim of the tea cup and ran tests for blood group abnormalities. I was looking for anything significant like congenital conditions. It took all night because there are over 600 known blood group antigens. But, there weren't any. Had I not known otherwise, I would have thought that you had given me Cameron's samples by mistake. They were that similar. Both men appear to be perfect specimens - of what I am at a loss to know.

'I did manage to lift several really good fingerprints off the teacup, however, but it's outside my sphere of expertise. I expect you'll be able to identify them from police records.'

'Thanks, Max. This will be very useful,' said Seymour.

'So have you got round to staking out Pascoe's house yet?'

'Haven't had time,' replied Seymour. 'Too much happening, too fast. But I will as soon as I get a chance.'

'Well, you know, I have plenty of time on my hands now. The forensics are all but completed and Doctor Grant can deal with what few things are still outstanding. So I'm not essential to the work at university. I could watch the place, if you like.'

'It's a kind offer, Max,' Seymour replied. 'But that's my job, not yours, and sitting around in a car all day is not exactly fun. Surveillance is mostly drinking crap coffee, dozing off and boredom, you know. It's a bit of a menial task for a university Professor, and frankly, you're a little overqualified for the job. Besides, nobody might turn up at the address for days, even weeks or months.'

'I understand that. But it's not exactly the best use of your time and if it's only a matter of observation, I'm sure even I could manage that. Anyway, I'd quite like the chance,' said Fosse. 'I always fancied trying my hand at sleuthing. Different to my usual work anyway.'

'You're mad Max, (no pun intended). Surveillance is a bloody awful job.'

'Go on, Charlie, be a sport and give me a chance.'

'I don't know.' Seymour hesitated. 'How sure are you that you're up for this?'

'I'm sure.'

'Okay. On two conditions,' insisted Seymour. 'First, you must keep your mobile switched on at all times. Second, if there's any movement ... anything at all mind you, call me immediately. And don't try to do anything yourself.'

'That's three conditions. But okay, I promise. Phone you and do nothing. Got it.'

'Right. But let's be clear. I don't want you rushing into something from which you can't extricate yourself. Leave heroics to the professionals. You will have no legal authority. You will be just observing, okay?'

'Yes, Charlie. Just observation, nothing else.'

'And keep this between us, okay?'

'Understood. Loud and clear. That's settled then.'

As they continued sipping tea, Seymour's attention was drawn to the photographs that hung around the room. 'Are these pictures of your family, Max? I understood you to say you were single.'

'Well, I am, now. But I was married. Once.'

'I would never have guessed it,' said Seymour. 'You seem like the stereotypical bachelor.'

'Most people think of me that way. The fact is, I was widowed many years ago, long before I came to live

Twelve

up here. That photograph is thirty years old.'

'Sorry Max. I apologise if I've been too inquisitive. It's just that you've never spoken of your wife before.'

'No, it's okay. It was a long time ago. I still have all the memories, of course, but time has passed and we all have to go on living.'

'May I ask how she died?'

'It was pancreatic cancer. It had become inoperable and irreversible.'

'Must have been awful,' said Seymour. 'Who's the little girl in the other picture?'

'My daughter, Susan.'

'Your daughter? So where is she now?'

'She lives down south in Kent. Married, with teenage children of her own.'

'That's a fair distance. Do you get to see them often?'

'I've hardly seen her at all since her mother died. Just occasionally at Christmas or Easter, but we're not close, and we don't get in touch very often. It's been almost a year since I saw my grandchildren. Things are what you might call strained.'

'Why's that?'

'She could never forgive me for not being there while her mother was dying. I can't blame Susan. I was young and working in the laboratory all the hours that God sent. Sometimes I'd be doing a thirty-six hour stretch and catching brief catnaps in the staff room when I could. I wasn't at home as much as I should have been, you see. And, when I was, it was at some unholy hour in the morning. Not exactly good for a marriage. My wife died late one evening while I was fast asleep in an armchair. When they did manage to rouse me, she had already passed away.

'The effect on my daughter was really bad, as you can imagine. She felt abandoned. She was the image of her mother, and for that very reason I couldn't bear to look at her for a long time; it just hurt too much. The family blamed me. I know that's ridiculous, but I still have those guilt feelings, even after all this time. Anyway, Susan went to live with her grandparents in Kent and has remained there ever since. I was in no fit state to look after a young child anyway. As the years passed and the status quo became normal, she just never moved back up here to be with me and I didn't send for her. I suppose I should have, but the occasion never seemed opportune. Kent was probably the best place for her, all things considered. Then she went off to university in London and the gulf between us became unbridgeable. And that, as they say, was that.'

*

Seymour went to police central records next morning. If Pascoe had ever had fingerprints taken, then they should be in the database. DVLA files had established that he had obtained a UK driving license, though there was no record of his ever having taken a driving test. After several hours in front of the monitor scrolling through countless files, the search routine finally concluded with an unequivocal message.

"No matching files found."

'Shit!' said Seymour out loud. Dead end! Frustrated, he sat thinking for a while, when the archivist walked over.

'Not found what you're looking for, detective?' she enquired.

'Nothing. Waste of bloody time! Excuse my French.'

'Oh, I'm used to it – no need to apologise,' she replied. 'Have you tried the Europol and Interpol databases,' she suggested.

'Are they available?' he asked.

'Yes. We have access to both from this terminal.'

Seymour had not considered this option and his

Twelve

countenance immediately brightened. He snapped up the offer and spent most of the remainder of the day examining both databases. By late afternoon he found just two matches for Pascoe's fingerprints. One had been taken within the last year in the Camargue Region of southern France and another recorded in Bosnia-Herzegovina in the early 1990s. Pascoe had entered France using an American passport and passed through several Balkan countries as a Swiss national. Records identified his full name as Arthur Donald Pascoe. This name had been used for many years, so it was reasonable to assume it was his real name. But what, Seymour wondered, was the American or Swiss connection? Pascoe sounded decidedly English.

He decided that, while these databases were available, he might as well run a speculative fingerprint search for Patrick Cameron. As luck had it, he found just one reference. It was for entry into the Somalia-Eritrea Region of East Africa from the Sudan in 1992 - a war zone that had already been flagged up by Caroline Massey.

*

He met up with Fosse at home later that afternoon.

'There's nothing known for Pascoe in the UK,' Seymour began. 'Not to any British police force at least, but I have found two fingerprint matches for him abroad. One in France quite recently and the other in Bosnia during the Balkan Wars in the mid-1990s. Here's the interesting thing. While I was at it, I also did fingerprint searches for Cameron, and found one also in the 1990s, in the Sudan and Somalia of all places. MI6 had already mentioned his having been in that region, but not that far back.'

'Intriguing,' Fosse replied. 'What was he doing in East Africa?'

'Apparently he was working with Médécins Sans Frontières, and like Pascoe, he used a Swiss passport. But here, read it all for yourself.'

He handed Fosse the printouts of the database search with a few handwritten notes that he had made in the margins. 'I must say, these two men certainly have been getting around,' remarked Fosse. 'Somalia and Bosnia in the nineties. Both were the locations of disastrous wars and the resulting tragic human crises.

'If memory serves me right, before Eritrea achieved independence following years of civil war in the early 1990s, the country suffered a major famine. That war had claimed several hundred thousand lives and there was international concern over the widespread abuse of human rights. You probably saw it on television; it dominated the news for months.'

'Can't really say I remember. There have been so many civil wars and famines in Africa,' Seymour replied with dispassionate cynicism. 'They all merge into one big catastrophe and I can't distinguish one from another.'

'Well, the drought that followed spread across the whole of East Africa,' Fosse continued. 'Governments in both Eritrea and Somalia were slow to act and it deteriorated into a disaster of Biblical proportions. Aid relief was prevented from getting through and material often fell into the hands of the terrorists and insurgents. When bands of militia became involved, the region degenerated into a war zone. Borders were ignored or non-existent. The International Red Cross and United Nations peacekeeping forces withdrew and supplies dried up. Many thousands starved or died unnecessarily of disease.

'Neighbouring Somalia saw the emergence of private armies, powerful warlords and militant sectarian groups including jihadists like al-Shabab and Hizbul-Islam. Many still hold a grip on large areas of that country and it's fair to say that Somalia is probably one of the most dangerous places in the world today.'

'So what do you think Pascoe and Cameron were doing in these war zones? They were hardly tourist

Twelve

destinations at that time.'

'Well, you did say Cameron was working with Médécins Sans Frontières?'

'Yes, I did, but the trail goes cold there. He disappeared completely and there's no record of him ever leaving Somalia. He was presumed dead at the time, probably a casualty of war.'

'But clearly he did get out. We know he died here, a few days ago.'

'That's true, and even more mysterious.'

'Bear with me a moment, I may also have something about Bosnia while we're on the subject of war zones,' said Fosse. He rooted among one of the bookshelves and brought out a large volume – *"Sarajevo under Siege"*.

'Just as I thought. Here it is.' He licked a finger and thumbed through a few pages.

'In 1992 the battle for Sarajevo was in full swing,' he began. 'It followed the break-up of Yugoslavia. Following the death of General Tito, the former Communist Bloc completely fell apart and the country soon degenerated into civil warfare. Before that, Sarajevo had been a beautiful city and a popular holiday resort. But after the war the city was little more than a bomb site, and hasn't fully recovered to this day.'

'I remember the conflict but not really what it was all about,' Seymour confessed.

'It started when Serbia invaded Bosnia-Herzegovina in an attempt to create a new Greater Serbian state. Their forces subjected Sarajevo to continuous bombardment for more than two years. Over eleven thousand people lost their lives, many of them children. Genocide was carried out in Srebrenica and Zepa, where thousands of men and boys were killed and around thirty thousand Bosnian Muslims were expelled. It was yet another human catastrophe with serious war crimes on both sides. Legal process is still going on in international courts of justice, though many of the perpetrators are still at large.

'Thanks for the potted history lesson, Professor,' said Seymour, somewhat sarcastically. 'But what does all that have to do with our investigation?'

'I'm not exactly sure,' he replied. 'However, these two seem to crop up in disaster zones regularly, and I know how you feel about coincidences.'

'That's true. But, talking of unlikely coincidences, something else occurred to me regarding what you told me about Cruikshank,' Seymour continued. 'You said you worked with him at Porton Down.'

'That's correct. Initially we were recruited to work in the Common Cold Unit.'

'I thought Porton was an MOD chemical weapons establishment.'

'It is. At least, that's what it's best known for, but it also does a good deal of other stuff. I was very happy there until we were put to work on biological and chemical weapons. Then I felt I needed to get out, and left as soon as I could. But I'm not sure whether Cruikshank stayed on or not.'

'That's my point,' said Seymour. 'Maybe Cruikshank continued working for them, possibly on genetics. Alzheimer's and dementia could have been a cover for military weapons research. Something a lot more pressing than research into the common cold or dementia has kept MI6 interested in him.'

'That may be. But I assure you that Cruikshank's published research on dementia is quite genuine. It's well authenticated and proven.'

'Okay, I'll grant you that. So maybe he is best known for that research, but he could have been working covertly on chemical weapons. In which case MI6 would still regard him as a valuable asset, worth keeping an eye on, wouldn't they?'

'Possibly. But this is pure supposition.'

Twelve

'Maybe so, but it would explain their continued interest. If Cruikshank's work at Porton Down was highly sensitive, or posed a potential vulnerability in their security, they would want a lid kept on it. They would need somebody to plug any embarrassing leaks, wouldn't they? An outsider, like me. A throwaway, kept in the picture just enough to be useful, but not knowing what's really going on. I think they might have recruited me, not as a copper, where my findings would be well reported and in the public domain, but as an MI6 agent, gagged by the Official Secrets Act. Cameron and Pascoe might just be a smokescreen to divert attention away from what Cruikshank was really working on for the military.'

Chapter 10: Jeddah

It was early in the morning when the motorcycle courier arrived at the front door. He was clad from head to foot in black leathers and wearing a full-face crash helmet.

'Parcel, sir. Are you Mister Charles Seymour?' He addressed him curtly.

'Yes, I'm Charles Seymour.'

Seymour could not see the face through the gold mirror finish of the visor that remained fully closed throughout. The courier took out a sealed package from the knapsack around his shoulder, presented it to him and requested a signature. Then he wished him a pleasant day and returned to his machine. Seymour stood watching from the doorway for a time, as the motorcycle sped off down the road. Then, he went indoors to open the parcel.

The small package was fastened securely with brown tape and an outer strong ribbon tied tightly and, somewhat incongruously, sealed at the knot with red wax. When he finally managed to open it, Seymour found that it contained a small flash memory stick and an accompanying note. It had been sent direct by Caroline Massey and it was rubber stamped in red ink.

"For Your Eyes Only - Erase After Viewing."

It was both cryptic and, as it turned out, unnecessary. The message began:

"Seymour.

We have come into possession of this news bulletin from Pakistan. The memory stick contains short CCTV clips that may be relevant to your investigations. Two of them show that Cameron was at the scene of the failed bombing attempt in Lahore, but in a role we had not anticipated. The other captures his arrival at the airport in Jeddah, talking to the man you have identified as Arthur Pascoe. Make it a priority to find out what these two had to do with each other and what they were doing there.

C.M."

Twelve

After getting dressed, Seymour placed the memory stick into his laptop and ran the first of the three film clips. It contained a recent report from the international news service of Pakistani Television. The excerpt showed a handcuffed man being roughly bundled into the back of a police van. A noisy frenetic crowd of onlookers and protesters were kicking and spitting at him. The strap line below read:

"TERRORIST ARRESTED IN LAHORE AFTER ABORTIVE CAR BOMBING."

He had assumed that Cameron was the would-be bomber, but, as the clip progressed, it became clear that his assumption was erroneous. Far from it - Cameron was not the perpetrator. He could be seen clearly in front of the crowd of onlookers, not dressed in a suit as he had been at the fatal accident in England, but in traditional Pakistani dress. He merged perfectly with the indigenous population.

As the clip progressed, it showed Cameron lifted shoulder high, while those nearby pushed forward to shake him by the hand. He was being acclaimed as a public hero. His reaction was modest and, clearly embarrassed by the accolade, when he became aware of the newsreel camera focussed upon him, he covered his face with one hand. Not modesty, thought Seymour, more an attempt to remain unrecognised. Evidently he did not relish being thrust into the public limelight.

It was a complete turnaround. All the assumptions based on profiling were wrong. Cameron had foiled the attempted bombing.

The second sequence showed a press conference in a Pakistani police station. The high room temperature was evident from the waving of makeshift fans or folded newspapers and by the constant mopping of foreheads with handkerchiefs. The station was packed with journalists and photographers, and a senior police officer, who sported a magnificently curled black moustache, presided against the constant clatter of camera shutters. His shirt was wet with perspiration, despite the cooling fan above his head. Eventually, he stood up and called the meeting to order. The audience settled and when the room had fallen silent, he addressed them in Urdu. His words were subtitled on screen in English:

"Had it not been for the quick thinking and noble act of daring carried out by this passer-by, the potential bomb blast would have devastated an area of many hundreds of metres surrounding the square, with a catastrophic outcome involving severe casualties and deaths. We have no way to identify this honourable man, who seems to have completely disappeared into the crowd. We would like this local hero to come forward to accept our thanks and those of the parents of the schoolchildren whose lives were spared as a result of his prompt intervention."

Seymour loaded the next sequence. It showed the busy arrivals concourse at Jeddah Airport. It was in low resolution and the picture was blurred, but as the security camera zoomed into the crowd at the gate, he could make out the figure waiting there as that of Arthur Donald Pascoe.

He paused the clip several times, to assure himself that this was the unmistakable profile of the man whom he had met briefly in the Lake District.

Cameron emerged from the arrivals control gate. He was dressed in the traditional long white robe typically worn by men in Saudi Arabia, and over that a cloak, which was trimmed with gold. His headdress was the Saudi gutra, a square cloth held in place by a plain black cord. Pascoe greeted him with a warm handshake and followed this with a bear-like embrace as brothers might. Perhaps Fosse's assumption was right – maybe they were related after all. At last, Seymour had photographic evidence that the two

Twelve

men worked together, as he had already suspected and as Jameson had predicted.

Finally, the two men walked out from the terminal building beyond camera range. Seymour ran both video clips back and forth several times, pausing and slowing them to confirm that he had not been mistaken in his identity of both figures. It was the first time he had ever seen Cameron alive and it took a few moments to sink in.

*

It was the day after Pascoe and Cameron's airport meeting that Aisha Halabi had driven the bright yellow school bus from Jeddah city centre down King Faisal Road towards the southern suburb of As Sarawat. Aisha was new to the job. School buses for girls were a recent innovation in the nation's education system, and in keeping with Islamic tradition they were chaperoned by a female driver. Aisha was proud that she had been selected for such a prestigious and emancipated role. It was an honour for her and for all Saudi women.

As she drove on, leaving Jeddah city centre far behind, the chattering noise of some twenty-five schoolgirls filled its air-conditioned interior with a din fit to burst her eardrums. Or it would have, had she not been wearing earphones connected to the iPod in the breast pocket of her uniform shirt. She was so completely engrossed in the loud music that, even had she been prepared, she would not have heard the loud explosive crack as the offside tyre on the front wheel of the coach blew out.

Her first realisation of the impending calamity was the sudden sharp wrench of the steering wheel, almost torn out of her hands by force. The wheel spun uncontrollably to the right and the whole vehicle careered over onto its side, ploughing sand before it and carving a fifty-metre long furrow alongside the asphalt at the edge of the carriageway.

What seemed an eternity must have been no more than a few seconds. At that moment, all time and space seemed to stretch like soft elastic, played out in slow stop motion and devoid of all form or structure, as if it were happening to some other disembodied person, and not to herself.

But she was dragged rushing swiftly back into the present as her earphones fell away in the impact. There followed the crunching, grinding clamour of sheering metal and breaking glass as the bus skidded groaning along the ground before shuddering to a halt against the mound of sand which it had bulldozed ahead of it. The rest of that split second saw her head forcibly smash into the front windscreen as her unrestrained body shot forward, and she had a brief microsecond to reflect on the inadvisability of not wearing her seatbelt.

The steering wheel airbag failed to inflate with sufficient rapidity but the windscreen resisted, cushioned by the bank of sand that had built up in front. It held in place and withstood complete shattering, as a growing network of crazed fractures spread across its entire surface.

When the bus finally came to rest, its engine began to race at ever-increasing revolutions and higher frequencies as the rear drive wheels continued turning, no longer slowed by the inertia of the carriageway.

Aisha fought to maintain conscious throughout, but, dazed and bruised, she became aware of the blood trickling down from the blunt trauma wound on her forehead. Then, as the initial shock subsided, she was mindful of the screaming and moaning of injured girls in the body of the bus behind her. She stood as best she could but her right leg was badly sprained and painful when she placed weight upon it. She turned to look back. Figures lay around in contorted heaps against what had been the side window, but which now formed the floor of the overturned vehicle. Students had been thrown around

Twelve

the interior, a mangle of arms, legs and schoolbags; many were injured and bleeding, while others fought to disentangle themselves from the chaos.

As she struggled to stand upright, Aisha detected the creeping pall of black smoke and the stench of fuel oil in the air. Crackling sparks were coming from the engine compartment at the rear of the bus. Then, looking back through the rear window, she saw and heard the explosion as the engine burst into full flame and caught fire, projecting innumerable small splinters of glass into the compartment, eliciting a fresh round of screaming from the terrified schoolgirls.

Sharp glass shards peppered Aisha's arms and shoulders and several small islands of blood oozed out through her tunic top. Then, holding tightly onto handrails she made her way through the increasingly smoke-filled cabin back to see what help she could offer to the injured. None of her training had prepared her for this and the dawning realisation that they were effectively trapped inside an incendiary tomb made her shudder.

She held her nerve and looked for an exit. The way forward was impassable because of the build-up of sand against the windscreen; the rear of the bus was now a raging inferno; the side window, which was supposed to serve as an emergency escape exit, lay buried in the sand on the floor. She raised her eyes heavenwards. A silent mimed prayer flickered across her lips. Seeing that the uppermost side of the bus offered a clear view of blue sky through the remaining unbroken windows she knew that this was the only way out. But it was three metres above her head and almost beyond reach.

Aisha stood on an upturned seat as best she could, removed one of her shoes and tried repeatedly to smash the glass above her head. But to no avail - the toughened laminated glass did not yield and the dull flat sole of her shoe proved less than useless. She thought that they would all now most certainly perish and prepared to make peace with her maker. Suddenly a voice boomed out above her.

'Stand clear!' it shouted in perfect Arabic.

'Who's there? Please help us,' she screamed.

'Hold on. We have come to get you out.'

'Allah is praised.'

'Move away,' the voice continued. 'I'm about to break the glass. Cover your face.'

She tumbled backwards as the loud crack of a metallic impact was followed by showers of glass fragments falling into the compartment. Immediately hands reached down into the cabin and she was lifted clear of the blazing vehicle. Two men stood on top of the bus and pulled out the girls from the smoke-filled interior, one by one, before lowering them into the arms of waiting helpers.

By now, a crowd of villagers from nearby As Sarawat, who were alerted by the noise of the accident, had gathered around the overturned vehicle. Emergency services had already been alerted and within minutes police, fire and ambulance vehicles arrived on the scene to the accompaniment of flashing blue lights and the wailing of sirens.

Paramedics immediately began to treat the injured that lay spread around on the sand clear of the burning vehicle. Many were blooded and lacerated, a few had suffered smoke inhalation, others had broken arms and legs; but none was injured critically and miraculously, none had perished. Fire fighters quickly got to work putting out the blaze, foaming down the burning bus till all flames had extinguished and it resembled some great meringue sitting incongruously on the hot red sand.

Aisha's cuts and abrasions were treated and the blood flow on her forehead staunched, but, like many of the other casualties, paramedics thought it best that she be checked over in hospital, particularly in view of her head wound. Despite the look of her injuries, somewhat exaggerated by the many bloodstains on her tunic and the gash on her forehead, they were slight. She had been lucky.

Twelve

Before she was taken off in a waiting ambulance, the commanding police officer questioned her concerning the sequence of events leading up to the accident. She confessed that it was all over so quickly that she had little time to take it all in, but went on to recount the quick thinking and speedy actions of her two rescuers as well as the high risk they took in climbing up onto the burning bus. They had, she insisted, saved the lives of everyone on board and without their brave actions all of them would now be dead. They were intervening angels sent from God, she concluded.

All later attempts to locate the two heroes proved fruitless; neither of the men could be found. Arthur Pascoe and Patrick Cameron had already disappeared into the crowd of onlookers and sloped away secretively into the narrow back streets of As Sarawat.

Chapter 11: Acquisition

Seymour was summoned once more to Vauxhall Cross. He was shown directly into Caroline Massey's office. Another man was present, standing, arms folded, at the back of the room. He looked like any one of the many other plain clothes agents that frequented the building, but Seymour had not seen him before. By the ubiquitous dark suit, the necktie clipped tightly into the shirt collar and his close-cropped hair, Seymour guessed him to be American, probably CIA.

Initially, Massey did not refer to the stranger.

'Thank you for your report, Seymour,' she began. 'We have now positively identified Arthur Pascoe as the second man in the airport security camera footage. It seems that he has used several different passports and assumed a variety of nationalities, passing himself off variously as American, British, Swiss, and possibly Spanish or Saudi Arabian. We also believe that Patrick Cameron used similar multiple identities, consequently both Interpol and the CIA have got wind of it.

'Your discovery of their presence in the two war zones has particularly concerned us. The Somalia connection has flagged up special departmental interest, in view of the emergence of al-Shabab insurgents, and the proliferation of piracy in the Indian Ocean. Although the war has technically ended in Eritrea, their conflict has migrated into Somalia and our latest intelligence suggests that a civil war may already be brewing in South Sudan.

'Cameron apparently entered the region on either a Swiss or American passport. The CIA documentation found in the car wreck has been verified as genuine. How he got such papers is a mystery, which has concerned them sufficiently for the Agency to join the investigation. They have indicated a willingness to share information with our security services. We are also speaking to Swiss authorities and Médécins Sans Frontières to see what they can tell us

Twelve

of his involvement in East Africa, and how he acquired authentication.

'This brings me to the Bosnian connection. Due to the outstanding war crimes investigations, we are of the opinion that this does merit our attention, and we are sending you to Sarajevo as soon as we can arrange for the appropriate paperwork.'

Seymour was annoyed that arrangements had been made for him without consultation, but it seemed to be the way things were done in the service, and he said nothing.

Then Massey introduced the stranger, who had observed the proceedings in silent circumspection, his eyes not diverting once from Seymour.

'Can I introduce you to Agent Richard Dexter of the Central Intelligence Agency? Dexter has joined us following the discovery of the American documents.'

Seymour had been right; Dexter was a Company man.

'Pascoe is already known to us,' Dexter began. 'He's been on our Watch List for some time, but we've never come face to face with him, as I believe you have done. Your investigation has led us to re-examine his case, which had been on the shelf in Langley for some time.

'We first became aware of Pascoe during a hijacking incident in July 2005 at Denver Airport, where he turned up as a hostage negotiator. An American Airlines Boeing 757 inbound from Heathrow had declared an in-flight emergency when three armed men took control. The plane was ordered to taxi over to the Domestic Cargo Terminal at the far end of the airfield, well away from the main passenger terminals. Terrorists were holding more than 300 passengers and crew hostage and demanded the release of seven suspected Taliban Afghanis detained at the Guantanamo Bay facility. They threatened to execute hostages within the hour if we did not comply with their demands.

'The man we now know as Pascoe persuaded them

to stand down and give themselves up without a single shot being fired or any loss of life. But alarms bells rang when he failed to show up for debriefing after the incident. Somehow he managed to slip away and leave the airfield unnoticed, despite the heavy security cordon we had thrown around the perimeter.'

Seymour interjected. 'Are you saying that he was authorised as an official hostage negotiator?'

'Well, no - not exactly.' Dexter looked decidedly embarrassed. 'That's the problem. There was no such authorisation. The guy just turned up at the scene. He was wearing a cop's uniform, flashed some kind of badge and paperwork before taking over and getting stuck in. He acted completely independently. Nobody had ever seen him before, but he seemed to know what he was doing. We have no idea where he came from, how he gained access to a secure airport, or how he learned of the hostage taking. There was a complete news and media blackout in place during the course of the incident. There have been a few asses kicked in airport security, I can tell you. We think he probably used the US passport as ID.'

'So how did he get hold of that? Surely they're not that easy to obtain?'

'No, they're not. His was perfectly legitimate. An American passport was issued to him on the basis of a birth certificate which was recorded at Grantsville in Clay County, West Virginia in 1959. Trouble is, Pascoe had assumed the identity of a dead infant. There was no reason to cross-reference it with death records, but had there been, it would have revealed that the genuine Arthur Pascoe died of diphtheria as an infant aged 16 months. The infant was buried in the local cemetery in 1961.'

'It appears that whoever he really is,' said Massey, 'He can slip into either British or American identities, and perhaps many others, at will.'

'Incidentally,' Dexter continued. 'Pascoe had also obtained other documentation based on that false birth certificate and the passport. He holds a US driving license, an American Express Platinum Card and has a social security number. He also has a bank account in Switzerland. We're trying to get access, but the Swiss are proving extremely uncooperative, despite international agreements. We are still working on that - eventually we hope to persuade them to allow us to look into his account.

'Pascoe, and most probably Cameron, spoke Arabic, possibly French, Spanish and who knows what other languages. According to eye witness accounts they speak many languages fluently. That's quite staggering in itself, but it gets even more impressive. At the Denver Airport incident, for example, according to ground staff, Pascoe spoke with a Colorado accent. And from what Miss Massey tells me, you reported that Pascoe has an educated British accent.

'But that's only part of it. The Agency has evidence that both Pascoe and Cameron have made appearances in conflicts in Libya and Syria over the past few years as well as the Balkans and East Africa as was reported earlier. So you can see why we're interested in these men.'

'They seem particularly attracted to war zones,' commented Seymour.

'They do indeed. But time presses on,' said Massey. 'Now, as to your trip to Bosnia. It's a relatively safe environment now, unlike Eritrea and Somalia, though Bosnians are still a little wary of Western Europeans. So we have arranged for you to liaise with a local police officer. Inspector Sasa Terzic will be meeting up with you at Sarajevo Airport. He's worked with the European Police Mission in Bosnia since 2002. Apart from his native Bosnian, he speaks Serbo-Croat, a little Albanian and is fluent in English, so you should experience no language problems. He will act as interpreter as well as your guide. Terzic lived through the Balkan conflict and is therefore very familiar with some of the more sensitive issues. More importantly, he should be able to overcome any local reticence in talking to you, a foreigner.'

*

Back in Manchester, Seymour immediately went round to see Fosse at the university.

'It's been confirmed' he began. 'Cameron and Pascoe worked together, Max. MI6 sent me the security camera footage of them meeting at the airport terminal in Jeddah as well as in Manchester. It was crystal clear; both men can be identified on it. Cameron had flown into Jeddah, Pascoe was waiting to meet him and they made a two-day stopover.'

'So now you've made the connection, all that's left to do is to find out what they were doing in Jeddah for two days.'

'The CIA is dealing with that end. But they have no more idea than we do, nor where they went to afterwards. I think the gesture is more to do with politics than cooperation.'

'I see. So the CIA is now involved?'

'Yep. I already met one of their operatives in London. But enough about me. How did your surveillance go? I'm assuming that as you didn't phone, nothing significant happened.'

'Not a sausage. I spent all day and a night watching. Nobody came or went. You were quite right. It was very boring. Next time I'll take a book or some music to pass the time.'

'Sorry, Max, but I did warn you, that's just the way it goes sometimes.'

Just then, the office phone rang. Fosse picked up the receiver and listened intently. 'Yes, DI Seymour is here,' he said. 'Would you like to speak to him?'

He handed the receiver to Seymour. It was Chief Inspector Forman.

Twelve

'Yes, sir,' said Seymour. 'What can I do for you?'

Fosse could not make out what was being said by Forman but Seymour's face was troubled as he listened in silence. Eventually, he replaced the handset. 'Well?' Fosse queried. 'Don't keep me in suspense.'

'It's Cameron,' he replied. 'His body has been taken from the university mortuary. Somebody has acquired it!'

'Acquired? Who?' demanded Fosse.

'They don't know, but it's disappeared.'

*

The constant commuting between Manchester and London was becoming exasperating, but Seymour held his impatience in check and responded the next day to yet another summons to Vauxhall Cross.

'I've brought you and Agent Dexter back in,' said Massey. 'In view of recent developments relating to the disappearance of Cameron's body from the university in Manchester and the new element that has materialised, I thought we should meet again.'

'Any clues as to where the body's gone?' asked Seymour.

'Its current whereabouts are unknown, but we have been able to obtain all the CCTV recordings for the university campus last night. These cover the main reception area, as well as the front and rear entrances. We also have images of the two people who removed the body. Unfortunately, they're impossible to identify. They came totally prepared and took steps to avoid direct facial exposure to the cameras. We believe that they may have spent some time surveying the building in advance, probably posing as students.'

The recordings showed two people alighting from a black Ford Transit van and entering the university building.

'That's the delivery goods entrance and leads directly to the refectory kitchens,' said Massey. 'From there on we lose all trace of them. There are no cameras in this area and they obviously knew that. Cameras are mostly concentrated on the exterior entrances to the buildings and in the main reception foyer. We assume a third person may have been driving, but he or she is not in either shot.

'Now, if I fast-forward the clip six minutes, you can see the two of them leaving the building carrying a black body bag.'

'But how were they able to remove a body from a secure building unchallenged?' Seymour queried.

'They had the right documentation,' said Dexter, who had thus far sat in silence. 'Again. The paperwork they presented to the night guard was convincing and appropriate. But we've been unable to find any agency, either British or American that could have sanctioned the removal. It's just like the Denver incident. Whoever these people are, they seem to obtain apparently legitimate documentation at the drop of a hat. According to the security guard, the authorisation was countersigned on behalf of the Joint Intelligence Committee and on official government notepaper.

'We had no active assets anywhere in the UK last night,' Dexter continued. 'They were not CIA, so as you can imagine, the Company views this incident with a degree of seriousness and urgency. Miss Massey also confirms that according to the JIC, the British had no operations in progress last night either.'

'That's correct,' said Massey. 'Neither of our Security Services gave authorisation for the removal of the body from university premises.'

'So who the hell are they?' said Seymour.

'On the face of it, these people appear to be part of the same cell as Pascoe and Cameron. It's possible that someone may have infiltrated one or more of our departments. As for their identities, we know that one of

Twelve

them was a woman. It's not much, but I think we might have seen her before.'

'It looks like the woman at the hospital,' said Seymour.

'We have run the tape over many times, and the woman does indeed appear to be the same person who visited the hospital. You may remember that she claimed to be his sister. Her physical build and clothing appear to be similar, if not the same, and if you look at this one frame...'

She paused the clip to reveal a profile of the female's head as it could be partially seen beneath the hood of her sweatshirt.

'A blonde. It is the same woman,' said Seymour. 'Whoever she is.'

'She doesn't match anything we have on file,' said Massey. 'She's a new face to us, judging by what little we can see of it.'

'Do we have any idea why the body was taken?' asked Seymour.

'No,' said Massey.

'But the guard insists she sounded Russian, or Polish,' said Dexter. 'We have been able to enhance the image to identify the van. The number plate is quite clear.'

'Well that should give us some kind of a lead,' said Seymour.

'It does. We identified it very easily,' Massey replied, somewhat embarrassed. 'I'm afraid it's one of ours!'

'Ours?' asked Seymour incredulously.

'It's an MI6 vehicle. It was taken out from under our noses. It's presently parked in the garage below this very building. Somebody took it to Manchester and drove it back again completely unchallenged. They signed it out, and back in again, but the signature is indecipherable. We are questioning the garage staff and already have a team going over the vehicle with a fine toothcomb, but don't expect to find anything. If experience is anything to go by, their attention to fine detail will be faultless and there will be no clues left behind.'

Chapter 12: Assignation

The family had just finished their weekly shopping. Seymour was returning the trolley back to the storage bay while Sarah loaded the groceries into the back of the car. Suddenly, a car flashed its headlights at him from across the parking lot. He looked over and saw a hand waving at him through the windscreen. Curious, he walked over and tapped on the driver's window. It lowered and Katherine Chaplin looked out at him with a wide beaming smile.

'Hello, detective,' she said.

'Katie,' he replied. 'I didn't know you shopped here.'

'I don't.'

'So what are you doing?' he asked.

'What d'you think?'

A slight shiver ran down his spine and he looked back towards his own car. His wife sat observing them and waiting impatiently.

'Christ, Katie. Are you stalking me?' He looked terrified.

'Anything's possible, Charlie,' she replied. 'What if I was?'

He hesitated, at a complete loss for words. Could she be serious? How could he explain away her appearance at the car park to his wife? No time to think.

'I must go,' he panicked. 'Sarah's waiting. We'll talk some other time – not now.'

'Okay,' she replied. 'I'll be in touch.'

He walked back to the car as nonchalantly as he could.

'So who was that?' asked Sarah, as they drove away.

'Katherine Chaplin,' he replied. 'She's Doctor Grant's assistant at the university. She's sat in on a few meetings about this Cameron case.'

'I see.'

'I hardly know her really,' he excused himself unnecessarily.

'She's a very pretty girl,' Sarah remarked.

'Is she?' Seymour replied in as deadpan a tone as he could muster. 'Can't say I'd really noticed.'

Sarah *tut-tutted* loudly and lightly chided her husband. 'Oh do grow up, Charlie. It's perfectly okay to admit that she's pretty and that you've noticed her.'

'Okay, okay. She's pretty and I've noticed her. Are you satisfied now?'

'Well I am,' she ended. 'Just make sure you are.'

*

Later, as Seymour answered his office telephone, he recognised the voice instantly. 'Katie.' He replied. 'You really put the wind up me showing up at the supermarket like that. What did you want anyway?'

'Just to meet up and talk a little,' she replied.

He paused a while and against his better judgement, agreed to a meeting. 'Okay, but briefly. The Crazy Horse Bar, then?'

'Yes, that'll do.'

'After work. Say around seven o'clock?'

'I look forward to it. Kiss, kiss!'

She rang off.

*

When Seymour arrived at the wine bar, Katherine was already seated in a side booth and had ordered drinks. Opposite her on the table, stood a regulation glass of sparkling water.

'I did get the drink right didn't I?' she asked as Seymour sat down.

'Yeh, that's fine,' he replied. (More bloody sparkling water, he thought. Last thing I need.) He was

Twelve

about to begin a prepared speech, but she pre-empted him.

'I've wanted to see you ever since our last meeting ended so abruptly,' she said with a hint of self-consciousness. 'I feel I need to apologise - yet again.'

'No need. Just don't turn up unannounced again.'

'I promise. And I'm sorry about the outrageous flirting the other night. Forcing you to kiss me like that put you in an awful spot. I regretted it immediately.'

'Well,' he continued. 'I was taken off guard, but as for the kiss, well ... you have no need to apologise.'

'But I do. I shouldn't have thrown myself at you like that.'

He took a sip of water. 'Katie,' he continued. 'Can I talk straight?'

'Uh-oh. Sounds like a brush-off is coming.'

'No, it's not that. It's just that gorgeous young women don't often come on to old coppers like me.'

'So you really do think I'm gorgeous?'

'Of course I do. You're beautiful,' he continued, 'and, it was obvious something was going on between us. But whatever that something is, it just can't happen. Under different circumstances who knows? We might have taken it to an inevitable conclusion.'

'So you think there was an inevitable conclusion?'

'You knew where it could lead. You were willing it.'

'So what if I did want something to happen? I think you would have too, if you weren't so afraid.'

'Too bloody right I was afraid, and I still am. People's happiness is at stake. Not just my family but also your own. Like I said, this is going nowhere.'

'You don't need to worry about me.' Her voice became stronger and increasingly determined. 'I'm a grown woman, Charlie, not a silly girl, whatever you may think. I can take care of myself. I'm not asking you to risk your marriage and I don't want you to leave your wife. I'm happy with my life as it is. It's just that I haven't been able to get you out of my mind since the other night and it's driving me crazy.'

'I don't know what to say, Katie.'

'Just say yes,' she urged. 'We can be very discreet. Nobody need ever know.'

'But I'd know, that's the problem. And sooner or later the secret would be out.'

She emptied her glass and reached for her handbag. 'In that case, will you take me back home please?'

'Of course I will.'

They walked back to her apartment block in stony silence till they arrived at the front door.

'Just a little one for goodbye then,' she said.

He stepped forward and meekly placed a dry peck on her cheek, with the lightest of contact, hardly touching her skin. Then he stepped away. Her eyes, however, looked directly at his mouth as she held on to his sleeve and drew him into her so that he pressed her hard against the wall. Unwilling to resist further, he began to kiss her mouth feverishly, as her response became equally impassioned. Eventually, they separated and stood looking at each other for a while, astonished by their unbridled fervour, before she turned and went indoors.

'Good night, Charlie,' she said, and through the glass of the closed door she blew another kiss to him.

*

'Sorry to call you so late, Max,' said Seymour. 'Can I come round?'

'Of course, old man, I'll put the kettle on.'

Fifteen minutes later, the two men sat opposite each other in Fosse's library. 'I need to talk to somebody, Max,' said Seymour, 'and you're the nearest thing to a friend that I have.'

'I'll try to take that as the compliment I'm sure you intended.'

Twelve

'Sorry. That didn't quite come out as I meant it to, but you know what I mean. It's just that you said that if I ever needed someone to talk to ... '

'Quite so,' Fosse replied. 'What's the problem, Charlie? Drink?'

'No, it's not alcohol. Not this time. There's this woman, you see.'

'Ah ... Katherine Chaplin.' Fosse cut directly to the chase.

'Why do you assume it's Katherine Chaplin?'

'*Cherchez la femme*, Charlie. It's was pretty obvious.'

'Was it?'

'Of course. You could hardly take your eyes off her when she was around. And why not? She's a pretty girl and you're a red-blooded man in the prime of mid-life. Add two people thrown together by circumstance into the mixture and it's a no-brainer.'

'I suppose so. Trouble is, I am finding her absolutely irresistible,' Seymour confessed. 'And I'm fighting it all the way. Just not doing very well.'

'So how far have things gone between you?'

'We've kissed a couple of times.'

'Is that all?' said Fosse. 'So just stop before it gets serious. End it now if it's troubling you so much. Unless you really want to pursue it, in which case, you need to step back a little and consider the consequences.'

'I know all this. I've been through it repeatedly in my head. But it's not my head that's causing the problem.'

'How does the old maxim have it? *"Spiritus quidem promptus est caro autem infirma"*. The spirit is willing but the flesh is weak, old chap.'

'Exactly. I keep fobbing her off, but she just keeps coming on ever stronger. Nothing seems to stop her. She's voracious! I've never been in this situation before. Unfortunately, she knows full well that I'm infatuated with her and that just keeps encouraging her.'

'So you admit that it is just an infatuation?'

'Of course it is. I love my wife, I really do.'

'So this is just about sex?'

'I suppose,' Seymour admitted. 'What do think I should do?'

Fosse removed his spectacles, leaned over, and adopted a more serious countenance. 'It's not my place to tell a grown man what he should or should not be doing, Charlie. But you say you love your wife. If that's true then you already know full well what you ought to do. It seems to me that you have two options: you can go for this thing with Katherine, get this sex thing out of your system and face the consequences, or else steel yourself resolutely and walk away from her. It's a simple choice, really.'

'If only it were that simple.'

'But it is. Oh, I realise it's easy for me to say. Not quite so easy to do, though, and I wonder, were I in your position, would I be able to take my own advice?'

Chapter 13: Khartoum

It had been a typically humid day in November 1992 when Patrick Cameron's Emirates flight from Abu Dhabi arrived at Khartoum Airport. The scheduled airport transfer bus that was supposed to take him to his hotel never materialised. Cameron had telephoned ahead and they assured him that the bus had been dispatched, but after a further fruitless hour waiting, it had still not arrived. The hotel switchboard had insisted: "Shuttle is coming. Yes mister, shuttle come". But eventually he gave up and took what transport was available.

The taxi ride was a nightmare. What should have been a short uneventful journey into Khartoum was the most uncomfortable ride of Cameron's life. The cab window was permanently jammed open and clouds of fine dust blew in whenever another vehicle passed by, so that when they eventually arrived at the hotel, he was covered in a fine powdering of Sudanese sand.

He realised the moment he stepped onto the pavement that the Hotel Arosa Parc was a mistake. Its monolithic concrete structure may have been considered state-of-the-art when it was first built, but it now looked dated and sorely in need of a refreshing coat of masonry paint to cover the caked-on street grime, urine and graffiti that adorned its exterior. Inside, it was acceptably clean, at least by local standards, but it could not be considered of an international quality, despite its three star rating. The staff spoke no English. Fortunately, Cameron spoke perfect Arabic.

The receptionist, who also doubled as porter and switchboard operator, (and no doubt, thought Cameron, was probably the driver of the non-existent shuttle bus), was in complete confusion over the appropriate rate for the room, although the tariff was clearly displayed in a glass frame on the wall outside. Cameron pointed this out and the man dashed into the street to refer to it before returning, apologetically, and stating what the price for the room would be. He seemed like a nice enough fellow, despite his initial ineptitude and the over unctuousness of his manner. The hotel was not busy, and he was evidently employed as a general factotum. Judging by the level of attention extended to him and the absence of other people around the lobby, Cameron thought it likely that he would be the only guest staying at the hotel.

He was shown to his room and the first impression confirmed his worst fears; its entire fabric was coated in the same fine red dust that had blighted the taxi ride from the airport. Dust would likely be one of his abiding memories of Sudan.

Seeing Cameron's dissatisfaction, the porter hastily switched on the brass ceiling fan, which had the exact opposite effect than he intended. The sudden downdraught of its whirring blades immediately disturbed the settled layer and dust particles were whipped up spiralling back into the air. Like a shot he rushed over to open a window to let in some fresh air, but this admitted yet more dust, along with car exhaust fumes, a cacophony of street noise and the ubiquitous stench of the street. The porter went to close it again.

'Leave it. Leave it!' Cameron instructed sharply in English. The man understood perfectly, despite the language barrier. But, relenting a little of his irascibility, Cameron held out a twenty Sudanese Pound note as a gratuity, just to get rid of him. This was equivalent to about four British pounds sterling, which was perhaps a little over generous. The porter probably worked the whole week for a good deal less than that and hastily grabbed the cash before making a rapid exit.

As the dust gradually began to settle, Cameron pulled back the ornately patterned bed quilt and lay on the white dust-free Egyptian cotton sheet beneath. Surprisingly, it was fresh, crisp and clean. He began to plan how he could accomplish what he had come all this way to

Twelve

do, but he soon fell into a sweaty jet-lagged sleep.

*

The representative of the Médécins Sans Frontières organisation arrived at the hotel early next day to welcome Cameron.

'Bonne journée Monsieur Cameron,' he began. *'Je suis Guillaume Renard. Je crois que vous avez été en attente pour moi.'*

'Je suis enchanté de faire votre connaissance, Monsieur Renard,' Cameron replied in a perfect Parisian dialect. 'I'm pleased to meet you, Monsieur Renard. No, I haven't been waiting long.'

'Welcome to the Horn of Africa and to MSF,' said Renard. 'We have been expecting you for some time. I trust you had a good journey.'

'So-so,' replied Cameron. 'It was long and tiring, and I'm still getting used to this blessed heat and dust. But I am looking forward to starting work with your organisation.'

'One does get used to it in time, but it will take a day or two for you to become fully acclimatised to this humidity,' said Renard. 'Does your hotel not have air-conditioning?'

'I'm afraid not. Just an electric ceiling fan.'

'That's unfortunate,' he continued, with a touch of inevitability in his voice. 'Life in the Sudan makes one realise how privileged we are in Europe. Still, a fan is better than nothing and you're only going to be there for a couple of nights, so it's no great inconvenience. It does cool down significantly after dark anyway. Just take the day to rest and get your bearings. There's no great hurry; after years of conflict and civil warfare it will all still be there and waiting tomorrow.'

They sat down, drank a thick muddy coffee, and after exchanging a few pleasantries, arranged to meet the following day.

*

It was a small office on the ground floor of the Soba Medical Campus in the University of Khartoum, where next morning Guillaume Renard outlined Cameron's potential role with Médécins Sans Frontières.

Renard was a petite man, with a somewhat effeminate demeanour. His immaculate ivory linen suit had none of that inevitable creasing that is normally so characteristic of the fabric. Cameron thought it reminiscent of the last days of the Second Empire, when France once administered many settlements in North Africa, and such a style had been *de rigueur* for fashionable colonials. In spite of the heat, uncannily, Renard appeared not to sweat at all, but remained as cool as a proverbial cucumber. Conversely, Cameron could feel patches of sweat already oozing from his own armpits and an ever-growing stream of moisture trickling down his spine from the nape of his neck, even though it was still early morning.

Renard removed his wire-framed spectacles, took a neatly folded white handkerchief from his breast pocket, breathed on either lens and cleaned them before replacing the glasses on his head.

'Just to tell you a few facts about the place and what we do here,' he began. 'This is the largest and oldest university in Sudan. It has proved an advantageous base for MSF and for the distribution of aid and medical assistance throughout East Africa. It suits us because of the current relative stability of Khartoum, compared to that found in neighbouring Somalia and Eritrea. These are the areas where our current aid programme is directed.

'Our teams of volunteer and professional workers enable us to run hospitals and clinics in these countries, where we perform surgical procedures and vaccination campaigns as well as setting up food distribution centres

Twelve

for refugees. It is important to emphasise that in such conflicts Médécins Sans Frontières must remain strictly non-political. Therefore, our funding is sourced from private individuals, not governments, political organisations or factions, so that we are seen as completely independent. We provide our service to all who need our help most, regardless of colour, creed or politics. This well-publicised non-partisan policy means that all sides have grown to trust us as neutral and even-handed. As a rule, therefore, we are able to access those in need unhindered. I cannot emphasise too strongly that strict neutrality is essential to our work.

'You may be aware that the region has experienced prolonged warfare and our position here is tenuous at best. Sometimes the fragile peace breaks down, our work is interrupted and has to be either withdrawn from war zones, or else carried out as clandestine operations. This is never quite satisfactory, but there are times when it's the best that can be achieved. The position in Somalia is a case in point; our credibility is not as solid as it was and we do not enjoy the same freedom to operate as we formerly did. These are very dangerous times, but we are virtually the only suppliers of aid getting into the country.'

'So what exactly would be my role in the MSF?' asked Cameron.

'Whatever you feel best suits your talents. We have a variety of important roles that need filling, but what we need most is drivers. We are desperately short of men and women who are prepared to move medical supplies, clean water and basic foodstuffs through exceedingly treacherous terrains at considerable risk to themselves.'

'I see.'

'You don't have to make any hasty decisions. However, if you were prepared to drive that would be most valuable to us. Usually, we allocate two drivers to each consignment. Nevertheless, it is by no means an easy job and few are willing to operate in such hazardous conditions, without any form of backup. Sometimes it is necessary to evacuate severely wounded patients from battle zones, often under fire. Drivers need to be ready for many such unforeseen eventualities; to think and act with initiative and speed.'

'That was what I understood when I volunteered.'

'All well and good, but to be fair, there are also plenty of less perilous functions that have to be carried out here in Khartoum. There are administrative, warehouse and management tasks that have to be done, including packing, storage and dispatch of medication, tents and foodstuffs. In their own way these jobs are just as vital to our work.'

'No, I'm happy to drive.' Cameron insisted. 'That's what I came out here to do.'

'That's excellent news, Mister Cameron. Then I think we will be sending you into Somalia.'

*

Cameron was shown over to the truck by a Somali whom Renard introduced as his co-driver. He guessed that Yusuf Mosi was about 30 years of age and stood a towering six and a half feet tall in his sandals. His smooth body and classically shaped head was close-shaven so that it shone in the sunlight. He had that typically lean physique, common on the African continent, where the svelte muscled build of the bushman still predominated and the flaccidity of Western obesity had not yet made inroads into their ancient cultures.

Yusuf stood proud and handsome. His long neck gave an air of great natural dignity and he held it high; the deep black hollow face with its high cheekbones acted as a frame for the pure white of his eyes and the pearly brightness of his teeth; his face was clean-shaven apart from a neatly trimmed goatee beard. He broke into to a wide welcoming smile as Cameron walked up and cordially

Twelve

shook hands with him.

'Yusuf will be accompanying you on this trip,' said Renard. 'He knows the way in, and more importantly, the way out. He is a native Somali, so speaks its language as well as good English and passable French, so you will find him to be an invaluable asset. Get to know each other well. You will need it.'

With that brief introduction concluded, Renard wished them both *"Bon voyage et bonne chance"* – 'good journey and good luck,' and left the two men to get acquainted.

*

The old Peugeot truck, in which they were to make the long overland journey, was painted white to stand out in high profile against the red sands of East Africa. This had so far proved an effective protection against unwarranted attacks. Traces of khaki drab still showed through its scuffed and grazed paintwork, revealing its former military ancestry. A large distinctive MSF logo was emblazoned on its sides and on the canvas canopy to afford protection from unwarranted and periodical air attacks.

Cameron and Yusuf spent much of that first morning loading the truck with medicine packs, food parcels and tents as well as shrink-wrapped plastic bottles of water – all clearly stencilled with MSF identification.

'This is important,' said Yusuf. 'What we don't want is American insignia or branding anywhere on the load; that would be fatal for both of us.'

'Fatal, how?'

'Because if we get stopped by the rebels, or even certain rogue elements of the Somali Army, and they thought we were American, or even just bringing in American aid, they'd confiscate everything and probably execute us both on the spot. They might like drinking Coca-Cola, but that doesn't translate into a love of the

USA. So we replace any trace of American insignia with our own MSF logo.'

Yusuf explained that after midday it was too hot to work and that they should aim to get the load stowed aboard before noon. During the journey they would sleep through the afternoons and early evenings; the cool hours of night and mornings were the preferred times to travel. Desert temperatures could be extreme, often reaching forty degrees Celsius. Parts of Somalia had recorded the highest annual temperatures anywhere in the world and posed a serious risk of heatstroke.

'Besides' he said. 'It's much safer to travel by night; even insurgents have to sleep some of the time.'

When the truck was full to its tailgate, Yusuf pulled down the tarpaulin to protect it from the elements, and the loading was complete.

'We are expecting severe storms sometime over the next few days,' he said. 'In the desert it's not good to be caught up in one, but we have to go on. Our entry papers have limited dates, and we must be in and out before they expire.'

'So where are we heading?' asked Cameron.

'We are going to Burcoma in Somalia,' Yusuf answered. Then he looked Cameron full in the eyes. 'This is the last chance to change your mind, Mister Cameron. Once we leave Sudan and enter Ethiopia and Somalia, we will be committed. There is no turning back.'

'No,' Cameron assured him. 'I'm good to go. So what time do we leave?'

'Dusk is the best time. The roads will be less busy.'

'I suppose I'll get a little coaching on driving that old truck before we set out?'

'Don't worry about that. There's a long way to go and you'll get plenty of practice. I'll drive in the first place. You can spell me after a couple of hours. I'll talk you through it all. It's not exactly a high tech vehicle; controls are pretty basic, just four gears and a floor shift. You'll

Twelve

pick it up as we go on.'

Cameron had now met up with one of the two people he had come to East Africa to find.

*

Their journey began at six o'clock that evening. Khartoum was soon left far behind, and after a few miles, the hard metalled road surface gave way to a deeply rutted dirt track. Many such so-called highways would be negotiated before they reached their destination. By dusk, they were in the open expanse of the South Sudan countryside.

'So how did you come to get involved in MSF, Yusuf?' Cameron asked after a few hours on the road.

'It's a long story,' replied Yusuf, his voice raised over the noise of the smoky diesel engine.

'We have plenty of time,' replied Cameron.

'Well ... I left my home town of Qardho in northern Somalia in 1986 on a UNESCO scholarship to study in England. I was just a teenager. I was on my way back here after completing my studies and spending some time as an intern in London just as the war started.'

'So that's where you learned English?'

'Yes. I studied Law at UCL and worked for three years in Gray's Inn. It was hard, being a foreigner, and black, so I had intended to return home to set up my own legal practice, probably in Mogadishu. But that didn't quite work out. I hoped to return in triumph with my London degree and articles of law, like some local big shot who'd made good. However, the Somali government had collapsed, the country was in chaos and constant battles were taking place between rival militias. Any formal judicial system was non-existent, national law and order had completely broken down and what remained was a clan-based civil and religious law applied at a tribal level.

'For a time, a sort of peace was maintained by a few self-appointed Somali alliances. But there are now so many, most not peaceful at all, and some are prepared to exert power by any means. United Nations peacekeeping forces have had little effect; they are regarded as an invading army, and have become targets in their own right. They will probably withdraw completely from the country soon, as they are already sustaining heavy casualties from rebel militia. Men with guns rule Somalia now and it's no place for young lawyers. I'm also a Sunni Muslim, and that was the wrong ethnicity at the time. So I fled to Sudan and got a job driving for MSF. I've been working for them almost two years.'

*

During the hours of darkness they drove southwards on the main highway to Wad Madani. By early morning, they had reached Al Qadarif where they made an unscheduled stop to allow the overheated engine to cool down. Such enforced breaks occurred with monotonous regularity, though on the upside, they afforded welcome breaks from the prolonged driving spells and inhospitable terrain. During these times, they dined frugally on small portions of hard-crusted flat bread and their limited ration of dried meat tack. Cameron thought it to be some type of Biltong. It was extremely chewy, hard on the teeth and gums, but when it had finally softened, it was surprisingly pleasant to the taste. No doubt, it was eminently nourishing.

'Eat up,' said Yusuf. 'To a Somali, this is a feast!'

Chapter 14: Somalia

Dawn was breaking as they arrived at Matema on the Ethiopian border. A long procession of trucks and other vehicles were already queueing to cross. Roof racks were piled high with luggage and border guards examined everything, clambering aboard trucks and systematically rifling through their contents. Car drivers were forced to unload for themselves so that close inspection could be carried out at the roadside. It appeared to be the most laborious and intrusive procedure that the guards could devise. Ethiopia did not seem to extend a particularly cordial welcome to visitors.

'Why are they being so thorough?' asked Cameron.

'They're looking for guns,' replied Yusuf.

'Thank god we're not carrying any.'

Yusuf looked across at him edgily.

'What?' said Cameron.

'We're carrying one,' said Yusuf. 'It's hidden beneath the chassis. For protection. You never know when you'll need one out here.'

Cameron looked at him incredulously. He said nothing, but the prospect of being caught with a weapon on board filled him with trepidation. The border guards didn't look the sympathetic types.

'It's taking a hell of a long time,' said Cameron after they had waited for an hour in the stifling heat, with little appreciable forward movement. 'At this rate, I doubt we'll get through till late afternoon.'

'I think you're right,' replied Yusuf. 'Let's pull over. It makes more sense to park up until sunset, rather than sit exposed to the midday sun.'

Cameron jerkily reversed the truck back a few hundred metres until they came to an off road lay-by out of sight of the border post. Yusuf lifted the truck's bonnet to allow the engine to cool while Cameron attached the lean-to canvas to the shadow side of the vehicle so that they could shelter beneath it.

*

They slept through the afternoon and once rested, they set off again. Yusuf drove up to the barrier just before the crossing closed at sunset. There was no longer a queue and the solitary border guard showed only a cursory interest. It had been a long day, he was coming to the end of the shift and the MSF logo on the side of the truck weighed in their favour. He stamped their passports and they drove on, at last, into Ethiopia.

Despite the delayed entry, once into the country, they made good progress and driving was unhindered, so that by the small hours of the next day they reached the massive inland sea, known as Lake Tana. Its waters invited another unscheduled rest stop, and it was an opportunity to relax for a few hours, swimming and savouring the luxury of its cool water in the darkness. It was a relief to wash away the sweat and dust and a temporary respite from the truck's stifling heat and the unremitting noise of the diesel engine.

When well rested, they resumed the journey, driving along the western edge of the lakeside, flanked by the mountains on the east. Eventually the truck arrived at the turn-off for the narrow pass that went over the top to Tabor. The slow gruelling climb up severe gradients and the prolonged driving in low gear to the summit, made the engine scream under the effort and spout steam from beneath the bonnet once more, forcing yet another stoppage. As they waited for the engine to cool down, Yusuf asked Cameron how he came to volunteer for such a hazardous operation.

'Altruism, I suppose,' he replied, hiding his real motive with a deadpan expression. 'It seemed like a great idea at the time and it's a good way to see the world.'

'I can think of easier and less dangerous ways to

Twelve

see it.'

Yusuf knew nothing of Cameron's true purpose in coming to Somalia, or what had brought him to this land at such a perilous time in its history.

He would never know.

*

At the little town of Dessie they took a cross-country detour through the Yangudi National Park. According to Yusuf, this way avoided passing through Eritrea and Djibouti, which he said was the most dangerous route. Though the park terrain had no established roads and they could expect some uncomfortable driving, it would be free of other traffic, especially hostiles. 'It'll take us longer, but it's safer,' Yusuf insisted.

'I am in your hands,' said Cameron. 'You know best.'

There was no moon that night, but as they proceeded into the open parkland, the landscape was dimly illuminated by starlight. On several occasions they were so distracted looking up at the open sky, that they narrowly avoided rolling the truck, as it lurched into one of the many deep ruts. On one occasion it almost stuck fast in a muddy river crossing. At a painstakingly slow pace, they made progress negotiating the unspoiled wilderness, the faint glow of their tarnished amber headlamps barely impacting on their meandering path.

At one enforced stop Yusuf took out a mat and knelt down to pray, while Cameron topped up the radiator and replenished the fuel tank from one of the jerry cans. Then, he stood looking up, still overawed by the magnificent nocturnal splendour of the heavens, as if seeing them for the very first time. Periodically, the sky was illuminated by spectacular displays of shooting stars, a common occurrence over the continent in mid-November, and he reflected on his own insignificance.

Yusuf finished his prayers and they continued on their way again. Before long the truck reached the edge of the park reservation where it re-joined what passed for a major highway.

As they approached the Somali border they began to meet up with increasing numbers of heavy-laden vehicles coming the other way. Small groups of people were also fleeing the country on foot, refugees carrying everything they could of what little they still possessed. Some rode bicycles in their flight, one or two had camels or donkeys, but most walked.

Eventually, the truck reached the Somali border. The checkpoint appeared to be unmanned. A small hut, which once served as a border post, had been abandoned for some time, judging by its state of dilapidation. The striped pole barrier was permanently raised upright and a hastily scrawled chalkboard a few yards beyond announced 'Somalia' in English, French and in Arabic. On the ground beneath lay the original enamel sign, now riddled with rusting bullet holes.

They approached warily, uncertain whether a guard was still on duty, but no-one came forward and after a moment's hesitation they drove through, unchecked. The road led directly into Burcoma. Yusuf said the encampment would be located beyond the township. That was to be their eventual destination.

*

The Burcoma road was littered with abandoned vehicles and maize plantations on either side had been scorched black. Nearby houses were razed to the ground and those that remained standing bore the pock marks of heavy shelling and automatic weapon fire. Here and there, the rotting carcasses of goats and cattle lay strewn about.

'Between the soldiers and the rebel militias, my poor people don't stand a chance,' cried Yusuf. 'Who

Twelve

would slaughter cattle and burn crops when people are hungry? It's a crime! Soldiers and militiamen take what they need for themselves and destroy the rest. What they can't use or eat, they burn. May these sub-human animals be cursed forever ... Allah forgive me!'

Cameron knew that there was nothing he could say that would not be trite or clichéd. Therefore, the truck continued rumbling on down the road deeper into the Somalian interior, and he remained silent.

*

An hour after daybreak they arrived at a temporary road block, manned by armed men in camouflaged battle fatigues. Cameron brought the vehicle to a standstill a hundred metres away. For a few moments they sat considering their options, the silence only punctuated by the tick-over of the truck's engine.

'Army or militia? What d'you think?' asked Cameron.

'They're militia,' replied Yusuf. 'The worst. You stay in the truck and I'll do all the talking. Say nothing, but if you have to, do exactly what they say. Do you speak French?'

'Yes, I speak French. Why?'

'If they address you at all, they'll expect it. Most MSF people are French. Whatever you do, speak no English.'

Cameron was glad that his birth parents had chosen the dark skin colour for him. Hopefully, here and now, he would not be mistaken for a European.

A militiaman stepped forward and beckoned them to approach, raising a hand to halt them when he considered them close enough. He was apparently a leader of some kind, and carried a Russian assault rifle slung over his shoulder. His mirrored Ray-Ban sunglasses exuded an incongruous air of menace combined with high fashion.

He seemed to possess all the characteristics that might qualify him as a psychopath.

A large Nissan pickup truck was parked some yards further back, behind the barrier. It had been converted into a mobile gunship and sported a DShK 1938 Soviet heavy machine gun. Nicknamed the *Dushka*, it was colloquially known as 'the sweetie' because of its readily available parts for maintenance and how little time it took to master. It had no doubt been captured from Somali Army forces and was being operated by a young boy who looked no more than twelve or thirteen years of age. He exhibited that same dispassionate weary expression of a soldier who had seen too much, and for whom every trace of empathy had been totally expunged.

The child soldier swivelled the gun barrel round to point directly at them. With a loud metallic click, he advanced a round into the firing mechanism; it was as if some other reinforcement were needed, and the mere presence of the ordinance insufficient warning. The boy looked perfectly prepared to use it, at the slightest pretext, as he had already done so, judging by the several shot-up vehicles at the roadside.

Two other armed men watched as they sat on the running board of a troop carrier, casually sheltering in the shade of a burnt-out house, chain-smoking and fanning themselves. Yusuf dismounted, approached the officer and presented his papers. The soldier scrutinised them for a few moments. He looked back towards the truck and shook his head negatively. Cameron observed the proceedings intently. Something wasn't right, something bad. A heated discussion began between Yusuf and the soldier, in Arabic, so far as he could tell, but too far off for him to hear what was being said. The argument grew increasingly animated until finally, Yusuf threw up his arms in a gesture of desperation, before making his way slowly back to the truck.

'What's going on?' said Cameron.

Twelve

'They want half our load,' replied Yusuf.

'What?' exclaimed Cameron in disbelief. 'Can they do that?'

'Who's going to stop them out here? They can do whatever they like. I told you before, the man with the gun rules in Somalia.'

'Can't we at least bargain with them?'

'No. If we give them the slightest pretext, they'll line us up against that wall.'

Cameron looked towards the side of the house where Yusuf had indicated. It was spattered with blood and peppered with bullet holes. On the ground beneath lay the dead bodies of several men and women, whose corpses had already begun to darken in the blazing heat of the late morning sun.

'There's no guarantee that they won't execute us anyway,' said Yusuf. 'Even if we give them what they want, they may still shoot us!'

*

Several other militiamen had come over to watch, and sat idly observing as Cameron and Yusuf struggled to unload packages from the tailgate of the truck in the intense dehydrating heat of midday. Throughout, the boy soldier continued pointing the artillery in their direction and not one of the soldiers offered any form of assistance.

After more than half the contents had been off-loaded, their leader seemed satisfied with the quota. He handed back their papers and indicated that they could continue on their way. It was with a deep sense of relief that they saw the barrier pole descend behind them and they sped away as fast as the old Peugeot could manage, short of blowing a cylinder head gasket. They dared not look back; glad to be clear of the checkpoint and almost at their destination, although with less than half their original load.

When it felt safe to stop, they drove out into the desert, far enough away from the road not to be seen by any other hostile traffic that might pass by. They could ill afford to lose more of their cargo.

They slung the tarpaulin underneath a solitary acacia tree and Yusuf laid out his prayer mat beneath its cover, away from the intense burning of the desiccated surface, while Cameron dozed in its shade, hot and exhausted. So far they had survived the journey, but tomorrow they would arrive at Burcoma.

*

It was an hour before sunrise and not a soul stirred in the Burcoma Township. The tell-tale evidence of a hasty retreat was all around them. Streets and alleyways were littered with ransacked cases and trunks, as fleeing residents had abandoned their homes and possessions. Evidence of the panic was clear from the incongruity of the discarded detritus that had been left behind. An upturned table, an upholstered settee, a flat screen television, an old Singer sewing machine – all bizarrely disowned in the middle of the road.

As they picked their way cautiously around innumerable forsaken obstacles, the air hung heavy with palls of black smoke and the nauseating scent of decaying human and animal corpses. So pungent was the stench that they had to close the cab windows and pack air intake vents with whatever came to hand, preferring the stifling heat of the interior to the foetid air that pervaded outside. But the odour of rancid putrefaction persisted and they speeded up to get through as quickly as possible. It was not until dawn, when they reached the far side of the town and emerged into clean fresh air, that they were able to open the windows and vents to breathe freely again.

*

Twelve

Burcoma refugee camp sat on an open plain – an enormous makeshift settlement that stretched out before them as far as the eye could see. Its scale was unimaginable, a shanty town conglomeration of more than three thousand temporary dwellings. Hundreds of tents had been donated by the Red Crescent and Oxfam, but most were hastily thrown together from make-do tarpaulins. And it was hot, very hot. The daytime temperature on the plain was so intense that there was a danger that any white skin exposed for more than twenty minutes would suffer heat stroke or serious sunburn and dehydration would soon set in. Dark-skinned Somalis, on the other hand, better adapted to the high temperatures, seemed content with only the thinnest of head coverings. Yet still they died.

The plain was entirely devoid of trees. Those that once existed had long since been felled for cooking or warmth during the chill of desert nights. A tall flagstaff rose high above the settlement, limply draped with the black colours of the rebel forces, in whose hands it was currently held. It marked what passed for camp administration. At other times, it had been under the control of Somali government troops, but in the unstable politics of the region, flags of different colours had changed on an almost month-by-month basis, as one or another opposing army retook the area.

The truck drew up outside the administration tent and both men stepped out into the blazing sun. A dozen or so corpses were unceremoniously stacked against the wall of the huge marquee, crudely sewn up in muslin shrouds like so many mail sacks awaiting collection. Interment was customarily done on the outskirts of the camp on the same day that death occurred. Sometimes that did not happen, and this was just such a day. Thick swarms of blowflies were already busily seeking ways through the thin shrouds, attracted by the promise of a macabre meal.

The camp had swelled continuously over many months. As a result, earlier cemeteries had been overtaken by the outspread of ever more dwellings and were currently marooned in the middle of the encampment. The dead now lay buried among the living, surrounded by ever-later arrivals of refugees.

Cameron thought that if there was a place called Hell, then it was here and now.

*

More than a dozen armed men idly loitered around the administration marquee. They watched suspiciously, as Yusuf went in, followed closely by Cameron. At a large table sat a senior officer, fanning himself with an ornate ivory fly swatting whisk. He said nothing as they approached. For what seemed an eternity, the two men stood waiting for some acknowledgement of their presence or an indication that they should speak. Eventually, the officer enquired what their business was. Yusuf explained that they had come with food supplies and medicines.

'Never mind medicine!' the officer said brusquely. 'You have any guns?'

'No guns. Just food, water and medicines.'

'Show me.' He stood up from behind the desk and motioned them out to the truck. He followed them out, flanked by two armed men. Yusuf unfastened the tarpaulin and lowered the tailgate.

'Is that all?' asked the officer.

Yusuf explained that half of their consignment had been confiscated at the checkpoint earlier. At this, the officer's manner became a little more irritable.

'That would be the Amin mob. Bastards and scum. They spoil things for everyone. Okay, you had better unload the truck. You can put it in there,' he said, pointing to the back of the marquee. 'We'll distribute it tomorrow.'

Twelve

Then he reached into one of the packages, breaking the shrink-wrapped seal with a large knife that he had withdrawn from a belt scabbard and took out a bottle of water.

'Is this it? You got no fucking Perrier?' he snarled.

'No, sir, just plain still water,' replied Yusuf.

The officer grunted, twisted off the bottle cap and without pausing for breath, drank down its entire contents. A group of refugees gathered around, eyes wide and tongues thickened with thirst. Not one uttered a word as they watched him drink. When he had emptied the bottle, he casually flung it to the ground. Immediately a dozen flailing hands fought to acquire it, hoping for a chance to get the last dreg, before it evaporated.

When the unloading had finished, the officer ordered Cameron and Yusuf to go with one of the armed guards. 'Follow this man,' he said. 'He'll take you to a place where you can park the truck and there's a tent where you can stay tonight. But you must get the fuck out of here tomorrow, first thing.'

The soldier jumped upon the running board of the Peugeot and guided them to an emplacement at the very edge of the camp. They stepped down and he ordered them into the tent. He stood guard outside, an unequivocal indication they were not allowed to wander around the compound. They were effectively prisoners for the night.

*

Despite the stifling heat, both men managed to snatch a few hours' sleep. By six o'clock, the night began to draw in and Yusuf awoke first. He fumbled around for his shoulder bag and pulled out a small flashlight. Then, he took out a bottle of water and some food that he had brought from the truck. He woke Cameron and they began to eat. The bag also contained an MSF standard emergency pack with a basic first aid kit, a pair of binoculars and salt tablets. Yusuf had done this before – he knew to be prepared for any eventuality.

They had almost finished eating when a slight figure surreptitiously lifted the brailing at the back wall of the tent and crawled in, slithering beneath in a snake-like fashion. Yusuf turned on the flashlight. The beam illuminated the face of a young woman. She had the most piercing opalescent eyes that Cameron had ever seen. In any other place, he would have thought her extraordinary, but such colouring was rare in Africa and even more startling because of it. Though she was strikingly beautiful, her expression was fearful and apprehensive. She recognised Yusuf as a fellow African, and spoke directly to him.

'Speak French?' she said. 'American?'

'Somali ...' replied Yusuf, '... and English.'

She looked relieved. 'Have you come to deliver us?'

'No,' Yusuf replied. 'We've just brought food, water and medical supplies.'

'You must take us away from here. They bad men – do bad things.'

Yusuf shook his head empathetically and offered her the half-empty water bottle. She grabbed it roughly, thrust it up to her cracked lips and gulped it back in such haste that she began to choke in her impatience. Yusuf sprang forward and clasped a hand tightly over her mouth to stifle the outburst. The guard might have heard the commotion – had he not been fast asleep outside.

When she stopped spluttering, Cameron offered her the remaining fragment of bread, which she crammed into her mouth with equal haste and wolfed it down hungrily. He realised that this was the real face of famine at very close quarters, the first that he had personally witnessed. After she had swallowed the last crumb, she thanked both men and praised god for the small life-saving meal.

Twelve

'I am afraid there is little more we can do to help,' said Yusuf. 'There are thousands of you here. Our truck could only carry a few people even if the militia would allow it, which I very much doubt.'

'No. We are not thousands. There are just a few of us.'

'How many are you?' asked Cameron.

'Sixteen, maybe a few more,' she replied. 'They keep us for sex. We are slaves, beaten, violated daily and raped continually.'

Cameron looked at Yusuf with a mixture of horror and disbelief.

'Sadly, it's not unusual,' said Yusuf. He turned back to the girl. 'Go on.'

'Some of our number have already died; others committed suicide. My friend killed herself in the latrine only yesterday. She couldn't face it anymore and held her head under the shit. Another girl died by her own hands last week; she slashed her wrists and bled to death. We are so weak from hunger and ill with malnutrition that we die easily.'

'How old are you?' asked Yusuf.

'I am seventeen, I think, or perhaps eighteen. I cannot be certain,' she replied. 'Two of our number are even younger than I. The soldiers don't care. They take us anyway. They threaten to kill us if we refuse. It's either that, or they don't feed us until we agree to their demands.'

'By what name are you known?'

'I am called Samiila – Samiila Ghedi.'

In the silence that followed she looked imploringly first at one and then the other and Cameron knew exactly what had to be done.

'I can't leave these young women at the mercy of these thugs, Yusuf.'

'I understand your concern, Cameron. But exactly what do you have in mind?'

'We have to take them back with us. They can be

hidden in the back of the truck.'

'It would be a great risk, to them and to us,' Yusuf replied.

'I know,' said Cameron. 'But we cannot allow this barbarity to continue. The truck is empty, so I doubt the militia will check again. If we leave at dawn, before everybody is awake, we might be able to make it.'

*

Just before daybreak, Samiila escorted the young females to the truck, one by one, stealthily through the twilight. By some act of providence, the sentry had sloped off and they were no longer guarded. Yusuf helped each woman climb aboard, while Cameron signalled them to remain very quiet. When they were stowed aboard at last, Yusuf dropped the tarpaulin and secured the tailgate. There were several more females than Samiila had accounted for.

One final whispered request for absolute silence and both men crawled back under the tent wall. They had not been observed. Yusuf knelt to pray as he customarily did, but on this occasion, he made special prayers for the girls' safety.

Cameron was too tense to sleep. 'You realise we don't have enough food or water for all these women?' he whispered. 'And some of them badly need medical attention.'

'I know, but we must trust in god. He will provide.'

'I admire your optimism, Yusuf, but I think we might need to give him a bit of a helping hand.'

Chapter 15: Exodus

At dawn, Yusuf cautiously looked out through the tent flap. There was no sentry and few people were stirring so early in the morning.

'Okay. All clear,' he signalled to Cameron. 'Time to go!'

The two men climbed into the truck, started the engine and slowly made their way out of the encampment. They drove in low gear to attract as little attention as possible. As they passed a solitary militiaman, Yusuf waved nonchalantly to him; he waved back with no hint of suspicion. Why should he? After all, this was just another charity truck leaving after delivering an aid consignment.

Once the camp was out of sight, Yusuf stepped hard on the accelerator pedal to put as much distance between them and the settlement as possible. They had agreed that it would be wise to take a different route than that by which they had arrived.

'We will go another way to the Ethiopian border,' said Yusuf. 'Nobody might look for us in this direction. It's a longer route and very few people use it.'

*

Their preferred crossing was about a hundred and fifty kilometres from the Burcoma camp. According to the map, the border lay just north of the Amar Mountains separating Somalia from Ethiopia and the road led directly to Addis Ababa. Somewhere along this route, Yusuf had been told, there was a shallow ravine, the remains of an ancient riverbed. It was to be found some way off the highway, perhaps seventy-five kilometres south-east from Burcoma. They could make it there in less than three hours ... if all went well.

Reputedly, even in times of prolonged drought, residual stretches of water remained from the monsoons that seasonally swept across the plain down from the Gulf of Aden in the north. These small pools had been used by camel drivers and goat herders for centuries and many travellers had survived severe deprivation thanks to the elusive waters.

It was in places where the ravine was deepest, according to what he had heard, that even in the driest times, a little water could sometimes be found. Though it was scarce and said to taste like camel piss, it was good enough to drink. A man could survive on it. It was also, he thought, a safe place to rest for a while.

'We have hardly sufficient food for them, but with water they can last for a couple of days till we reach Ethiopia,' Yusuf assured Cameron.

'Perhaps it makes sense to lay low there for a while anyway,' said Cameron. 'Just in case the militia are following us. I don't fancy meeting up with them out in the open. They will be looking for us, I expect, especially when they discover that we have taken their women. We can also take time out to rest up, tend to some of the womens' cuts and bruises and consider our next move.'

A few hours later, at a place that he judged most promising, Yusuf pulled the truck off the road and drove across the stony terrain until they arrived at the ravine. As they had anticipated, it was little more than a shallow sandy depression. They shadowed its course south for a few kilometres and eventually they found water. It was not much, but it would do. It would save their lives.

Cameron went round to release the women from the truck. No sooner had he dropped the tailgate than the entire complement leapt out and ran headlong down to the meagre pool of water. Immediately, as one, they knelt down in the sand and began to drink from their cupped hands. Typically, in Africa, where water was often in desperately short supply, not a single woman had entered the pool. When silt was disturbed, it often took several hours, before it was clear enough to drink the water again.

Twelve

Following their lead, Cameron and Yusuf crouched at the water's edge alongside the women and began lapping as if they had been thirsty cattle or a herd of goats.

*

They spent two days and nights at this secluded encampment, sleeping under the stars, as meteors continued to stream spectacularly across the firmament. During the daytime, they were thankful for the shade of the truck and the acacias. Several women made use of Yusuf's mat to pray beneath the shelter of the lean-to tarpaulin.

Food proved less of a problem than Cameron had anticipated, for many of the girls were gifted foragers – no doubt born of necessity. Some managed to unearth tubers and edible roots with their bare hands. The few acacia trees also provided flowers and leaves that were edible and nourishing, though unpleasant to taste.

Yusuf was also adept at trapping small lizards and desert mammals or bringing them down with a slingshot that he had fashioned from the torn fabric of one of the girls' garments. Although he had spent recent years training as a lawyer in London, he had lost none of his skills in bush craft and could still make fire.

Desert creatures were elusive and scarce, and much of the day and night was spent scavenging and trapping whatever could be found. All told, however, during the two-day stopover, they cooked and ate several hedgehogs, abeeso python, monitor lizards, striped mole rats and a quantity of pygmy gerbils. What could not be eaten immediately was dried for the coming days' nutritional needs. It occurred to Cameron that the tough Biltong, which he had shared with Yusuf for the past week, probably began life as one of the creatures that now hung drying over the open bush fire.

In late afternoon of the second day, Yusuf

emerged from the back of the truck. 'I thought these might come in handy,' he said triumphantly. Cradled in his arms was a collection of empty water bottles. 'I guess these must be from an earlier consignment,' he said. 'Either drivers or militia must have emptied them. No matter, we can fill them for the journey. Did I not tell you that God would provide?'

*

Cameron estimated that the youngest of the women could be no more than eleven years old, and that the eldest looked to be in her late-twenties. Their number included Somalis, Eritreans and Ethiopians, and they told stories of forced imprisonment as well as the sickening details of their treatment at the hands of rebel militia bands. Some had been sold into marriage or passed from one group to another, while many others had died or been murdered.

Samiila gradually emerged as the chief spokesperson, as few of the women would speak or communicate directly to either Yusuf or Cameron. Despite the charity of their rescuers, most of them still regarded conversation with strange men to be immodest, in keeping with Islamic tradition. Avoiding all eye contact with either Yusuf or Cameron, they lowered their heads or pulled a headdress down to cover the face, and only when necessary did they make an acknowledgement with the slightest tilt of the head.

However, Samiila spent many long hours talking with Yusuf and describing her life during and before her abduction. She seemed unbound by false cultural modesty or religious prohibition. She was intelligent, forthright and spoke with an emancipated candour that Yusuf found captivating. The deep blue of her wide eyes shone incandescently in the midday sun and he had become completely enamoured of her. Little did he realise what history they would share together in the years ahead.

Twelve

Cameron said nothing, but watched their burgeoning relationship develop. He already knew who she was and who she would become. Samiila and Yusuf were the reason he had come to Africa.

*

'Everyone be quiet. They're here,' said Cameron. It was the morning of their third day in the ravine and he lay at the top of the embankment observing the highway in the distance.

Yusuf crawled up and lay alongside him, prostrate on the sandy bluff. Cameron handed him the binoculars. He took a moment to refocus on the moving dust trail from a distant column of military vehicles driving south along the highway. The convoy was led by an open-topped staff car, followed by a large truck loaded with armed militia. Bringing up the rear was another ubiquitous gun-carrying pickup truck.

'I knew they'd be looking for us,' Cameron said. 'It was bound to happen.'

'They may not be. It could be a coincidence.'

'No,' replied Cameron. 'You said yourself that this road is hardly ever used. They're the militiamen from Burcoma. They're after us all right.'

Yusuf handed back the binoculars and rolled over onto his back. 'What do you think we should do?' he asked.

'Well, we're not going anywhere just yet,' replied Cameron. 'That's for certain.'

*

As it happened, nature was to intervene. By late afternoon, a fierce dust storm had blown up, and visibility was down to an arm's length. The windblown sand cut into the face and stung the eyes with such intensity that moving about proved impossible. Women and girls huddled together in the back of the truck, covering their heads and faces, while the men lay beneath the tarpaulin. The storm raged for several hours, during which time Cameron had formulated a plan.

'I have an idea,' he shouted to Yusuf above the noise of the storm and the interminable flapping of the tarpaulin sheet. 'Do you think you could make it out on foot with the women, if you had a head start?'

'I don't know. Why, what have you in mind?'

'We can't risk driving along the highway now that we know for certain there are militia about. We'd never make it. But you could lead them out on foot. Are you up for it?'

'So what will you be doing in the meantime?'

'I'll be driving along the highway in the opposite direction as a diversion, hopefully drawing them off and giving you a chance to get the girls away safely,' Cameron replied.

Yusuf considered the proposition. 'It's about eighty kilometres to the border and the territory is very hostile, even without militia on our trail.'

'I realise that, and it won't be easy, but I know you can make it.'

'You can't be certain.'

'Yes I can.'

'How can you possibly know that?'

'You'll have to take my word for it. Let's just say I have a compelling reason to say so. It'll be three or four days hard walking in this heat, but it can be done. You're a good man, Yusuf, and resourceful. You know the terrain and have already demonstrated your survival skills. You will need to ration the food, but I dare say you'll be able to hunt for more on the way. Stick to the ravine. You say it runs south all the way to the border and well into Ethiopia. With luck you may find more water on the way.'

'It might work,' said Yusuf after some

Twelve

consideration. 'It's a long shot, but I suppose it's our best chance.'

'Exactly! I can't see any other options. If you set off when the storm dies down a little, it will cover your tracks. And as you said, God will provide, so you can't lose your faith now.'

'My faith is strong and I know we can't stay here indefinitely,' said Yusuf. 'But what if they catch up with you out on the highway?'

'I'll just have to make sure they don't,' replied Cameron.

*

As the storm abated, they began digging the truck out of the sand and unclogging the engine's air filters. It took a good half hour before they were ready to leave. All preparations completed, Yusuf shook Cameron by the hand and they stood hugging each other for some time.

Presently, Yusuf moved away. 'May your God go with you,' he said. Then, he turned and headed southwards along the river bed, the women and girls following closely behind him in single file. Several women, who had shown such modest reticence earlier, ran over to shake Cameron's hand and utter expressions of gratitude, before the column disappeared into the dying sandstorm.

When the last of them was out of sight Cameron climbed aboard the truck, started the engine and drove off northbound into the abating storm. It would be the last that they would ever see of him.

*

Three weeks later Yusuf and Samiila sat in the Médécins Sans Frontières office in Khartoum, recounting the details of their epic journey out of Somalia to Guillaume Renard. Yusuf told how, once safely across the border, many of the women and girls had been taken in by medical and charitable aid agencies in Ethiopia. Some had been found new homes, others were being helped locate their lost families and one or two had gone their separate ways. Sadly, two of the party failed to make it - one had died of dysentery and the other, too weak to continue walking, had fallen and died in her tracks from heat exhaustion. But all told, twenty-four women and girls had made it out of Somalia to safety.

'What became of Cameron I do not know,' explained Yusuf. 'But he was a brave man. I suppose he was also a little foolhardy, but I doubt we would have made it without him. I am also embarrassed to have to inform you that we lost the truck. We have no idea what became of it after Cameron drove away. But I do have some good news.'

Yusuf paused, his face beaming widely. 'Samiila has graciously agreed to be my wife. Of course, she is Shia and I am Sunni. Such unions are not common, but as neither of us has any family still living who might object, we are unencumbered by such restrictions. We would also both like to continue working for MSF, if that is possible.'

Renard smiled. 'I think you will make an excellent match for each other. May I be the first to congratulate you? As for MSF, of course we will be happy to offer Samiila an administrative position here, if she'll take it. Your own job is secure as it always has been.'

They thanked him and sat happily holding hands. But the smile faded gradually from Renard's face and he adopted a graver expression. 'As for the fate of Patrick Cameron, we have some news,' he continued. 'But sadly I have to inform you that it is not good news.'

Yusuf leaned forward apprehensively in his chair.

'The Peugeot was found at the roadside in Somalia,' said Renard.

'So is Cameron safe then?' asked Yusuf.

'I am afraid we cannot say. The truck was

Twelve

abandoned, its engine destroyed by some form of artillery and its sides riddled with bullet holes. Of Cameron himself, nothing is known. Neither his body, if he is dead, nor his whereabouts, if he survived.'

Chapter 16: Italian Connection

Seymour decided that he was long overdue a visit to the local residence of Mister Arthur Pascoe. Vehicle Licensing had confirmed the address, and Fosse had already made his first foray into amateur surveillance of the property, even though that had proved fruitless.

The house was located in a residential district that had once been popular with the prosperous Victorian middle classes. But it had seen better days. Over decades the area had deteriorated into a less than salubrious dormitory, comprised of low rent housing and flats to accommodate the city's large student population. Small shops and fast food outlets had sprung up to keep residents well provided, so that young would-be academics could satiate themselves in saturated fats, sugars and alcohol, well into the early hours of every morning.

Pascoe's house stood in the middle of a long terrace, in a street lined with urban plane trees. Typically, much of the row's original uniform terracotta brickwork had been overpainted in lurid colour washes, while several other facades were hidden behind imitation stonework. Doors of every colour proliferated so that the street had degenerated into a pot-pourri of styles, and was none the better for its kaleidoscopic diversity.

Seymour did not want to attract unwarranted attention, so he parked in a quiet back street and walked the short distance to the Pascoe property. He had decided that mid-morning would be the best time to investigate, as most residents were likely be at work. He stood observing the property from the opposite pavement, biding his time until he was certain that nobody was about. One solitary car was parked some way off, otherwise the street looked deserted.

It was a two-up, two-down dwelling, like countless properties in similar terraces throughout the city. The curtains were drawn and there was no obvious point of

Twelve

entry. Getting inside would be problematic. The front entrance was in open view of the whole street and direct access was out of the question. Seymour was reluctant to break a window or force an entry, but unless something better offered itself, he would have no choice. All things considered, the back of the property might be a more promising option.

He walked a few yards further on till he came to a narrow passage, which led to a cobbled alleyway running along behind the terrace. It was enclosed, not overlooked, and offered potentially good cover. So, Seymour counted his way along until he came to a high wall with a large wooden gate, at what he judged to be the back of the Pascoe house. He tried the latch, but it was securely bolted. He would have to climb over the wall. Nearby were several dustbins. He selected one that he thought robust enough to bear his weight, leapt upon it and sprang quickly over the wall.

The small enclosed back yard had been bypassed by time, unlike the refurbished and modernised properties on either side. Untouched for more than a century, it still retained the outside privy and washhouse.

Curtains were drawn, just as they were at the front of the house. He tested the ground floor window, but, sealed tight by successive years of over-painting, it held fast. The back door was equally unyielding. There was nothing for it - he would have to pick the lock. The use of pick keys was strictly against regulations, and quite illegal of course, but almost every copper seemed to have a set. So why not, he thought? He had not used them in years, but it took only a few minutes fiddling before the lock gave a gratifying *click* and the door could be pushed open. Like riding a bike, he thought. Some things you just don't forget.

Before entering, he put on a pair of rubber gloves. The drawn curtains made the interior dark and dingy, and it took a few moments for his eyes to acclimatise to the low light level. He tried a light switch beside the door, but nothing illuminated. Perhaps the bulb had blown. He took out his flashlight and began to look around.

First, he opened the refrigerator. The interior light worked perfectly, and he knew that there was electrical power in the house after all. Evidently, it had not been entirely abandoned. Although Fosse said nobody had entered or left the property, signs suggested that someone planned to return. The fridge had very little in it: there was an unopened carton of milk, six eggs, butter and two of tins of tuna. The freezer compartment held a half dozen frozen ready-meals. That settled it. Pascoe, or whoever, would be coming back.

The living areas were singularly devoid of personal effects - no photographs, ornaments or mementos of any kind. This was not a comfortable or permanent residence. The entire house was starkly minimalist – the ground floor sported a small microwave oven, a solitary chair, a settee and a television set with an indoor aerial. Little else. Foil food containers in the waste bin indicated that somebody had eaten recently.

On the hall carpet by the front door, Seymour estimated there to be the best part of a hundred unopened letters, mostly publicity leaflets or unsolicited junk mail. Several utility bills addressed to Pascoe and one telephone bill to Cameron. Footprints on some of the envelopes suggested that they had lain there for some time.

He made his way up the stairs and went into the front bedroom. It was similarly devoid of comforts, except for an unmade bed, an old utility chest and a small wardrobe. The drawers held several neck ties, a selection of underwear and handkerchiefs, most monogrammed with the initials 'A D P'. In the wardrobe there hung a large black overcoat and a grey suit. Beneath them, a pair of highly polished black leather shoes. Seymour examined them all carefully. The garments were expensive, well cut and hand sewn. The overcoat was of pure cashmere wool.

Twelve

No doubt about it, these were Pascoe's clothes. All the labels had been removed, exactly as Cameron's had been.

Seymour continued searching, but found nothing significant. He had seen enough. On his way out he tripped the back door lock behind him, and left.

In the yard outside, he moved another dustbin and propped it against the padlocked gate. He was about to climb upon it, when an idea struck him. As the bin had been locked inside the yard, it had probably not been emptied for some time. It was worth a look inside. He tipped it over, spilling garbage out across the yard and knelt down to examine the contents. It was general household refuse in the main, but amongst it were many torn papers and envelopes. He picked out a typewritten scrap, addressed to *"Arthur Pascoe Esq"*. Another damp stained letter was attached to its sticky underside. He carefully separated the two items to reveal a smudged and almost obliterated address - he could barely make out a few words. Just a few almost indecipherable characters - *"Si.n.r A P...oe"*... and another fragment read: *"Cap..la da Cam.., T..can., Ital.. 52...3...0."*

He grinned with disproportionate glee, placed the torn fragment and the envelope into a sample bag and tucked it into his coat pocket. It was incomplete, but a second address that Pascoe may have used. Looked like an Italian address. As he knelt among the garbage, suddenly, a voice called out his name from the top of the wall. It brought him upright with a jolt. He turned and saw Fosse's head peering over the coping.

'Christ! You scared the shit out of me, Prof!' he exploded. 'What the hell are you doing here?'

'Sorry, old man. I was in the car watching the house from down the street,' replied Fosse. 'I saw you arrive, but hadn't been able to work out where you'd gone. So I wandered round the back and down the alley. I heard the bin go over and thought I'd take a look.'

'How long have you been surveying the place?'

'On and off for several days. Ever since I agreed to do the stakeout.'

'But I thought you were only going to do it once. I had no idea you were still at it.'

'Well I found it a little tedious at first, but I've actually quite enjoyed catching up on my music while I was playing detective. I've also managed to do some reading without all the distractions. Anyway, why are you rummaging in a dustbin?'

'I've found something that might be important.'

'I see. But, would you mind awfully if I got down, Charlie?' said Fosse. 'I'm afraid it doesn't feel very safe perched up here on a wheelie bin.'

'Perhaps you're right. It would be better if we talked about this in more comfortable surroundings rather than discuss it over a brick wall.'

*

Back at the Crazy Horse Bar Seymour retold what he had discovered at the Pascoe house.

'It's as we thought. Pascoe stayed there and Cameron certainly did, at least for some of the time. I don't think either of them lived there on any long-term basis. It's hardly habitable for permanent occupation, but it's definitely one of their properties.'

'What d'you mean, one of their properties? You think they have more than one?'

'It seems so. I found this fragment of a business letter addressed to Pascoe ... it looks like it might be in Tuscany.'

'Tuscany? You mean the one in Italy?' Fosse examined the soggy envelope.

'Well yes. Unless there's another Tuscany that I haven't heard about. It seems clear that Pascoe, and possibly Cameron, also have a place in Italy.'

'This is completely unexpected, isn't it?' said

Twelve

Fosse, when he had taken another sip of whisky. 'I must say, Charlie, Tuscany sounds an infinitely better place to stake out than a terraced house in Manchester. Don't you think?'

'Too right, Max,' replied Seymour. 'But I'd like to know what connection they have to Italy. It's a clue we haven't come across before. It may not be significant, of course. Pascoe may just have been on holiday there.'

'Possibly. But this is definitely part of a business letter. Who receives business mail while on holiday? I doubt that's the explanation.'

'Perhaps you're right. Maybe I need to visit Tuscany, Prof,' said Seymour.

'It's Max!' insisted Fosse.

Chapter 17: Geneva

Seymour had often said to his wife that air travel was the most unremittingly boring way to travel. Despite his pathological fear of flying, Caroline Massey had ordered him to Geneva, which necessitated an urgent air trip. As things turned out, the flight served only to reinforce Seymour's negative attitude. Though he left the house ten hours earlier, just over two and a half of those actually involved flying – more than seven had seen him waiting around in overcrowded airports. There was also a long inter-flight connection between terminals at Heathrow. No question, he would have preferred a long leisurely drive through Europe, where he could enjoy fine wines and cuisine enroute, instead of the inevitable nerve-racking air turbulence and unidentifiable microwaved food.

'I need you to check out Pascoe's bank account in Geneva,' Massey had told him two days earlier. 'While everything points to him having access to a large personal fortune, so far as we have been able to determine, neither he nor Cameron have any visible means of support.'

'So how have they funded themselves?'

'That's what you're going to find out. Neither has ever held down a job or submitted tax returns in Britain. Or anywhere in the European Union, for that matter. Revenue and Customs are understandably interested. And, as funds held in Switzerland are frequently associated with money laundering and crime, the Police Serious Fraud Office have requested to be allowed access to the results of your investigation. A lot depends on this, Seymour. For the time being, both of those agencies are happy for us to handle things, but you'll need to dig deep and find out where their money comes from.'

'I understood Swiss bank accounts were virtually inaccessible. Isn't that the whole point? Away from the prying eyes of the tax man?'

'That's certainly been true for many years.

Twelve

Switzerland has been a notorious tax haven for a very long time,' she explained. 'But Swiss frostiness is gradually thawing in the light of new European legislation on bank transparency. In an increasingly globalised world it's not as easy to conceal accounts as it used to be. We have also pulled a lot of strings with Swiss banking authorities, and along with a few favours the Americans have called in, we think we have made some progress.'

'So can I expect the Swiss to co-operate?'

'We have secured authorising documents for you,' she continued. 'So we're fairly confident that they will open some doors. However, the BrenSchweiz Bank International, is a private affair, and it's by no means certain how willing they will be to recognise the documents, or if they do, how much weight they'll give to them. There's just an off-chance they may not be forthcoming at all. You'll just have to use your best judgement. Interpol and Swiss financial authorities have supplied these documents, so hopefully they will allow you full access to Pascoe's account. There are one or two other things in your favour.'

'I'm glad to hear that there are a few things in my favour,' said Seymour.

'Well, there has been a lot of international pressure on Swiss banks regarding tax evasion of late. They refuse to admit it, of course, but they remain embarrassed by accusations of Nazi gold in their vaults. Consequently, they have signed up to a convention with the OECD and agreed to exchange more information with member countries. Tax collection agreements with Great Britain are already in place and international pressure from America, France and Germany has prompted a relaxation in their traditional culture of banking secrecy.

'Also, in January the Swiss Bankers Association agreed to the US led International Agreement on Bank Disclosure on behalf of its six hundred members. There is no doubt that this has softened attitudes and some banks do seem to be leaning over backwards to be co-operative. In fact, some appear unusually keen. Whether this is real or they're just going through the motions we can't say, but you'll no doubt find out while you're over there.'

*

The Swiss International Airlines Airbus had departed London Heathrow after making the routine scheduled connection with the Manchester shuttle. As ever, Seymour was petrified as the aircraft made its landing approach into Geneva. He fell into a state of panic at the alarming screech when the rubber undercarriage wheels contacted the concrete runway, and he struggled to avoid throwing up over the seat in front. To say that he was not a good flyer would be an understatement. As he used to tell his wife, 'It's not fear of flying; it is fear of crashing that I suffer from.'

Throughout the descent, he gripped the crease of his trousers tightly and his hands sweated profusely. The engines reversed and the aircraft's rapid deceleration propelled him back into the headrest. It was with a silent prayer of 'thank you' to some unseen deity that he unclenched his fists and the plane came to rest, before taxiing slowly over to the disembarkation apron. So great was his relief that when the illuminated sign indicated that he could unbuckle his seat belt, he sprang to his feet, hastily grabbed his briefcase from the luggage rack, and rushed headlong to be first off the plane. He had landed safely, with no loss of life. Once outside, he walked briskly into the terminal building of Geneva International Airport.

Seymour cleared customs quickly, collected his baggage from the carousel and took the first available taxi at the kerbside rank.

'Wo Sir?' asked the driver.

Not speaking a word of German, but grasping his meaning, Seymour tore off his luggage label and handed it

Twelve

to him. The driver uttered a curt *"Bitte"*, and set off on the short fifteen minute journey to the Hotel Warwick in the Rue de Lausanne overlooking Lake Geneva.

*

Seymour's appointment with the president of the BrenSchweiz Bank International was at 11 o'clock next morning. The moment he walked into the building, he was awed by the grandeur of the spacious interior. It's extravagantly patterned marble floor, the detailing of its furniture and the bronze caryatid light fittings were all expensively elaborate and of a high order of art. The coloured stained glass of the tall windows and the echoing coffered ceilings gave it just that air of affluence, immense strength and time-honoured security, that it had been designed to do. He was no expert, but even an ordinary copper could see that. His father would have appreciated such fine craftsmanship.

'This,' Seymour thought, 'Is exactly where I'd want to keep my ill-gotten gains.'

He walked over to the long desk in the lobby. The receptionist had been expecting him. She escorted him to an anteroom outside the president's office where he waited, sitting uncomfortably on one of the German-made black leather and chromium steel chairs that he knew his father would have hated. In stark contrast to the main hall, these were examples of a style of industrialised modernist design that he always detested.

Displayed on the glass table beside him was a selection of promotional brochures, in a variety of languages, including English.

He began to read the mission statement on the inside page:

> *"At BrenSchweiz Bank International every client is of unique value to us and guaranteed integrity,*

*confidentiality and loyalty in handling their private
affairs is paramount among our core values ... "*

It continued in a similar vein, but there was no need to read further; Seymour got the idea. He replaced the brochure on the table as the office door opened and he was ushered inside politely.

The bank's president sat behind a huge glass-topped desk at the far end of a large room. Its surface was devoid of any clutter, except for a laptop computer, a pristine blotter pad, (which was probably for effect and never actually used, thought Seymour), and a telephone. Swiss efficiency, combined with the slightest trace of extravagant decadence, oozed from the very fabric of the room, as it had done in the anteroom. Yet another plaque, smaller, but located precisely at the epicentre of the desktop, identified him:

"Gunter von Steinmann, President"

Seymour walked over and the banker came round the desk to greet him. They shook hands jerkily.

'Good morning Detective Seymour,' he said. 'Or would you prefer me to address you as Agent Seymour?' News evidently got around fast.

'Either will do, Herr Steinmann,' he replied.

'So how may I help you?'

Seymour took out the documentation from his briefcase and spread it over the desktop. 'I believe these will explain the purpose of my visit,' he said.

Steinmann was visibly irritated at the sudden appearance of unsolicited and randomly arranged papers on his otherwise scrupulously tidy desk. He raised an eyebrow, but said nothing, picked up a sheet, took out his spectacles and began to read.

'So what have we here?' It was a rhetorical question. He leafed through a few sheets and looked up.

Twelve

'I see,' said Steinmann. 'This is all very irregular. You must appreciate that the BrenSchweiz maintains the strictest confidentiality as a matter of operational policy. We have long subscribed to a duty of absolute silence regarding accounts held by us.'

'I realise that, Herr Steinmann, but I think you will find that all the papers are in order. Permissions have been granted by the highest authorities and it is our understanding that the BrenSchweiz is a signatory to the International Bank Disclosure Initiative.'

'That is correct. We are co-signatories to the agreement, but I believe it only concerns accounts held within the last thirty years. While I accept that your papers appear to be in order, I cannot say that I am happy, Detective Seymour.'

He examined several papers again, taking a little more time to digest the contents, before he continued. 'You understand that the Agreement was primarily initiated by the IRS to deal specifically with American clients, and your request appears to relate to the account of a British subject.'

'We are aware of the sensitivity of our request, Herr Steinmann, and realise that while it may exceed the precise terms of the Agreement, a spirit of co-operation and good faith between us may make it possible for you to accede to it. Also, you have our assurance that whatever information you provide will remain in-house and will not to be for general distribution.'

'Can I have that in writing?'

'I believe you will find a confidentiality letter to that effect contained in the file.'

This seemed to go some way to satisfy Steinmann's reservations.

'I will, of course, require some proof of identity.'

'I would have been surprised had it been otherwise.' Seymour handed Steinmann his passport and warrant card.

'May we make photocopies of the documents?' asked Steinmann. 'You will understand the need for caution and prudence on our part, of course.'

'Yes. Naturally,' Seymour agreed.

Steinmann pressed a buzzer beneath the desktop and an assistant entered the room. He whispered a few instructions and handed over Seymour's documents.

Steinmann resumed. 'I note that this authority extends to just one account.'

'Yes, that of Mister Arthur Pascoe. He is believed to have travelled under several nationalities, but the account in question was probably established based on British documentation. We cannot be certain, but we believe that the UK was his country of birth.'

'Precisely what level of access do you expect from us?'

'Ideally we'd like to examine everything relating to the account, but we would be grateful for whatever you feel able to allow us to access.'

Steinmann continued inspecting the documents thoughtfully. 'May I ask what it is about this particular account that has aroused your department's interest?'

'It concerns an on-going case that we have been pursuing for some time,' replied Seymour. 'Mister Pascoe appears to have operated across several countries, including East Africa, the Balkans as well as in the United States. However, he has no apparent means of support, despite the considerable expenses that these operations must have incurred. Her Majesty's Revenue & Customs and the Metropolitan Serious Fraud Squad have also expressed an interest in this man's finances. It is possible that monies came from illegal sources and perhaps are even going to fund terrorist training in the Middle East.'

'You have evidence to back up this supposition?'

'Only circumstantially. Indeed, his funds may have been acquired perfectly legitimately. However, without access to the account we cannot be certain. We are

Twelve

especially interested in statements of deposits and withdrawals on the account over the last five years. Perhaps even further back if that proves necessary. Either way, such details will help explain the discrepancies, even if only to eliminate him from our enquiries.'

Steinmann seemed satisfied with the reasons Seymour had given, but he was slow to respond. 'I need to consult with my directors before I can agree to your request. I hope you will understand, Detective Seymour, but I cannot sanction it without further consultation.'

'Naturally, I understand,' said Seymour. 'How long do you envisage it will take?'

'I shall convene a meeting with the board later today, and should have an answer for you tomorrow. Say around late morning?'

'That would be excellent,' said Seymour. 'I hope you feel able to accommodate our request fully.'

'We shall do our very best, detective.'

'I look forward to meeting again. Good day, Herr Steinmann.'

'*Auf wiedersehen*, detective.'

*

At eleven o'clock next morning, Seymour sat once again before the great glass desk of Gunter von Steinmann. Resting upon it lay a slim Manila file secured by a large rubber band.

'We have agreed,' announced Steinmann, 'that within certain bounds, we are able to grant you access to the account of Mister Arthur Pascoe. However, as the account has existed for many years, certain ... how shall we say ... certain more sensitive details have been thought necessary to withhold.'

'I am delighted that you feel able to accommodate us,' replied Seymour.

Steinmann slid the file across the polished desktop.

When Seymour opened it, he found that significant portions of the content had been redacted. Dense black blocks obscured substantial paragraphs. He had not been afforded absolute carte blanche. Nevertheless, after he had flipped through a few pages he found what he was hoping for.

Seymour was astonished to see the balance of the account. It currently stood at more than forty-seven and three-quarter million dollars. Curiously, page after page of statements showed no evidence of any money being paid in. 'There are no deposits being made into this account,' he said aloud. 'Is that right?'

'Quite correct,' replied Steinmann. 'In fact, if you look back through the file you will discover that there have been no monies paid in since it was originally set up in 1769.'

'Surely there must be some mistake,' said Seymour. 'Are you certain about the date?'

'Absolutely,' Steinmann assured him. 'There is no mistake. The original sum of six hundred guineas was transferred in 1768 from the Dale End branch of Lloyds Bank in Birmingham. There is no record of the name of the depositor, as few records still exist from that time. But Lloyds may be able provide you with that information, if they still have it.'

'That's astonishing,' said Seymour incredulously. 'So how did it end up here?'

'The sum was transported overland and deposited in gold coinage, according to what few records still exist. The BrenSchweiz was a small family bank at the time and this was a substantial sum, as you can imagine. Herr BrenSchweiz, our founder, extended considerable privileges to such an important customer, and he was granted a very high level of personal confidentiality. Hence, the depositor's name went unrecorded. However, the account is very active as you may see from recent statements. Today it totals many millions of dollars and

Twelve

sums are regularly withdrawn - the last just two weeks ago. Though none is ever paid in, as you say, the balance has grown into a sizeable amount over the years, through accrued compound interest and the dividends from several investment portfolios which we maintain for the client. My directors considered some of these details to be so confidential that they have been redacted, as you can see. But we believe these are not relevant to your enquiries.'

'So have you ever personally ever met the current account holder?'

'No I have not,' replied Steinmann.

Seymour produced copies of the camera images of Pascoe and Cameron taken at Jeddah Airport. 'Have you ever seen either of these men?' he asked.

'I can't say that I have,' replied Steinmann. 'No I'm certain. I have never seen either person before. But that's not unusual. We rarely come face to face with account holders these days; most financial transactions are completed online, by card, or from an ATM. One thing is certain, whoever they are, this group of people has substantial funds at their disposal.'

'You speak of 'this group of people'. So not just the one account holder?'

'No. If you take a look at the authorised signatories, you will see that there are twelve names listed for those who may draw on the account.'

Seymour looked down the list. 'There are twelve joint account holders?'

'There are, yes.'

Pascoe and Cameron's names were listed, which came as no surprise to him. But he had not anticipated ten others. The very last page of the file contained an address where quarterly statements of account were sent:

"Stradina della Chiesina 1,
Capella da Campo, Toscana
50230 Italia."

At last, the Italian connection was confirmed and identified.

Chapter 18: Capella da Campo

The budget flight from Liverpool John Lennon Airport was considerably less comfortable than that to Geneva had been less than a week earlier, but the landing at Pisa was equally traumatic for Seymour. He vowed that next time he would travel the long way round by car.

Unlike the swift Swiss border controls, Pisa's were leisurely and time-consuming and he found himself at the tail end of an earlier flight arrival. Several hundred people queued ahead of him and it was almost an hour later that he cleared the terminal building. Formalities complete, he walked out into the airport complex and a throng of Italian travellers.

Pisa was pleasantly warm. The early days of autumn had seen the last of the sticky humidity and soaring temperatures that had dominated the Tuscan summer that year. Violent electrical storms and heavy rainfall had cooled the land and occasional thunderclaps still rumbled around the valleys. He made his way directly to the car rental desk where a vehicle was awaiting collection. It took a few moments to get his bearings, before he picked up direction signs for Livorno-Genoa motorway and the Florence turn-off enroute to Lucca.

The forty kilometres to the City of Lucca took just forty-five minutes on the fast E76 autostrade, but by the time he reached the city outskirts, the relative ease and flow of the uncluttered motorways was a fading memory. He soon realised that driving around Italian cities was going to be a nerve-wracking experience.

European driving was still a nervy occupation for English first-timers. Everything was either the wrong way round or on the *wrong* side of the road. There was also the constant cacophony of car horns, bumper-to-bumper queues of near-stationary vehicles and screeching tyres on polished asphalt. Such distractions, though they appeared to leave the indigenous population unfazed, made British motorists grit their teeth. They travelled more in hope than any certainty of arrival. These alien encounters accompanied any route through urban Italy, where motorists seemed to regard the rules of the highway as guidelines rather than legal constraints. In order to survive the journey, Seymour concluded that he must abandon his inherently defensive driving technique and go native. Thus, he settled into a more aggressive mode that would only be moderated by the occasional speed camera or the ever-vigilant Carabinieri parked up at the roadside in their highly-tuned Alpha Romeos.

His route though Lucca followed the ring road clockwise around the fortified walls, along a wide tree-lined avenue and past several major portals into the old city. Overhead banners honoured the city's most famous and celebrated sons. Among these were numbered Giovanni Arnolfini, counsellor to the Duke of Burgundy, subject of Van Eyck's *Arnolfini Portrait* in London's National Gallery, and Giacomo Puccini, Lucca's much-loved world-famous composer of operas like *Madame Butterfly* and *Turandot*. However, Seymour found driving too stressful to spare a thought for the city's cultural history.

Once clear of the suburbs, the road branched off towards Abetone and Castelnuovo, following the valley of the River Serchio northwards out into the open Tuscan countryside and on towards the Apuane Alps. He passed through the village of Borgo a Mozzano with its spectacular arched Ponte della Maddalena footbridge, which spanned the river just above the weir. Perhaps he would stop and look on his return journey, but this was not the time for tourism either.

*

It was late afternoon by the time he passed Fornacci de Barga and reached the village of Capella da Campo. Its

Twelve

main street was already jammed solid with extensive traffic tailbacks as the local school-run was in progress. However, he made better time once he had turned off the main highway and began ascending the almost traffic-free Strada Principale up into the mountains. He drove past the turn-off to Castelnuovo, leaving the river valley behind and the road began to climb steeply. Progress was slower on the numerous hairpin bends, and frequent gaps in the roadside barriers slowed him even further, as he reflected on his own mortality. At one such place, a memorial had been erected, decorated with wreathes and a makeshift wooden crucifix, where some poor soul had gone over the edge and down the mountainside.

These were not the easiest of driving conditions at the best of times. Here and there, road signs indicated that snow chains were required during winter months, but even had he been so prepared, he would not have attempted the climb at that time of year.

Presently, he came to the Stradina della Chiesina. It was a narrow unpaved track, barely wide enough for a single vehicle. It led steeply down an incline to a hillside terrace on which stood a large villa. At a wider passing place half way down, Seymour pulled in and parked the car. Immediately he stepped out of the vehicle, his senses were met with heady perfume of wild lavender and an aroma of roasting chestnuts.

He was still taking in the pungent atmosphere, when, as if from nowhere, a huge wolf-like dog came running up the track towards him, barking noisily. Seymour's immediate instinct was to get back into the car, but when he saw the animal's tail wagging away excitedly, he knew that it would not be necessary. The dog came to heel beside him and looked up for approval, nuzzling Seymour's thigh for attention. He stooped to stroke its thick long coat and the beast licked his hand. Thus having bonded in a new and unexpected friendship, they strolled amiably together down the remainder of the track and onto the patio in front of the house.

As they approached the villa, a matronly woman, alerted by the commotion, emerged from the front doorway. She came over and addressed Seymour in Italian.

'*Mi dispiace per il cane, signor,*' she said, '*... è del tutto innocuo e non avrebbe fatto male a una mosca.*'

'*Non parlo molto bene l'italiano,*' Seymour replied. 'I don't speak very good Italian.'

Then she smiled and repeated herself in English. 'I'm sorry about the dog, signor, but he's quite harmless and wouldn't hurt a fly; unless you are a porcupine or a snake, that is, in which case he will go for you!'

'No, I see that he's very friendly, despite initial impressions.'

'So what can I do for you today?' she asked.

'I've come to see the owner of the house,' he replied.

'The master is not at home at present.' Her tone was apologetic.

'Do you know when he'll be back?'

'We can never be sure. Sometimes it's weeks, even months before he returns.'

'Do you know where he's gone?'

'I'm sorry to ask, signor,' said the woman, 'but without wishing to cause any offence, may I ask who you are and what is your business here?'

'I should have said. I'm an old friend,' he lied.

'Ah, I see,' she replied. 'The master rarely says where he's going or when he'll be back. He often jets off on business and is away for some time. I believe he is currently in the Camargue region of southern France. He hardly spends time here at all these days'.

'So you act as caretaker while he's away?'

'Yes, together with my husband,' she replied. 'We manage the day-to-day running of the estate. Sandro does any odd jobs that are needed around the place.'

She had not yet actually said that this was Pascoe's

Twelve

property, but Seymour needed to confirm that he had arrived at the right address. 'This is the house of Mister Pascoe isn't it?'

'It is indeed the house of Signor Pas-a-coe.'

'Arthur Pascoe?'

'Yes, I believe that's his given name, but to us he is simply the master.'

'I'm sorry to have missed him. I've intended to visit for some time. He has spoken about it often,' he lied again. 'I wonder would you'd think it impertinent if I asked to look around the place?'

'Not at all,' she replied. 'I'm sure the master would have shown you around himself had he been here.' She went back inside and Seymour strolled leisurely around the grounds.

It was a large house, typical of Tuscan villas, distinctive in its terracotta rendering, painted window shutters and the overhanging pantile roof. Three storeys high, it was built on a wide terrace, one of a succession that covered the whole of the steep hillside. The villa's high vantage point offered panoramic views across the Serchio Valley to the mountains opposite and the dense plantations of trees that covered the lower slopes. Alongside the house, the large lawn was scorched brown with prolonged exposure to the summer sun. Upon it stood a light helicopter, sheltered beneath a canvas cover, its rotor blades roped to pegs driven into the lawn. Compared to the cropped brown lawn surrounding it, the long green grass growing under the landing gear skids suggested that the machine had not been moved for some time.

Beyond, a man stood waist deep in a small swimming pool and was cleaning it with a large pole net. Seymour assumed that this was the housekeeper's husband, Sandro. The man looked up from his labour and clambered out of the water.

'Signor. Can I help you?' he asked.

'The housekeeper said I might look around the property.'

'Ah that would be my wife, Assunta. It's no problem. People are coming and going all the time. But may I enquire who you are, signor, and why you are here? I am afraid the master has gone away.'

'So your good lady tells me.' Seymour thought quickly to maintain the pretext of his visit. 'Signor Pascoe is an old acquaintance of mine, and I thought it about time I paid him a long overdue visit. I hadn't given any notice and your wife informs me that he's away on a business trip in France. I guess it's just bad timing on my part.' Despite the feebleness of the fabrication, Seymour hoped it would be convincing.

'Indeed he is. But when he returns I shall tell him you called. If you will leave your contact details. I'm sure he'll be sorry that he missed you.'

'It's a very fine place,' said Seymour. 'So how long has your master lived here?'

'His family has owned it for a very long time. I was told that they came from England many years ago and have been here as long as anybody can remember. Some of his family also stay with him from time to time, brothers and sisters I think, or maybe cousins. At any rate, they are all very close.'

'I must say the whole place is immaculately kept. I suppose it must be very expensive to maintain.' Seymour already knew Pascoe's financial situation, but thought he would press the point to see how Sandro would react.

'Well, we understand that the master has some family money. An inheritance or some such. But the estate. covers more than twelve hectares and is virtually self-sufficient. Five of these are chestnut woods, which is our main cash crop. Chestnuts are a regional specialty; we roast them on site and export them all over Italy. A few go to countries abroad. The master is also seeking a market for the timber.'

Twelve

'Well, there seems to be plenty of it around.'

'More than enough for our own needs. We also have olive trees, several hectares of bamboo and a modest vineyard, as well as the beehives,' Sandro continued. 'We are reputed to produce the very best chestnut honey. Most is sold locally, but some is exported and a little is kept for the master's personal use. We have just harvested the chestnuts which are being roasted in the barn as we speak. It's a good time of year, what with wine, olives and chestnuts.'

'So you are not related to Signor Pascoe, then?'

'No, we're not part of the family – merely employees. We receive a small salary, but we live here rent free and have few food costs, as you can see.'

'Well, I mustn't keep you from your work any longer. Many thanks for talking to me. Is it okay if I look around a little more?'

'Of course. Please call me if you need anything further.'

Sandro resumed cleaning the pool while Seymour continued his tour of the grounds. At the back of the house was a wooden pergola, heavy with large trusses of ripe tomatoes. Next to it apricots, figs, lemon and kiwi fruit trees were in abundance, as well as aromatic herbs of rosemary, oregano and basil. There was no doubt about it, thought Seymour, Signor Pas-a-coe lives very well ... very well indeed!

*

Seymour was about to take his leave when Assunta reappeared at the door.

'Do you have a place to stay, signor?' she asked.

Seymour said that he had made no arrangements for the night, but that if he couldn't find lodgings, he would sleep in the back of the car.

'Nonsense,' she said. 'I feel certain that the master

would expect us to offer you a bed for the night.'

'I wouldn't want to be an inconvenience,' replied Seymour.

'It's not a problem. Quite the contrary, it would be our pleasure. No friend of the master can leave without being offered hospitality. He would never forgive us. Besides, the night is beginning to draw in and you'll have difficulty finding anywhere at such a late hour.'

'Well, as you are so very kind, how could I refuse?'

'That's settled then. I shall make up a bed in the guest lodge. It used to be a cattle shed, but the master has converted it to a modern apartment. I think you'll be very comfortable there.'

In view of their hospitality, Seymour was already beginning to feel guilty at his deception. He followed the housekeeper across the patio to the lodge.

'We never bother to lock it,' said Assunta. 'Besides the hound usually wards off any would-be intruders. His barking is usually enough. But there are keys if you'd prefer it,' she said. They entered, followed by the dog, still furiously wagging its tail.

'I'm sure it will be fine,' replied Seymour. 'I've put you to enough trouble as it is. I really am most grateful.'

'There are towels and toiletries in the shower room; please feel free to use whatever you wish. If the hound is a nuisance, just put him out. He is a yard dog and not allowed in the main house anyway, but he will take every opportunity he can to sneak in, especially if he thinks you are easy-going. He's very clever, that dog.'

'No, it's fine. I quite like his company.'

'Very well. But you must join us for dinner. We usually eat in the kitchen at eight o'clock. It will not be much, but you are most welcome to join us. Just make your way over to the house when you are ready.'

*

Twelve

Assunta had prepared a meal of pasta and porcini mushrooms dressed in olive oil and a fragrant fresh basil pesto. It was accompanied by a green salad and a crusty cottage loaf from southern Italy, a Pane Pugliese, which Assunta broke with her hands and distributed with all the solemnity of a Eucharist. Meantime, Sandro poured out copious quantities of the estate's own Sangiovese wine. Seymour had no idea, nor cared much what sort of wine he was drinking, but it tasted good, and to refuse would have been unthinkable. So he drank. Tomorrow would be soon enough to deal with the inevitable guilt and its consequences. When the meal was over, Seymour commented on the superb location of the estate.

'Tell me,' he asked. 'How old is the house?'

'I believe the family took ownership of the land many hundreds of years ago,' said Sandro. 'As far as we know, the Pas-a-coes built the house and cut the terraces by hand. We believe his ancestors also planted the chestnut trees. They probably intended them for fuel back then. The chestnut business came later. Much of late summer and early autumn is spent felling some of them and stacking wood to fuel the stove. It heats the whole house through winter.'

'You never need be cold with such forests of timber around you.'

'No. We are pretty well provided. Being so isolated, we need to be, and at this altitude, we are regularly snowed in through winter. I expect you will have seen the signs regarding tyre chains on your way up here. When it's really bad, cars can't make it at all and we use the tractor. You can get around pretty well in that. Unless it gets really bad.'

'I couldn't help noticing you also have a helicopter,' said Seymour.

'That's the master's, of course. My wife and I don't fly,' said Sandro. 'He pilots it down to the airport in Pisa, or Florence, where he can make connections to anywhere in the world. It tends to be wrapped up for the deepest part of winter – we're getting it ready just now. Helicopters don't fly well in very cold weather or poor visibility, he says, and with steep mountainsides, you have to be careful. Strong side winds can be a real hazard.'

'So how did Signor Pascoe get to the airport?'

'He drove,' replied Sandro. 'He also drives a small pickup truck, and uses the helicopter when the roads are completely impassable.'

Assunta began to clear away the dishes and Seymour felt that he had taken the interrogation as far as he could without becoming intrusive. Sandro seemed to sense an end to the conversation.

'I'm about to do my rounds and feed the dog,' he said. 'If you'd like to look around the house I'd be happy to show you.'

'Yes, go signor,' said Assunta. 'You might find it interesting.'

'If you're certain I wouldn't be in the way,' replied Seymour.

'Not at all.'

He thanked Assunta for her hospitality and praised her cooking before the two men began the tour of the house.

A central corridor ran the entire length of the ground floor. Its plain white walls and red quarry floors were elegant and simple. They would have been thought too cold for the English climate, but in this Tuscan mountain retreat, they would provide a cooling interior for hot days of summer.

A gallery of family portraits hung on the corridor walls, apparently representing many generations and dating back several centuries. They appeared to record an unbroken line of landed aristocracy that would not be out of place in a Florentine Palace. However, when Seymour inspected the paintings more closely, the unmistakable Pascoe features looked out from every canvas. Sandro

Twelve

noted his curiosity.

'All the master's ancestors had those distinctive Pas-a-coe features in common, don't you agree?' he commented.

'Indeed. Quite remarkable,' replied Seymour. 'As you say, it is a very strong family resemblance. One could easily mistake them for the same person.'

Sandro failed to react, but as Seymour compared one picture with another, he became more curious. The oldest portrait, perhaps from the eighteenth century, was of a young man in his early twenties, resplendent in a powdered wig and holding an ebony cane with a silver pommel. It could easily have been a young Arthur Pascoe himself. As he progressed along the gallery, costumes and hairstyles changed, but the likenesses remained uncannily identical. The facial features of every portrait were virtual facsimiles of the others.

At the far end, Seymour's attention was drawn to a small photograph, the only one in the whole collection. It was a faded sepia image, judging by the soft-vignette of the edges. It portrayed a family member in soldier's uniform. The figure had a rifle slung over his shoulder and a bandolier belt diagonally across his chest. He wore a beret, jauntily tilted back to reveal the same familiar Pascoe features. Though rough looking and unshaven, the moustache longer and unclipped, it was undeniably Pascoe's face. Standing in front of the soldier stood a small boy of perhaps eight or ten years old. He was wearing a long apron that reached down to his ankles and he carried a bowl of some sort.

'What can you tell me about the photograph, Signor Sandro?' asked Seymour. 'Who's the little boy?'

'I'm not exactly certain, but I believe the soldier may have been the master's grandfather. I am told it was taken in 1936, when he volunteered to fight in the Spanish Civil War. As for the boy, I have no idea who he is, except that he will be a very old man by now.'

'I notice that there are no women represented in the collection,' said Seymour.

'No, only the male line of the Pas-a-coe family are represented,' explained Sandro. 'The tradition goes back hundreds of years.'

'Even so,' said Seymour. 'It is odd. Has your master never been married?'

'No, signor, he was never so blessed. He is a man who is content in himself.'

*

It has been said that for the alcoholic, one drink is too many and a hundred are not enough. This old maxim ran around Seymour's head the following morning, as his dry mouth and the craving persisted unabated. He fought the dehydration, courteously declined the hot ciabatta toast and chestnut honey that was offered at breakfast, and settled for several cups of freshly percolated black coffee.

'You cannot possibly drive back to Pisa on an empty stomach,' rebuked Assunta in a motherly fashion.

'I'll get a pizza or something at the airport,' he replied. 'Food is the very last thing on my mind just now. Too much of your very fine vino.' He laughed.

He had decided on an early departure to catch a return flight home, but before he left, Seymour handed Sandro a slip of paper on which he had written a fictitious telephone number. Sandro said that the master would be sorry to have missed him.

As he made the long drive back through Tuscany, Seymour could not get out of his mind the almost identical features of the portraits that were displayed at the villa. It could simply have been a strong family resemblance, as Sandro had said, but the more he thought on, the less tenable the point became.

Twelve

Chapter 19: Covent Garden

The Tuscany debriefing at Vauxhall Cross lasted well into the afternoon.

'Your report is very detailed, Seymour,' Caroline Massey began. 'We have already spoken with Lloyds confirming the initial bank setup and the transfer of gold to Switzerland. It looks genuine enough. The BrenSchweiz's account of Pascoe's involvement also checks out, so we have concluded that it would have been a great-grandfather, several times removed, who facilitated the transfer. The money seems to have been a legitimate family inheritance. Of course, we cannot know the source of the original funds - records no longer exist. In any case, after so many centuries, it's not pertinent to our current investigation and would be a waste of time and resources to pursue further.

'However, I note that several other names are attached to the account - people who can also draw on funds, including the late Patrick Cameron.'

'Yes. Cameron's name on the list was not altogether unexpected,' said Seymour. 'The connection between Pascoe and Cameron was already well established. But it hadn't occurred to me that there could be others.'

'Nor to us, either. But, given that both Cameron and Pascoe assumed bogus identities, we are no closer to knowing who they really are, despite having a list of their names. They could all be similarly assumed identities.' She paused. 'Now as to this Tuscan residence. What is this place called? Capella de something or other ...?'

'Capella da Campo.'

'That's right. You have reported in great detail what you saw there, but I'm having trouble understanding some of your conclusions.'

'Which conclusions in particular?'

'I refer to a note at the end.' She began to read a fragment aloud. 'You wrote, and I quote, *"I formed the impression that these might not have been portraits of different generations, but of the same man – of Arthur Pascoe himself'.* Can you explain how and why you came to that conclusion?'

'Can't really explain – call it more of a gut feeling. I know it makes no apparent sense, but there are such strong facial similarities in all the portraits.'

'So what are you saying?' asked Massey.

'I'm saying that, in my opinion, they were not all just very similar ... I think they were portraits of the same man!'

'That doesn't make any sense, Seymour.' She sounded irritable.

'I know it seems preposterous, but I believe Arthur Pascoe may have posed for all of the paintings.'

'But what would be the point?'

'I don't know. Perhaps he has illusions of grandeur, or aristocracy. Maybe to create an ancestry or a fictitious history for himself - maybe.'

'Maybe? Is this the best you can come up with? This is all unsubstantiated guesswork! I have to say, Seymour, I'm very disappointed.' She was now showing visible impatience.

'I have no other explanation,' he continued. 'But there was another odd thing that led me to this conclusion. There were no female portraits in the house. None at all. What happened to all the women of the family? The caretaker spoke of brothers and sisters, or cousins, who visit the villa sometimes. It was a collection of a single male line. Don't you think that's a little strange?'

'It doesn't really matter what I think, Seymour,' she replied. 'An interesting theory, but it's all speculation. That's not the function of this department. We do not deal in hypotheses here, but in evidence. You really need to get to the heart of this. Bring me facts, Seymour. Facts!'

*

Twelve

The early evening London rush hour was in full flow and the lengthy meeting had all but exhausted Seymour. He found a small bed and breakfast place, just a short walk to Euston Station. He would catch a train back to Manchester next morning. After showering, he decided to call his wife Sarah.

'Hello love,' he began. 'How are things?'

'Fine, everything's fine. Glad you're back safely. How was flying?' she asked.

'You know me and flying. Least said about that the better.'

'So how did it go in Italy?'

'Well, Tuscany's very beautiful and Italians drive like maniacs, of course. Apart from that, I only found out a few things – less than I'd hoped for. Otherwise, it was just routine.'

'Hardly routine! More like a short holiday break! When will you be home?'

'Hopefully tomorrow, or the day after. It all depends whether they want me back for further debriefing.'

'So where are you now?' she asked.

'I'm staying at the Tasman Hotel in Gower Street. It's cheap and cheerful, but they only do bed and breakfast, so I'm about to go out for a curry or something.'

'Okay, see you soon. Enjoy your curry. Take care. Love you.'

'I will. Love you too. Kiss Daisy for me.'

He had hardly finished speaking to Sarah when an incoming text message arrived on his mobile. He could not identify the number. It simply read:

"Where R U? Still in Italy or in London yet?"

He cautiously responded. "London. Is this who I think it is?" His reply had still not been sent when it was pre-empted by an incoming call. He answered immediately. It was Katherine Chaplin.

'So when did you get back?' she asked.

'You're still stalking me, Katherine. 'Got back yesterday. How did you know where I was?'

'I wheedled it out of Professor Fosse. He's a big softie really, and a girl only has to flutter her eyelashes at him. He told me you were in Italy and that you were expected back any day soon, so I thought I'd just try ringing you.'

'I must have words with Max when I get back.'

'No, I'd prefer you not to,' she replied. 'I wouldn't want to embarrass him.'

'So where exactly are you now?'

'I've just got off the train,' she replied. 'I thought I'd risk a text, on the off chance that you were back. I'm at Euston Station, just up the road.'

'You're in London?'

'Yes. I have a tutorial at LSE tomorrow morning for my Open University course. And, as I have some time off due to me, I thought I'd take a couple of days down here in London.'

'It's a bit of a coincidence that your tutorial appointment is while I'm in town as well,' he said.

'It's not a coincidence,' she continued. 'I knew you were already here, or soon would be, and I managed to get a last minute slot so that we could meet up. I'm staying at the Palace Hotel in the Strand. I've got a seat for a West End show this evening. Bit of a treat. Why don't you join me?'

'I'm already booked in at a B&B on Gower Street. It's a bit late to get a last minute ticket in the West End anyway. Besides, I'm a bit knackered, so I think I'd best pass up the offer. Maybe some other time.'

'Oh come on, Charlie,' she chided. 'Live a little dangerously.'

He thought for a while, and relented. 'I suppose I could grab a few hours shuteye and we could meet up for dinner afterwards. I know you'll only pester me otherwise.'

'Yes, I would,' she replied. 'Do you know

Twelve

somewhere nice?'

'There's a little place I know in Covent Garden called Brasserie Bougival. It's just off the Strand, quite near where you're staying. We could meet there later.'

'The show ends around ten-thirty. I could probably make it soon after that.'

'Okay, I'll book us a table and I'll see you there.'

*

The Brasserie Bougival was located about fifty yards from the heart of Covent Garden. Seymour had arrived early after catching a few hours' sleep. It was a fine evening and he had walked from his hotel across town to the restaurant in Wellington Street. By 10.45 he was sitting at a small window table, impatiently watching the theatre crowds going home or making their way to one of the many chic bistros and trattorias that surround London's West End theatres. Occasionally, people would stop to peer in at the window or to peruse the menu.

He was drinking a large glass of Rioja, when Katherine appeared outside and strummed on the glass pane to attract his attention. He stood up as she came in and walked over to him. Without a word, she planted a kiss firmly on his cheek, leaving a bright red lipstick smear. He was not prepared for that.

She sat down, leaned forward, took the folded handkerchief from his breast pocket and proceeded to rub his cheek as a mother might wipe the face of a child. He looked around self-consciously, but the place was still quite empty and no-one seemed to have noticed.

'Don't be so nervous,' she said, taking off her coat and gloves. 'It was an innocent kiss, and besides, nobody knows us down here. Relax, and pour me a drink.'

*

Katherine talked enthusiastically about the show at the Adelphi Theatre. Seymour could not take his eyes off her as she described her Business Management course at the London School of Economics. In turn, he told her what he could of his Italian trip, of the Tuscan landscape, chestnut woods and a wolf dog. He said nothing of the purpose of his visit. 'Just routine work,' he said. 'Nice place, but a wasted visit really.'

She pressed him no further.

Seymour had given little thought to how much wine he had drunk; he had taken for granted that he would be able to handle it. But when they stood up to leave, he swayed unsteadily and realised that his system was not as used to alcohol as it was. But he felt good. Overcome by a profound sense of wellbeing, he regained his balance, happy that it could be like this. Drinking openly and socially, in company. Not secretively, guiltily, or alone.

Katherine linked his arm and they walked down Wellington Street into the Strand. He felt a little self-conscious, but liked it. Had she not met up with him, he would have probably spent the night drinking alone until he passed out, or until daylight dawned, or both. Perhaps she would be a far better addiction than alcohol had ever been.

They reached the Palace Hotel, where she was staying. A liveried concierge stood formally outside and opened the door in readiness as they approached. 'This is my hotel,' she said, pointing to its large imposing entrance. 'You could come in for a nightcap.'

He looked at his watch; it was well past one o'clock in the morning.

'It's still early for London, you know,' she said. 'The hotel serves through the night – you can get anything, even a pot of tea and biscuits!'

'Okay,' he replied, 'Maybe just a quick one.'

Ten minutes later, they sat in the lounge, she with a fine Armagnac and he with a small pot of tea. She drank

Twelve

up quickly. 'Come upstairs with me,' she said, completely unexpectedly. 'Stay tonight. I have a huge king size bed. It's far too big for one.'

He paused thoughtfully. 'Are you sure?' he said.

'I am absolutely sure.'

He nodded; they walked hand in hand over to the lift and went up to her room.

*

It was the afternoon of the next day.

The great elevator rose up from the subterranean platforms of Covent Garden, creaking and groaning as it ascended the equivalent of fifteen storeys. Katherine chose to take it, despite its dingy antiquity and the crush of other bodies pinning her into a corner. The alternative would be to climb the never-ending staircase up from the depths of the old underground station.

She emerged from the gloom into the afternoon sunlight, turned into Long Acre and walked down James Street to the Covent Garden Market building. Seymour stood waiting beneath the arch of the Apple Market, as they had arranged. He came forward and they greeted each other in a long sustained embrace.

'How was the tutorial?' he asked.

'Not exactly awe-inspiring. But it's a mandatory course element. What you might call routine.'

They strolled around every stall and market stand in the Covent Garden complex for an hour or so, stopping occasionally to inspect a souvenir. Later they sat on a bench, drinking coffee from paper cups and eating thick minted lamb sandwiches bought from a street stall. Seymour was unusually quiet and withdrawn.

'Not regretting last night already?' she asked.

'No, not yet,' he replied. 'That might come later, but not at this exact moment.' He looked at his watch. 'But, all good things must end sometime, and I need to get back to Gower Street and check out. There's a train at six-thirty.'

'You're leaving, already?' She looked disappointed.

He thought for a moment. 'Well I was originally planning to return home today, but maybe tomorrow will be soon enough. And, who knows, I could be summoned to another meeting at Vauxhall Cross.'

'Do you think that's likely?'

'No, I don't. My business down here is concluded,' he replied. 'At least, for the time being. But it would be an excellent pretext to stay on longer.'

So, they spent a second night together in Katherine Chaplin's bed on the fourth floor at the Palace Hotel, and providentially, as Seymour had anticipated, there was no summons to another meeting with Caroline Massey at Vauxhall Cross.

*

The following day at Euston Station, they boarded the late morning train to Manchester. Seymour had collected his luggage from Gower Street and paid the bill for all the facilities that he had not used. At the station, they chose to upgrade to a First Class compartment, which would be more private, especially since it was almost empty.

'So is this it then?' said Katherine, when they had settled into their seats.

'I guess so,' he replied. 'It's been great, Katie, but it has to end here.'

'If you say so.'

'Sorry,' he apologised. 'It's just the way it has to be.'

'No need to be sorry. I suppose I expected it and I knew what I was getting into. You made it quite clear from the outset. But, for what it's worth, I would not have missed a moment of it. One brilliant weekend of passion! I can live with that.'

Twelve

He took her hand and squeezed it gently. Suddenly, a man passed through the compartment and interrupted their conversation.

'Detective Sergeant Seymour!' he proclaimed.

Seymour looked up and instantly recognised Superintendent Joseph Golding, his former superior officer. ('Shit!' he thought. 'Holy Joe. That's all I need.')

'You must introduce me to your lady friend, detective.' Golding's tone was sarcastic and laced with sufficient menacing innuendo to make Seymour wriggle uneasily in his seat.

'This is Katherine Chaplin. My liaison at the university.' Then he turned to Katherine. 'This is Superintendent Golding, my former station chief.'

'Yes, former is the right word. Least said about that the better,' said Golding. 'I must say you seem to be doing very well for yourself in your newfound privileged position.'

'Things are going well, thank you very much.' Seymour's response was curt.

'You appear to have come up in the world. Travelling First Class. Your new friends at Vauxhall Cross paying for this then, are they?'

'It's on expenses, yes.'

'Typical! Lucky for some.'

Seymour shrugged, and Golding turned to leave. 'Well I mustn't keep you,' he said with a threatening undertone. 'I expect you two would like to be alone. Please remember me to your wife.' With that, he continued along the carriage and disappeared into the next car.

'What an awfully unpleasant man,' said Katherine.

'That hypocrite wasn't called Holy Joe for nothing. He's a nasty patronising and unholy piece of shit! We all breathed a huge sigh of relief when he was moved on.'

He said nothing more of it, but the episode left Seymour with an abiding sense of foreboding.

*

Caroline Massey contacted Seymour at home next day by telephone.

'Check your computer,' she began. 'I've just sent you an email with a photograph attachment. Stay on the phone and let me know when you receive it.'

After a few moments, the email arrived. 'Yes, I've got it now,' he said. It took a minute for the image to load on screen and reveal a fragment of the photograph that he had already seen during his visit to Tuscany.

'Have you got it all yet?' asked Massey.

'Yes,' he replied. 'It's the photo I wrote about in my report, only a fuller version.'

'That's what I thought. It seemed to tally with what you had described.'

The screen image portrayed two ranks of militiamen, apparently International Brigade volunteers in the Republican army during the Spanish Civil War. It was an expanded version of the photo in the villa at Capella da Campo and was captioned *"Toledo 1936"*. Smaller captions below identified each figure by name. Most appeared to be Spanish nationals, but the last, on the far right, was named as Arthur Donald Pascoe. Before him stood a small boy who was identified as José Antonio Gomez.

'Where on earth did you come across this?' asked Seymour.

'Would you believe we just Googled it and it came up in the images?'

'It never occurred to me to do that,' said Seymour.

'It took us some time to think of it too. We sometimes look for complications where the simple solution is often staring us right in the face.'

'Apparently so. But what was the original image source?'

'It came from an old clipping in a Belgian newspaper called *"De Standaard"*; it's based in Antwerp.

Twelve

Apparently they had a war correspondent in Spain during the Civil War, and he took many photos during the siege of Toledo in the summer of 1936.'

'But the name is specifically Arthur Donald Pascoe. How can that be?'

'What's your point?'

'It's the middle name – Donald!'

'I can't account for that – I didn't write the caption, Seymour. But I don't regard that as necessarily significant. Traditional and recurring family names are not exactly uncommon.'

'No, but it's rare to perpetuate the same first, middle and surnames, don't you think?'

'You may have a point,' she replied.

'And who's the lad in the picture? This José seems particularly attached to Pascoe.'

'We are currently looking into records dating from the Civil War period. Perhaps that will throw some light on things. Pascoe seems to have enlisted under his real name, so there should be a record somewhere, as well as for this boy José. Records may remain in Toledo, though I understand much of pre-Civil War documentation was centralised in Madrid after Franco came to power. During the Fascist regime, many records were kept hidden, but with the monarchy restored and Spain being a member of the European Union, it might prove easier to get hold of information. I'll keep you posted, if we come up with anything.'

An oddly improbable thought was emerging in Seymour's head. Arthur Donald Pascoe had become a troubling paradox.

Chapter 20: La Mancha

It was in the very early hours of the 12th of June 1936 when Arthur Pascoe had come ashore just short of the harbour at Cudillero. The small powerboat from which he landed had departed from Biarritz in France a day earlier. It had made a wide sweep across the Bay of Biscay to avoid the rocky coastline of the Costa Verde, before turning inland for one of the few sheltered inlets on the northern Spanish coast. He had chosen to disembark at this quiet Asturian fishing village because of its relative remoteness and inaccessibility.

It was the height of a very hot summer and they were perilous times. The first rumblings of civil war had spread from the south as many Spanish towns had already rejected General Franco's Fascist Nationalists in support of the democratically elected Republican government. Major cities like Seville and Cordoba had declared for the Republic and resistance to the Fascists was well advanced in the Catalan stronghold of Barcelona. But, with alarming rapidity, the impetus had spread northwards through Castille, Léon and La Mancha, and had reached the southern slopes of the Picos de Europa. Resistance was in the air everywhere. Rumours abounded that Oviedo on the other side of the mountains had fallen to the Nationalists, but they were unsubstantiated. Reliable news was hard to come by.

With the bow of the boat beached and the engine still running, the pilot helped Pascoe manhandle ashore the motorcycle that he had brought with him. It was a struggle to prevent its dead weight capsizing the flimsy wooden vessel as they scrambled to land it safely on solid ground. But once it was hauled clear of the drift line, over the dry shingle and onto the firm asphalt of the coast road, they could relax a little. Presently, after catching his breath, the pilot shook hands and wished Pascoe *'Adieu et bonne chance'*, and cast off.

Twelve

Pascoe stood watching as the craft sped away, illuminated in the moonlight, its ever-expanding wake cutting through the otherwise placid seascape, and it soon disappeared over the horizon. The nocturnal tranquillity of the beach was resumed once more, broken only by the gentle lapping of the waves and the chattering of pebbles as they washed back and forth along the shoreline.

After he had looked about to check that his clandestine arrival had not been observed, he took out the soft leather helmet, goggles and gauntlets from his rucksack, primed the choke and kick-started the machine into life. Although the motorcycle was twelve years old, it had been given a clean bill of health by mechanics in Biarritz. The bike was familiarly known as the 'AJS Big Port' on account of its distinctive exhaust pipe, which was unusually large for the time. Originally it had been designed as a racing sports bike, but it was also regarded as a good long distance touring machine, which was Pascoe's reason for choosing it. To complete his mission he needed to travel more than half way across Spain and that required a transport that was robust enough for the endurance test to which he was about to subject it.

The AJS was a noisy brute of a machine, but many riders liked it for that very reason. It was a motorcyclist's motorcycle. Menacingly jet-black all over, with a polished chrome silencer and tailpipe, in years to come it would be eagerly sought after as a museum classic. Its large sprung seat was comfortable and forgiving, ideal for the long rough roads and cross-country routes that lay ahead.

Pascoe was travelling light with a few basics kept in a rucksack on his back - some bread, water, a few tools, spare inner tubes, a compass and a quantity of Pesetas to see him through.

Initially, he rolled along gently, in first gear, without lights, making slow headway into the centre of Cudillero. The village and its harbour had remained largely unchanged for centuries and in happier times it had been a popular place to vacation. This was not such a time, even though the Civil War had not yet reached its secluded cove. It was quiet, not a soul was about, but even at this early hour, oil lamps still burned at a few windows.

Cudillero's characteristic fishermen's cottages were stacked in terraces up the cliff face, and formed a virtual amphitheatre around the inlet. Even by moonlight they were colourful. Below, facing the harbour slipway was the small square. There were a couple of cafes, a fish market and a solitary gas street lamp - little else.

The whirr of the tyres on the cobblestones and the low-geared growl of the engine were the only sounds in Cudillero's square. Even so, their muffled sounds amplified and echoed around the enclosed village. Black headed gulls, roused from their night roosts, screeched their displeasure at the unwarranted disturbance, and flew several circuits around the bay before settling back down to the rooftops. Apart from that, nothing stirred.

When he had cleared the village, he began to accelerate up the winding road away from the coast, towards the Camino de Santiago, a kilometre inland. This ancient highway stretched more than eight hundred kilometres, starting from just over the French border in the east and followed an unbroken route to Santiago de Compostela in the Province of Galicia in western Spain. There, reputedly, the last resting place of Saint Iago, the apostle James himself, was to be found. As one of Christianity's most sacred places, peregrinos, as the Spanish called pilgrims, had walked the so-called Way of Saint James for centuries. For Pascoe, however, this was to be a completely different pilgrimage.

When he reached the Camino he stopped, consulted his compass and took bearings. Before him stretched the high mountain barrier of the Picos de Europa, that separated the narrow coastal strip of the Costa Verde from the rest of Spain. Centuries before, these same high peaks had halted the Moorish advance

Twelve

into the far north and enabled locals to boast proudly of the unmixed purity of their blood. In those days Asturian sensibilities were untroubled by the finer points of political incorrectness.

There were two possible ways over the mountains. On the one hand, the Camino went westward into Galicia. This would take him around the Picos via Ribadeo and Lugo; it was a fast major highway and the longest of two routes. But, ever conscious that political tides might turn at any moment, he thought it best to avoid densely populated areas. On the other hand, a dozen kilometres eastwards was a high mountain pass over the top. This was a steep, cold and tortuous route, but it afforded the best chance of travelling unseen. On the downside, the road led directly to Oviedo, a city that he would prefer to avoid. All things considered, the latter was his preferred option. Maybe he would be able to bypass Oviedo enroute. So, he set off eastwards towards Soto del Barco, where the road branched off, to climb the winding hairpin bends up into the mountains.

*

Dense mists and drizzle frequently descended the lower levels of the Picos de Europa. This particular morning was no exception, but by the time dawn broke, he was through the cloud base and the verdant coastal hinterland had given way to clear air and craggy pine-covered slopes. He passed through the two small hamlets on the way up, but they had been abandoned. Spain had effectively shut down and people were preparing for the worst. Anything approaching normal life had ceased and a claustrophobic siege mentality prevailed.

Higher still, as he approached the summit, the temperature fell sharply, so that, even though it was the middle of June, his fingers became numb. It was a welcome relief when he reached a side margin near the top, where he could rest and warm up. He held his hands close to the hot crankcase to revive the circulation, before taking out an oilskin waterproof from under the saddle, and pulling it over his head against the cold moist mountain air.

He took a few sips of water from a flask. Refreshed, and with full function brought back into his hands again, he felt able to appreciate the panorama of the high mountain range at last. Nearby, cattle lay sheltering among the large erratic boulders; the proliferation of dung on the roadway and verges indicated that they regularly spent time here. These native Tudanca cattle were untethered and free to graze over the entire mountain range, their whereabouts broadcast by large bells suspended around the neck by wide leather straps.

Pascoe left the motorcycle and walked a little way from the road, intent on taking a much-needed toilet break. Although completely unseen and apparently quite alone, he decided to stand behind one of the huge rocks in an act of redundant modesty. Suddenly, to his utter amazement, he confronted a skinny waif of a boy huddled against the underside of one of the cows, in the process of suckling milk directly from the beast's udder. Pascoe stepped back astonished, and the boy jumped up, equally startled.

'Señor!' exclaimed the boy.

'What on earth are you doing, young man?' said Pascoe. It was a pointless question.

'I am drinking milk,' the boy replied.

'But why are you up here alone? Where are your parents?'

The boy told him that his family had been shot by Nationalist soldiers in Oviedo. He had been living rough for a few weeks and the only refuge he had been able to find was among the mountains, surviving on milk and a few wild berries. He had narrowly avoided capture by climbing into a storm drain, and later made his way to the

Twelve

mountains, which he knew well. 'On fine days, before the troubles, my papa would bring us up here for picnics,' he stated proudly. 'We had a car.'

'How many were there in your family?'

'Just the four of us at home. Papa, mama, myself and my younger sister.' He explained that all three had been summarily executed as Republican sympathisers. 'I do not understand. My parents took no sides in this conflict. Now they're all dead and I am alone.'

'You have no other family who could take you in?' asked Pascoe.

'I have two older brothers, but they've gone off to fight – south to Toledo, I think. I also have an uncle and aunt who also live there.'

'I'm very sorry for your loss,' said Pascoe. 'So by what name are you called?'

'I am called José Antonio Gomez.'

It was the second surprise Pascoe had experienced in just two minutes. He had not expected to meet the young José so soon. The encounter had been expected somewhere later on this journey, or so he had thought. Most likely in La Mancha or Toledo.

'I am very pleased to meet you José Antonio Gomez,' Pascoe said calmly, shaking the boy by the hand. Then, seeing him shivering with cold, he took off his oilskin and placed it around the boy's shoulders and offered him what few provisions he had in his rucksack. José consumed the scraps hungrily.

'So where will you go now? You cannot possibly stay up here in the mountains.' Pascoe already knew the answer.

'I plan to go to Toledo,' José replied.

'How do you intend to get there?' Pascoe knew the answer to that one too.

'I shall walk,' said José with a great show of bravado.

How very Spanish, thought Pascoe. 'But do you

know how far that is?'

'Not really, señor. A great distance I believe. But I have no other choice.'

'Then I shall take you,' said Pascoe with a tone of finality. 'But first, we must sort out some better clothing for you. Your footwear has seen better days. You can't possibly wear those.'

The sole of one of José's shoes hung off loosely, held by a mere thread, while a large hole gaped in the other, so that his foot was completely exposed to the elements. Blue with cold, the boy offered no argument.

'Let's get down off this mountain,' said Pascoe. So saying, he placed the rucksack back over his shoulders, rolled his sweater into a cushion and placed it on the petrol tank. 'Up you get!' He sat José before him astride the tank. 'Is that comfortable?'

'Si, señor ... a little.'

'Then off we go. To Toledo!'

*

They made a brief stop at the village of Grado sometime around noon, a dozen kilometres short of Oviedo, to buy what scant food supplies they could get – a little bread, a small portion of goat's cheese and a few over-ripe tomatoes. The local blacksmith sold them what few litres of petrol he could spare, siphoned off from an old tractor. His wife, seeing José's footwear, brought out an old pair of leather work boots. They were oversized and heavy, but dry and fit for their purpose. She also provided a woollen jumper and a soft leather deerstalker hat to keep his ears warm while sitting exposed at the front of the motorbike. Finally, she presented him with a deep upholstered cushion, which was embroidered with an image of the Blessed Virgin Mary.

'That will save you from a great deal of arse ache!' she laughed bawdily. 'And Our Lady will forgive you for

Twelve

sitting on her face.' They all laughed out loud, if a little nervously at her irreverence.

Finally, Pascoe thanked the couple for their generosity and they sped off down the mountainside towards Oviedo and the central plains of Spain.

*

By mid-afternoon they had negotiated the last remaining hairpin bend. The relative remoteness of the mountains was left behind, and they had a clear view of the pastoral landscape stretched out below. However, Pascoe's appreciation of this bucolic tranquillity ended abruptly when he saw two armoured tanks straddled across the road, completely blocking the carriageway a few kilometres ahead.

Immediately he drew the bike to a standstill out of sight, behind a hedgerow. They were two T26 Soviet-built light tanks, and though he had not seen one before, Pascoe knew his history well, and by the end of the year they would be widely used in this conflict. Both tanks were well armed with a 45-millimetre gun; their only threat was from artillery or land mines. The Russians would go on to supply almost three hundred of them, to both Republicans and Nationalists alike, hedging their bets on which would be the eventual victors, and earning useful trade revenue in the process. The tanks were manned by Nationalist soldiers. Pascoe had not realised that they had made it so far north and their presence came as a surprise.

Rather than risk a confrontation, he would have to find an alternative route around the roadblock. Therefore, he cut the engine, forcibly thrust the machine through a thinner part of the hedgerow, and decided to freewheel silently off road, down the field. As the motorcycle gathered speed over the uneven pasture, José bounced up and down precariously on the fuel tank and only narrowly did they avoid colliding with a herd of grazing cattle.

Finally, they came to an abrupt halt just short of a drainage channel. On the other side, a narrow farm track ran in either direction. With luck, thought Pascoe, the right branch should re-join the main highway some way further on, and after lifting the machine across a shallow part of the ditch, they set off again. Fortune smiled. Pascoe breathed a huge sigh of relief when the roadblock was way behind them and they could continue their journey unimpeded.

Before long, they came to a fork in the road where a signpost indicated that a choice had to be made. Pascoe took another compass bearing. One branch went directly to Oviedo and the other pointed back to Cudillero, the way they had just come. Fate had decided. He had hoped for an alternative route, but none had presented itself. Reluctantly, he would have to drive through Oviedo.

'It should be okay by now,' said José. 'I think the Nationalists have left and it has been retaken by the Republican army, so it's safer than when I left a few weeks ago.'

*

As they made their way cautiously along the approaches to Oviedo, the carriageway gradually widened into a large boulevard. Before the war, this grand thoroughfare had been flanked by an avenue of luxurious fruit trees, but now they stood brutalised – charred stumps – evidence of the intense fighting that had taken place.

The battle of Oviedo first began when workers, mostly miners, joined by army factions loyal to the Republican cause, had taken the city after heavy fighting. They seized control of the arsenal with its several thousand rifles and machine guns. Despite better-equipped and more powerful opposition, they held the city for three months during the spring and summer of 1936. Socialist and anarchist factions among them had executed local

Twelve

politicians and clergymen and set fire to public buildings. However, the uprising had been short-lived and the town was eventually taken by Nationalist forces, and there were many executions following its recapture. It was to change hands several times over the following months. Oviedo was the largest and most important city in the region, the capital city of the Principality of Asturias, and unsurprisingly, both opposing factions wanted to claim it for themselves.

They made their way past the shell-marked and shrapnel-pitted west front of the great Cathedral of San Salvador in the city centre and Pascoe realised that José's assumption had been incorrect. There were no Republicans here. Nationalist soldiers guarding the cathedral confirmed that Oviedo was crawling with Fascist troops.

It was Sunday, the feast day of Corpus Christi, and ordinarily it should have been an important religious festival. Tradition had it that the large open plaza in front of the cathedral would be carpeted with rose petals and a procession of the Blessed Sacrament ceremonially paraded, accompanied by banners, flags and a civic brass band. An effigy of Santa Eulalia, patron saint of Oviedo, would lead children to their first communion, followed by city dignitaries and local police escorts, resplendent in dress uniform. On this particular holy day, however, the conflict had put paid to any kind of festive celebration. Instead, those few townspeople who dared venture out, scurried across the half deserted square, passing the cathedral speedily and averting their eyes away from the soldiers who guarded the great west front. Fascists or Republicans, it mattered little to them; equal cruelties had been meted out by either army and all military were feared, whatever their uniform, flag or politics.

Pascoe drove round the square warily, but to his great relief, they went unchallenged. Further on, they passed by the once-elegant Baroque façade of the Hotel de

La Reconquista, a former hospice and children's home. It now stood battle-scarred; all its windows blown out. It presently sheltered several hundred displaced persons and refugees.

By the time they had reached the southern outskirts, the light had begun to fade and Pascoe decided it was time to rest for the night. He drove on a few kilometres farther, till they were well clear of the city. A short distance before the village of Santolaya, on a remote stretch of highway, they came upon a truck, which apparently had been abandoned at the roadside. Pascoe pulled over, climbed in and checked it over – bullet holes peppered the driver's door, and there was dried blood on the floor and passenger seat, evidently several days old. Leading away from the truck, he could make out, even in the twilight, a dark red trail running across the adjacent field to a shack beside the railway line. Pascoe did not go over and check it out; he already knew what he would find. Fortune smiled again, however, for the fuel tank was three-quarters full and the engine fired after a few presses on the starter button.

'Okay, José,' he said, after he had wiped over the seats. 'This will do for the night. The previous owner has no further need of the vehicle, so we will commandeer it. The motorcycle will have to go in the back.'

Two grown men had struggled to offload the machine from the speedboat at Cudillero and with just one man and a small boy it proved an even more arduous undertaking. José tried to assist as best he could, but his efforts contributed more eagerness than physical strength. Patience and dogged determination prevailed, however, and eventually the motorcycle was securely stowed aboard. Pascoe tied it down and covered it loosely with a sheet.

Before settling down to sleep, José asked a question. 'Why is Spain at war with itself? What's it all about? Why do people have to die?'

'So many questions, José,' Pascoe replied. 'It all

Twelve

comes down to conflicting beliefs concerning how the country should be governed. You see, Spain had been run very badly for many years and under the old monarchy things were in quite a mess. Then, in a referendum, the people voted for the country to become a republic. The result was popular; it had widespread support, and the king abdicated. But some won't accept the result and want to restore the monarchy and the old power of the church. These Nationalists want to turn the clock back and return things to the way they were before the referendum.

Leading them is General Franco, backed by the army, large sections of the civil guard and the police. The Nationalists are intent on overriding the wishes of the people, and they maintain that the Republicans are under the control of Communists and anarchists. General Franco is determined to reverse the outcome of the election, whatever the cost, and many ordinary people have taken up arms to fight for the Republic, against his brutal dictatorship. Both sides are convinced of the justice of their cause and a bloody civil war has resulted.'

'But my parents were neither Republicans nor Nationalists. Just ordinary Spanish people. So why did they have to die, señor?'

'Ah, José. That's a really tough question to answer,' Pascoe continued. 'It's ordinary people like your father and mother who suffer most in wartime, caught up in the middle of the conflict. They were in the wrong place at the wrong time – collateral damage – the real casualties of war, like thousands of others. I know that doesn't really satisfy you – it's not fair, but it's just the way it is. It's all pure politics.'

'My little sister knew nothing about politics.'

'That's the real tragedy. Innocent children are dying or being orphaned.'

José considered Pascoe's words for a while, but had more questions. 'But I don't understand why you are here, señor. You are not a Spaniard. What does our civil war have to do with you, a foreigner?'

'Yes, it's true. I am not Spanish. But like many others, I have come to help fight for the Republic.' This was not the entire truth. He continued. 'People are coming from all over the world – from America, England, France and even Russia. Many are volunteering to stand up to the brutality and injustice of Fascism. Unfortunately, the tide is turning very much in their favour. General Franco controls a large Nationalist army, who are well trained and better equipped. They are overtaking towns and cities throughout Spain.'

'Why are you going to Toledo?'

'For two reasons. First, Toledo is still in Republican hands, but Franco's African Army is already advancing on the city and men will be badly needed for the battle that's coming. Secondly, since you have no other means of transport, I plan to reunite you with your relatives and your brothers, who you say are fighting there.'

'I hope they still live there. It is possible that they have fled the city.'

'With luck, we'll find them and you'll be back with at least some of your family.'

*

Over the next few days, in the new-found comfort of the truck, they continued south into the Province of Castille and Leon. On more than one occasion, when fuel reserves were spent, they were stranded temporarily at the roadside, waiting for some passing Samaritan who might sell them a few litres of diesel.

Pascoe decided to bypass the City of Leon - their experience of Oviedo had been warning enough, and he had learned the wisdom of avoiding large cities. Valladolid was swiftly driven through at night and apart from a few shelled buildings, it seemed to have got off lightly. Similarly, Avila and Segovia were strategically too

Twelve

unimportant for either side to be bothered – but in time, he knew that even they would be caught up in the conflict.

Madrid lay directly in their path, but Pascoe felt that the capital should be avoided at all costs. Consequently, he decided to divert westward and go the longer circuitous route through what he hoped would be the less hazardous open countryside. It would be time-consuming, but by taking the longer rural route through La Mancha, they would bypass Madrid, and if all went well, they would emerge unhindered south at Maqueda.

*

Pascoe was immediately struck by the vastness of the La Mancha plateau, stretching as it did from one horizon to another. Little wonder that the Moors had described it as wilderness – *'al mansha'* was Arabic for 'dry land'.

It was a summer of exceptionally severe drought, and as the kilometres rolled by, they passed through fields of withered wheat crops and dying oat plantations. Yet, vineyards and olive groves seemed to have survived in spite of the harsh conditions. La Mancha has an arid but fertile landscape and the brutal climate of the high plain is unsuited to all but the hardiest cattle. Conversely, the distinctive Manchego goats thrive under such conditions, able to obtain nourishment from the sparsest vegetation and to prosper under the unremitting temperatures. Goats were so common that with almost predictable regularity the truck had to make enforced stops as hundreds of these creatures were shepherded across the unfenced highway by goatherds or soldiers in combat uniform.

Here and there, they were able to purchase Manchego goat's cheese as well as small amounts of hard black bread. Occasionally a hamlet could spare some dried goat meat. Often it was old and almost inedible, but it was not a time to be fussy and they acquired as much as was available.

The long distances and the slow pace of their commandeered transport necessitated frequent overnight stops in the wilderness, and more than once they slept out in the open. Given such hazardous times, they camped well away from the highway, out of sight of passing traffic. On one such night, they found shelter beneath a solitary windmill among the wheat fields. These iconic structures had once been commonplace throughout La Mancha, but in an age of increasing mechanisation, many had shut down and growing numbers had been left derelict. Even so, their distinctive white cylindrical forms remained silhouetted starkly against the deep blue Spanish sky and their efficient skeletal vanes often continued to turn in the slightest of evening breezes, long after they had been abandoned.

After they had eaten their small rations and begun to relax before sleep, Pascoe entertained José with storytelling.

'I am going to tell you the tale of Don Quixote, a man of La Mancha. Every boy should know the story, because it was written by Spain's greatest author.'

'Who was this author?' asked José.

'His name was Miguel de Cervantes, and he wrote it over three hundred years ago.

'Long ago,' he began, 'in other troubled times, like these, there lived an old man by the name of Alonso Quijano, so the story goes. He was disillusioned at the way the world seemed to have lost all sense of decency and honour. So, he decided to embark on a quest to revive chivalry, accompanied by his companion, a simple farmer named Sancho Panza, who rode a donkey and was to become his squire. Alonso searched out an old suit of armour that had been rusting away in the barn and gave himself the grand title of *"Don Quijote de La Mancha"*. He named his own skinny nag of a horse Rocinante and the neighbouring farm girl that he fancied, he called Dulcinea Del Toboso. He declared that she was his lady love,

Twelve

though she knew nothing about this.'

Pascoe continued to recount the tale. He went on to describe how Don Quixote had tilted his lance and charged at windmills all over La Mancha, believing that they were dragons and that he must slay them, as the knights of old had done. By doing such brave deeds he hoped to win the hand of his beloved Dulcinea.

'Do you think he charged at this windmill?' asked José.

'Who can say?' replied Pascoe. 'I wouldn't be a bit surprised. Once, there were many like this around La Mancha.'

'But he was a madman,' said José. 'How could he hope to change anything by charging at windmills? It was quite pointless and very silly. No matter how determined, a man cannot change the world single-handed.'

Pascoe considered the innocent irony of José's statement. 'No, you are right. A man cannot change the whole world,' he continued. 'He can only work to change the things and the people around him. Each small deed that a man does makes the world a slightly better place. Don Quixote may have been foolish, but his heart was in a good place.'

But, his last statement fell on deaf ears, as José had already fallen fast asleep – his head slumped against Pascoe's chest.

*

Next morning they arrived at San Bernardo de los Molinos, a small remote hamlet of a half dozen farm cottages. Its inhabitants were keen to hear about the progress of the conflict in the country beyond. In exchange for news they offered small supplies of food and allowed Pascoe to fill his water flask from the well.

A village elder begged Pascoe excuse the meagerness of the supplies they could offer, explaining that most of their grain fields had lain untended since the young men of the village had gone to fight in Toledo. Yields were very poor due to the prolonged drought conditions and what remained had fallen prey to crows, jackals and field mice. Only vines, crocuses and olives had survived in the unprecedented harshness of the environment, he said, but nobody was buying either. Further, most of their goat herds had been commandeered. 'Stolen,' he said angrily, '...to feed troops in both Nationalist and Republican armies.' Only the weakest and scrawniest animals had been left behind. Commissioners had issued receipts for compensation, of course, so that it was all legal. But what good was that? They could not live on receipts, and who knew which side would be the victors, or who would honour such receipts after the war anyway?

These people seemed barely able to support themselves on a diet that consisted mostly of olives, supplemented infrequently by insubstantial scraps of goat meat and a little of their milk and cheese. The whole countryside was extremely depressed, trade was difficult and hunger widespread. As the grain crops had failed, bread was hard to come by. Yet, despite privation, Manchegos were invariably welcoming and generous. Under such conditions, Pascoe thought the kindness shown to them was quite extraordinary.

That night they were invited to share a modest meal at one small cottage, though the householder could ill afford the gesture. When they had eaten, a few other villagers crowded into the cramped interior, eager to know more about the uprisings. Pascoe described what he had witnessed in Oviedo and Avila, and of the roadblocks manned by tanks. He also spoke of isolated executions that they had witnessed. José told of his own family tragedy, at which a woman came over and threw both arms around him in a long maternal embrace. And, at the mention of the abandoned Corpus Christi procession in Oviedo,

Twelve

several women crossed themselves and uttered prayers to the Blessed Virgin.

Later, when they had all dispersed, Pascoe and José were offered a rough bed on the kitchen floor. A bale of straw spread on hard flagstones might not normally be considered luxurious, but they both slept as sound as contented babies that night. Pascoe had not lain under a roof in almost three weeks; for José it had been even longer.

Before taking their leave next morning, Pascoe offered money for his hospitality, but their proud host declined it, saying that it had been his pleasure, and that though the world had gone crazy and lost all sense of decency, he at least would maintain the Christian charity and humanity that his mother had taught him.

*

Pascoe's tale of Don Quixote seemed to have made a deep impression on José.

'Maybe you could be Don Quixote and I could be your squire, Sancho Panza,' he said completely unexpectedly.

'An excellent idea,' replied Pascoe. 'We'd make a fine pair of knights, you and me.'

'I think you are already a knight, señor,' said José. 'You have the knight chess piece pictured on your arm.'

'I do,' replied Pascoe. 'I have had the tattoo for many, many years.'

José thought for a moment. 'I quite like this Don Quixote knight,' he said. 'Though he was undeniably a strange man. But as you say, he tried to do his best, against all odds. He might have been foolish, but he was also very brave. No... I think I like him, after all.'

'I believe that's the point of the story,' Pascoe replied. 'I think I quite like him too.'

As their journey progressed slowly, over the days,

open fields grew less numerous and they began to descend from the high plain. By the time they passed through Maqueda, and re-joined the main road south, the landscape had softened. Settlements and villages grew more frequent, gradually the highway became tree-lined and hedgerows began to replace the open landscape of the plateau. On a few occasions, as road traffic increased, they had to dash quickly off road into the undergrowth to avoid passing military vehicles as well as several ominous looking Russian tanks. Better safe than sorry.

It had taken almost a month to make the eventful crossing from Asturias, but eventually they arrived at Torrijos just north of the River Tagus. Here they would spend their last night on the road, for tomorrow they would arrive at the fortified City of Toledo.

Chapter 21: Toledo

On the twentieth day of July they drove along the Tagus Valley and into the southern suburbs of Toledo. It was here that José said they would find the house of his aunt and uncle.

'There it is,' he shouted excitedly, pointing through the windscreen. 'The Carretera Alta.'

The house was set against the underside of the hill, across the river from the old city walls. José had said that the location was famous because it was the spot from where El Greco had made his famous painting of Toledo. Pascoe knew very little about the artwork of which this precocious ten-year-old boy spoke with such self-evident confidence.

The Carretera Alta, the so-called High Road, ran parallel to the River Tagus, high along its bank, facing the southern side of the city walls. It had been somewhere along here at the very end of the sixteenth century that the celebrated artist had set up an easel to paint his masterpiece, the iconic view of the city.

However, in this summer of 1936, the hillside proved an excellent strategic location for a Republican artillery emplacement, and ideal for the bombardment of the besieged fortress of the Alcazar. Not the time for art appreciation. As they drew closer to the house, every ear-splitting salvo from the field guns overhead made José cover his ears and cringe lower in his seat. Pascoe put on a brave face so as not to increase the boy's terror.

The truck drew up outside a roadside dwelling. On its ochre wall, crudely scrawled in chalk, were the words *"Ruta de Don Quijote"*. José jumped down quickly from the cab, and all fears of the bombardment going on around him were momentarily forgotten, as he ran over to the read the graffiti more closely.

'Look. See what is written here,' he shouted to Pascoe above the din. 'The Route of Don Quixote. He came this way. He was here!'

Pascoe had not the heart to remind José that the story was pure fiction, and feigned equal excitement. He thought that reality was hard enough for a boy to bear, without destroying the last vestige of his innocence. That would be lost soon enough during the coming days.

José ran over to the door and knocked excitedly, before Pascoe could join him. It opened and a woman answered.

'What do you want?' she scowled. 'No need to hammer the door in, boy!'

'I believe the boy's uncle lives here,' said Pascoe. 'Antonio Gomez?'

'No-one here of that name,' she replied curtly, and would have closed the door on them, had not Pascoe intervened by placing a foot smartly in the way.

'Are you sure?' he persisted. 'He has come a very long way.'

'Of course I'm sure!' she replied.

'There must be some mistake,' cried José. 'This is my uncle's house. I've been here many times!' Pascoe placed a comforting hand on the boy's shoulder.

'That may well have been so,' the woman continued. 'But that's not the way it is anymore. The house has been ours since they were taken away.'

'What do you mean, taken away? Where? When?' Pascoe fired questions at her in rapid succession.

'The militia arrested them. I believe they were both executed – the man and his wife. Suspected of being Nationalist Fascist sympathisers. They took a lot of others away in the big purge and the house was reallocated to us two weeks ago. Ours was made unsafe by the bombardment.'

José began sobbing loudly, and no matter how Pascoe tried to comfort him, he seemed inconsolable. 'We'll look for your brothers tomorrow. They're probably inside the city already.'

Twelve

'What if they're dead too?' he bawled. 'I will have no family and I really will be an orphan.'

'Then I shall be your family, José. From now on you may call me uncle.'

*

They slept fitfully in the cab of the truck that first night outside the walls of Toledo, but were glad of the respite from long days driving cross-country. However, they were awoken abruptly early next morning by the onset of the bombardment, which served as a pre-emptive alarm call.

The city gates had already reopened after the overnight curfew and they made their way across the monumental bridge of Saint Martin. Its massive stone structure led to the fortified barbican gate on the other side of the river. At the portal, several well-armed Republican militia of the Popular Front stood guard and checked people as they entered the city. One guard patted down Pascoe and another José, but seeing they were unarmed and posed no obvious threat to security, passed them through without ceremony.

The resumption of the artillery barrage heralded the regular daily interchange between Nationalist and Republican protagonists. Rallying gunshots and mortar fire could already be heard on the far side of the city, where besieged Nationalist sympathisers, under the command of Colonel Moscardó, had refused to surrender the Alcazar, despite threats to kill his captured son.

Hand-in-hand Pascoe and José made their way up the cobbled street that led to the centre of Toledo. Just past the Monastery of San Juan de los Reyes, in a back street wine bar, away from the immediate battle lines, militia had set up a command post. Volunteers were arriving to enlist every day. Many were native Spanish, but others came from around Europe and from the Americas – they would come to be known as The International

Brigade.

There was no great formality to the enlistment. A signature and a willingness to fight was all that was required. Messengers and orderlies busily dashed in and out of the bar going about their frantic business and an armed sentry stood at the doorway. Pascoe approached and spoke to him.

'Señor,' he began. 'Is this where we enlist?'

'Yes. Join the queue,' replied the soldier, pointing back into the bar. Then seeing José, he added, 'But the boy's too young to fight.'

'Yes, I realise that. It's just myself. He's only with me because he's been orphaned. He has no other family and for the time being I'm looking after him.'

'Poor little sod!' said the guard sympathetically. 'So many bloody orphans and displaced families. Where did he lose his folks?'

'In Oviedo. We believe his two brothers joined up here in Toledo. I'm hoping he can be reunited with them.'

'So you were in Oviedo. How were things going up there?'

'The Nationalists had control when we came through two weeks ago. They're everywhere, and I've seen a few Russian tanks on the way down here.'

'Tanks you say? First I've heard of that. Any news about the bombing in the Basque Region?'

'No, we've had no news for best part of a week. What's happened over there?'

'The bloody Jerries bombed the town of Guernica. Everybody's shaken by it. Even Picasso is staging a protest in Paris, so they say.'

'What does Germany have to do with all this?'

'They say Franco invited Hitler to give his new Luftwaffe a bit of bombing practice over Guernica. Unarmed civilians – killed from the air. It was a massacre, they say. Fascist Nazi bastards!'

'My god! Things just go from bad to worse,'

Twelve

replied Pascoe.

'You're telling me,' the sentry continued. 'So have you come far?'

'From Asturias.'

'Quite a way, then. Well good luck with finding the boy's family.'

The sentry waved them into the bar where they came face to face with a recruitment officer across a makeshift trestle table.

'Write your full name, nationality and sign here.' He indicated on the paper with the tip of his pen. 'What can you do? Any useful skills?'

'I have some medical experience, I can cook and I can drive,' Pascoe replied. 'I've brought a truck and a motorbike with me.'

'Humph!' grunted the officer disdainfully. 'Not much call for trucks or motorbikes in a confined city like Toledo. Most of the streets are barricaded or blocked with debris anyway.' Then he looked down at José. 'He with you?'

'Yes, he is. We're trying to find his brothers. They came here to join up.'

'What name?'

'Gomez,' offered José.

The officer thumbed through the enrolments. 'Rodrigo and Julio. That them?'

'Si,' replied José. 'They are my brothers.'

'Well, you're in luck, young lad. They are here. At least, they were when I last heard. You'll find them at the Alcazar. The fighting's been very fierce, so fuck knows how it's going. You'll be lucky if they're still alive up there.'

José was jubilant to learn that his brothers were nearby. He could hardly contain himself and jumped up and down excitedly.

'Stop that stupid boy!' the officer snapped. 'This is not a playground.'

Pascoe apologised. The officer scrutinised them

both intently before he allocated each to a task. 'Right. Medical orderly for you,' he said, pointing at Pascoe. 'Depending how things go you may still have to fight. Whatever and wherever you're needed most. You'll need to get in some rifle practice as well. We're expecting a big assault any time soon and we'll need every man we can get. Franco's Army of Africa is on its way to retake the city. I suppose the boy can help you around the kitchen.'

'I understand,' said Pascoe. 'What's the latest news about Franco's army?'

'I hear they've advanced from Cordoba and are encamped at Consuegra, awaiting supplies and reinforcements. Nevertheless, they'll be moving back to Toledo soon. They mean to relieve the Alcazar and to retake the city. I daresay fighting will be long and fierce, so you'd better collect your rifle and ammunition. Try and get some practice in.'

*

The fortified Alcazar held a commanding position, dominating the highest defensive point in Toledo. It was protected on one side by a steep escarpment overlooking the river. In the sixteenth century, for a time, it had been the residence of the Holy Roman Emperor, Charles the Fifth. Tradition also had it that an earlier building on the site had once been occupied by Rodrigo Díaz de Vivar, the famed El Cid, when he was governor of the city. Consequently, the building was a powerful symbol and whoever held it possessed great prestige. For that reason, General Franco ordered it to be relieved, despite the fact that it was of no great military significance. Many of his senior staff thought it a waste of men and resources. Madrid lay just sixty kilometres north and would be a far more important acquisition.

It was a monumentally massive building; five stories high with stone walls almost two metres thick in

Twelve

places and square towers at each corner. Nationalist supporters were trapped inside and refused to surrender to the Republican army and the militia who had laid siege on three sides. By now the stand-off was in its second week and the Alcazar's current occupants were intent on holding out until Franco's army advanced to relieve them. The besieged complement was believed to number around eight hundred persons all told, mainly Civil Guard, all Franco supporters, along with their families. Amongst their number were around fifty children and it was thought up to one hundred hostages. They had barricaded themselves in, armed with little more than rifles and machine guns, but reputedly were well stocked with ammunition and grenades. The opposing Republican forces had the advantage of tanks and field artillery, the latter guided on target by spotter planes that made regular sorties overhead.

The siege was at a virtual stalemate. It had become a war of nerves and waiting, though gunshot rallies went on all day and frequently throughout the night. Field guns and mortars constantly battered the building and its fabric was badly scarred and blackened in many places so that parts were already in a state of near collapse. But the bulk of the Alcazar had essentially held firm and all attempts to break through had failed. As a last resort, Republican miners had secretly begun to dig tunnels under the foundations in readiness to bury a huge cache of high explosive.

*

Pascoe and José approached the battle line warily, dashing across exposed clearings during breaks in the shooting and taking shelter where they could. Bullets whistled and ricocheted around them from snipers at windows on the upper floors. Gradually, they made their way up to the barricades where riflemen and machine gunners crouched for protection. The only indication that these informal ragtag combatants were Republican was by the black berets, which they wore to distinguish them from the red tassels of the Nationalist soldiers' forage caps.

Barricades had been thrown up from whatever came to hand. They had grown over the past two weeks, as upturned carts, abandoned vehicles and flagstones had been added as reinforcement. Periodically a militia man would raise his rifle above the barricade and take pot-shots at the building, but most fell harmlessly or rebounded off the hard stonework. It had become a futile expenditure of effort and cartridges.

Pascoe surveyed the scene for some time before he identified what appeared to be an officer of senior rank. He crawled over on all fours to speak to him, followed closely by José.

'Excuse me, señor,' he said. 'I'm looking for two brothers, Rodrigo and Julio Gomez. I was told they were up here. Do you know them?'

'Over there,' he shouted above the noise of a sudden artillery barrage. 'The guy with the periscope, that's Rodrigo Gomez.'

'Thanks.'

They crawled over towards Rodrigo, who instantly recognised his younger brother and handed the periscope to the next man. He laid down his weapon, squatted behind the barricade and held out his arms to greet him.

'My little me-oh,' Rodrigo shouted. It was a term of endearment he had used ever since José was an infant. 'What on earth are you doing here?'

They clasped each other in a long filial embrace. José began to tell him about their long trek overland to reach Toledo and the care that Pascoe had taken of him.

'This is Uncle Arthur, my protector,' José said. Rodrigo reached forward with a bandaged hand and the two men shook the other's cordially. But intelligible conversation proved increasingly difficult under the noise

Twelve

of incessant shelling.

'Sorry, I can hardly hear either of you,' shouted Rodrigo. 'We can't talk here, señor. Better withdraw to a quieter place of safety.'

He scrambled over to the officer to ask if he might leave the line. Permission was given and all three crawled back, away from the barricades and into the relative shelter of a nearby alleyway.

'I had to ask permission,' Rodrigo explained. 'Men have been shot by their own officers for leaving the line. Deserters get very short shrift out here.'

When they reached a doorway well clear of the battlefront, Pascoe reintroduced himself. They spoke further of their eventful journey from Asturias and he broke the news of the death of the family in Oviedo. However, Rodrigo continued to stare vacantly at the floor, stony-faced and apparently unmoved throughout. It was only when he raised a thumb to brush away the ingrained cartridge residue and sweat from his eyes that he betrayed the slightest trace of a reaction. It may possibly have been the beginning of a tear.

'My brother Julio also died here, two days ago,' he announced solemnly. 'A sniper's bullet took the top off his head! There was no time to mourn. Things were just too busy to think about the dead. Too many dead. Time enough for tears when this is all over. For now it's sufficient simply to stay alive.'

Rodrigo Gomez had become entirely battle hardened. Exhausted and fatigued, he had nothing more to say on the subject. Instead, he sat down and stared at his boots, reflecting on the mindless futility of it all. When he finally looked up and saw that José was sobbing bitterly again, he reached across to comfort him.

'But I have to thank you for looking after my little brother, señor,' he said to Pascoe.

'It was nothing,' Pascoe replied. 'We had a few happy times and were company for each other. The boy looked after me as much as I did him anyway.'

*

Pascoe was woken from his sleep the following day by a hefty kick to the shin.

The recruitment officer towered over him. 'Rise and shine, soldier,' he said. 'Looks like we have need of your truck after all.'

Pascoe and José walked back to reclaim the truck from outside the city walls and for most of that morning were conscripted into making trips to the suburbs to collect food. Two armed militia accompanied them, one standing either side on the running boards. Initially, Pascoe thought them unnecessary, but as things turned out, armed force proved essential on numerous occasions. They had been ordered to collect provisions wherever they could be found and often they had to seize materials forcibly when the owner was unwilling to 'donate'. The populace of Toledo was paying a high price in the battle for their city.

Such as they were, provisions consisted mainly of horse or donkey meat, potatoes, root vegetables and very occasionally, eggs. But they also collected many cases of small bore ammunition and mortars to replenish supplies at the front line.

When that task was completed for the day, Pascoe reported to the camp kitchen and began work as cook with José as his skivvy. The Republican authorities had taken over a restaurant just off the cathedral square. Kitchen work was a repetitive daily routine, as each day they peeled several hundred kilos of potatoes. There would only be one meal; it would consist of vegetable and egg tortilla, or patatas bravas, or a horsemeat stew, depending on whatever provisions had been requisitioned. Sometimes, ingredients came from dubious sources – Pascoe noted that there were no cats or dogs left in the proud City of Toledo – they had all mysteriously left.

Twelve

Nevertheless, food was available all day long, as soldiers took turns away from the barricades to rest, eat and catch a few hours' sleep.

Periodically, Pascoe was called out to administer first aid to a wounded combatant, but medical resources were limited, basic and frequently ineffectual. He saw men die outright, and many later from infection. This ritual repeated itself through the nights, days and weeks that followed. An endless round of preparation, cooking, eating, sleeping, administering first aid and preparing food for the next day again.

On their third Sunday in Toledo, Pascoe, who had not yet done so, was commanded to attend the shooting range outside the city walls. He duly presented himself and was ordered to lie down with others at one of the stations marked with wooden pegs in the sand. Shooting practice was supervised by a corporal of the Republican Army. He instructed him to aim the Mexican Remington rifle at one of the straw sacks located fifty metres away against an embankment. It was the first time he had held a loaded rifle in the conflict and he was allocated just ten rounds, to conserve ammunition.

When he was given the signal to commence firing, Pascoe advanced the bolt and took the first shot. He purposely aimed wide, high and slightly left. The bullet missed the sack and hissed harmlessly into the sandy embankment beyond.

'Again,' barked the corporal. 'Squeeze! Don't jerk the fucking trigger, man. It's not your bloody dick! Breathe slowly, compose yourself and take your time.'

The second shot fared no better. Neither did the next seven, which found their way into either the sandbank or the city walls behind.

Despite appearances to the contrary, Pascoe was actually quite a good shot, and missing the target was no accident. He knew perfectly well how to handle a rifle, even a veteran First World War model like this one. He had aimed wide intentionally, determined to play no part in the slaughter. He had not come to Toledo for killing, but for saving lives. However, he realised that he should get at least one bullet on target, if only to allay the corporal's suspicions. Therefore, he took aim carefully and his final round barely nicked the top outer edge of the target.

'About bloody time too!' snarled the corporal. 'Let's face it, man; you're pretty much shit at this. So please don't point that at anybody.' Then sarcastically, 'Christ knows why you enlisted. You had better stick to cooking. Remove the bolt and keep it separate in your ammo belt. Don't want that thing going off and shooting one of our own fucking men.'

Pascoe slung the decommissioned rifle over his shoulder and walked slowly back to the kitchen where he had left José doing the washing up.

*

Back at the camp kitchen, a group of a dozen or so militiamen had gathered outside, at the doorway, and were eating horse stew. In front of them, a press photographer had set up a wooden plate camera on a tripod. Seeing his approach, he invited Pascoe to join the group and he took up a position at the end of the front rank. The photographer raised a thumb of approval when he was happy with the arrangement and ordered everybody to stand very still. But, before he could complete the operation, José ran out, wash bowl in hand, joined the group, and stood immediately in front of Pascoe. The flash powder ignited with a short burst and the portrait was taken. Men broke ranks to finish their meal squatting and sitting on the doorstep of the kitchen.

'What's the photo for?' Pascoe asked the man standing alongside.

'Some Belgian newspaper,' he replied.

'Think we'll ever see the picture?'

Twelve

'Fuck knows. Can't say I really care to see my ugly mug in print anyhow.'

*

By September, the once impregnable Alcazar had suffered extensive damage from the constant artillery bombardment and intermittent tank volleys. Parts of the east wall were already in ruins, though the lower masonry was still intact and stubbornly defied all attempts to break through. Several times Republican forces stormed the breaches, only to be repelled by the fierce fighting of the defenders. A brief moment of relief came for the beleaguered Nationalists when an allied airplane flew over and parachuted fresh supplies into the central courtyard. A temporary truce was declared so that wounded Nationalist combatants could be brought out for medical attention, and Pascoe found himself treating men of both armies. Uniforms differed, he thought, but they were all men, and equally deserving.

Despite the rumours of Franco's advance and imminent relief, it had still not materialised and the besieged Civil Guard had begun to lose all hope. As numbers of wounded combatants grew, their women took up arms to join in its defence.

In the third week of September, the telephone line into the fortress was to be cut, and the commander given a final opportunity to surrender. Moscardó declined the terms and proclaimed that they were all prepared to die rather than give up. After this defiant gesture, he asked that a priest be allowed into the Alcazar to perform last rites. Little did he realise that the mine tunnels were complete and the explosives were already in place.

*

At eleven o'clock in the morning of the next day, mines

were finally detonated and the violent shock of their explosive force brought the whole of one side of the building crashing down. The sustained deafening discharge seemed to shake the city's foundations and rumbled on for a good ten minutes, reverberating through the fabric of its old cobbled streets.

Before the dust cloud cleared, a renewed attempt was made to storm the interior and bloody hand-to-hand fighting broke out in the courtyard. Despite overwhelming odds, the Nationalists succeeded in repulsing the assault, and finally withdrew back into the crumbling ruins of the Alcazar, blooded and less secure than they had been, but for the moment, undefeated.

Shortly after the abortive attack, news arrived that the army of General Franco had been seen only a few kilometres north of the city – already well within artillery range. They would probably arrive in Toledo the next day.

Pascoe knew that if he was to act, now was the time.

*

It was the twenty-seventh day of September, gone one o'clock in the early morning and guns had fallen silent across the whole of Toledo. The detonation of the mines had prompted a temporary ceasefire. Exhausted men slept at their posts, weapons in hand, glad of the lull, while others snatched moments of slumber behind barricades or in side streets. The sky was overcast and not a soul stirred.

Pascoe and José made their way surreptitiously through the pitch black streets, taking the roundabout route inside the walls, towards the back of the ruined Alcazar. As they approached, Pascoe waved a white kitchen towel aloft and a Civil Guard sentry stepped forward from the shadows.

'Quién pasa?' the guard challenged. 'Who passes?'
'Friends.'

Twelve

'Step forward. What friends?'

'Friends who would speak with your commander,' replied Pascoe. 'We are unarmed.'

Both he and José placed their hands on their heads and the guard called another over to join him. Thankfully, thought Pascoe, he wore nothing to identify him as Republican militia. Nevertheless, the guards frisked them both very thoroughly. Once it was confirmed that they were unarmed, their hands were bound and they were taken into the building, through its shattered corridors and the debris of collapsed side rooms. Wounded and dying men lay unattended everywhere and the monumental building that had once been the pride of Toledo, was now little more than a burnt out shell, fit only for demolition. In the central courtyard, they were presented to an officer. His uniform was dishevelled and torn at the shoulder and his sweat-stained face was darkened with smoke, blood and powder burns.

'What do you want of us?' he asked curtly. 'I have no time to waste, señor.'

'I have come for the children,' replied Pascoe. At that time the Alcazar held many infants, of whom around half were those of the Civil Guard, and the rest those of the hostages. Two babies had been born during the long siege. Pascoe explained that news had come that the Nationalist Army would arrive later that day and very fierce fighting would almost certainly ensue.

'It will not be a place for children,' he went on. 'Many brave men and women will die before the battle is resolved, and I believe there will be widespread reprisals and summary executions, whichever side is victorious. You know as well as I that no quarter will be given, whether they be men, women or children. But the children are innocent victims in all this - none of it is of their making. Therefore, I earnestly request that you allow me to take them out with a guarantee of safe passage. As a matter of common decency, I urge you to agree to this.'

'So how do you propose to achieve this miraculous evacuation?' asked the officer, his voice laced with self-evident cynicism.

'I believe that the children can be lowered by ropes over the city walls and down the cliff face to the river valley below. I propose to lead them along the shallow waters edge and away from the city. I will take them to Bargas, which is currently occupied by Nationalist forces under General Franco.'

The officer considered the offer for some time.

'You are a brave man, señor. You realise that both you and the boy could have been shot on sight?' he replied. Then after a moment's consideration, he continued. 'But it is as you say - the children have no part to play in this conflict. I will therefore consider your proposal and discuss it with the commander. Wait here.'

*

An hour passed before the officer returned leading a column of children and two nursing mothers.

'It is agreed. All the children may leave. Ours and theirs - you may take them all.'

'Thank you,' replied Pascoe. 'You are an honourable man.'

'We are all honourable men, señor. But I despair at the things honourable men may do to each other in the name of honour.'

'These are bad times, but it will not always be so.'

'I trust that you are right.'

The officer ordered two men to assist in roping up the children. Pascoe, made the first descent, with José close behind. The other children followed in turn, one by one, lowered down the hundred feet to the river valley below. The two women had swaddled their new-born in heavy shawls, and bound them tightly to their breasts. The whole evacuation took a full two hours, but when they

Twelve

were finally assembled on the river bank below, and all the children had been accounted for, they numbered seventy-four souls in all.

Pascoe placed both hands on José's shoulders, looked him directly in the eyes and addressed him solemnly. 'You must listen to what I have to say very carefully, José,' he said. 'The situation has changed. Now that there are two women in your party, I plan to stay behind. I want you to go on without me and take the children to Bargas.'

'You are not coming with us? What are you going to do?'

'I'm needed here in Toledo.'

'But why? This is your chance to get away. Don't you realise that the Nationalists are coming?'

'Yes, I know that, but my work here is not finished. There are dying men in the Alcazar and there will be many casualties on both sides in the battle ahead. They will badly need medics up there, and I cannot leave them at such a critical time.'

'But I don't want to leave you,' the boy protested.

'I know,' he continued. 'But you must be brave, José. The time has come for you to grow up and to be a man. I know you can do this. I have every confidence in you. Here is my compass - it will guide you along the river northwards until you are well clear of the city and then you can cut across country north-east to Bargas. It is only a few kilometres away and you will meet up with the Nationalist army long before then. They'll take care of you and the children.'

'But I'll be shot if they think I've been working for the Republicans.'

'These two women will vouch for you. They will tell them what you did and how you led the children out from the Alcazar.' Pascoe turned and spoke to the women directly. 'Make sure you tell them what the boy did,'

'Si señor, we will.' The two women assented.

Pascoe bade them all *"Adios"* and kissed José on both cheeks, before tugging on the rope as a signal to be hoisted back up again. Slowly he ascended the cliff face until they lost sight of him. By the time he had reached the top, the children were making their way along the riverbed, and dawn was already beginning to break.

'Goodbye little man,' he whispered under his breath. 'May your god go with you.'

That was the last time that Arthur Pascoe and José would ever see each other.

Chapter 22: Aranjuez

It had been some time since Seymour's return from London and the memories of nights spent in Katherine Chaplin's hotel bed were soon overtaken by mundane office routine. However, since the discovery of the Toledo photograph he had become obsessively preoccupied with the events of 1936.

Internet searches for *José Antonio Gomez* proved fruitful, and he was preparing to leave for Madrid. Among the millions of online records held by the Spanish National Archive he had discovered an entry for José's death in 2009. Birth and marriage records, national census statistics and Republican Army enlistment documents had also provided a great deal of additional information about his life. Seymour learned that both of the Gomez brothers had died in the battle for Toledo. José had fathered two sons. Formerly, they lived near Madrid, but had emigrated to America, and Seymour could find no trace of their current whereabouts. There had also been a daughter, last known to be living near Jerez, though she had died a few years earlier. However, Seymour was gratified to learn that José had eight living grandchildren, two of whom, Tomas and Mateo, he had already contacted by telephone. He had arranged a meeting with them at their home in Aranjuez, a short distance south of Madrid.

However, in view of his airplane phobia, Seymour decided on an alternative, and much preferred, mode of travel – he had booked an overnight sea crossing by the high speed catamaran ferry from Portsmouth to Santander in northern Spain. Nothing on earth would persuade him to board an airplane unless it was absolutely necessary, and this way seemed a sensible compromise.

He was about to set off from home, suitcase in hand, when his wife grabbed him by the shoulder and turned him to face her. He had anticipated a goodbye kiss at the doorstep, but what she said caught him completely unprepared.

'Can we talk about this Katherine Chaplin woman when you get back?'

Dumbfounded into silence, he realised he had no choice other than accept the inferred accusation as gracefully as he could. Anything less would be utterly pathetic, and his wife deserved better.

'Okay,' he replied eventually, and somewhat inanely. 'When I get back. I promise.'

'Drive carefully then.'

Her reply registered a degree of resignation. She placed an unanticipated kiss on his cheek, brushed a hair from the lapel and calmly closed the door after him. It was all over very quickly and was surprisingly painless. Seymour walked a few paces down the front pathway, but, bewildered by her unexpected composure, he stopped abruptly, turned and went back. When he opened the door, Sarah was still standing in the hallway.

'I can't leave it all up in the air like this,' he said. 'How did you know?'

'If you're going to cheat, Charlie, you should be more careful,' she replied. 'Lipstick on your handkerchief was a dead giveaway and your shirt reeked of a perfume that wasn't mine. I'd also phoned the hotel in Gower Street. They said you hadn't been in all night. That began to confirm my suspicions. Your mobile phone was switched off, which it never is, so I rang the hotel again the following evening. You were still unavailable. They checked your room. You didn't come down for breakfast either. I phoned repeatedly, fearing something awful had happened. Then, when I turned out the pockets before taking your suit to the dry cleaners, I found these.'

She brought out the receipts from the Bougival Brasserie from her dressing gown pocket. 'Expensive meals for two – at *our* restaurant. And wine, which you're not supposed to be drinking, by the way. Then, to cap it all, this Chaplin person telephoned the house.'

Twelve

'She phoned here?' Now shocked. 'When was this?'

'Just after you'd arrived back from Italy. You were still in London for that debriefing. It didn't take much to put two and two together afterwards.'

'She said Professor Fosse had told her where I was,' said Seymour.

'Well, she lied. It was I who told her. Quite naively, I said you were still in London. It wasn't till she rang off that I realised what I'd done. How stupid was that? I trusted you, Charlie.'

'Jesus,' said Seymour. 'I am sorry. I'm so very sorry. You must have felt awful.'

'The final straw came yesterday,' she went on. 'I received this text.' She handed him her mobile. It read:

"Ask your husband why he was in London with Katherine Chaplin. It might prove interesting".

'I didn't recognise the number. Who was it from?'

'Golding!' said Seymour. 'It had to be him. Bloody Holy Joe! He was on the same train at Euston. I felt uneasy about it at the time, but put it to the back of my mind.'

'So you're not denying any of this, then?'

'How can I?' he replied. 'It would be pointless wouldn't it?'

'Exactly.'

'But I swear to you it's over. Finished. It was just an infatuation. It meant nothing. Honestly.' He had exhausted all excuses.

'You had better go. You'll miss your sailing.'

'Promise me you'll do nothing till I get back,' he pleaded. 'I do love you, Sarah. We will talk and we can fix this.'

'We'll see. Now just go!'

*

In Seymour's opinion, the long sea crossing to Santander had all the advantages that were absent from air travel. For one thing, he was free to walk around the promenade deck at will, rather than shuffling around crowded airport lounges or crammed into inadequate airplane seating. He could enjoy dining, or even drinking, at his leisure – he couldn't imagine why it hadn't occurred to him to do this before. The sea voyage gave him the opportunity to reflect on all that had transpired before he left home, as well as time to brush up his Spanish vocabulary. At least, he had a comfortable cabin, and unlike the draining anxiety of travelling by air, he would arrive in Spain well rested. When the ferry docked in Santander almost twenty-four hours after setting sail from Portsmouth, he drove his car down the off-ramp and disembarked feeling unstressed and invigorated.

He could not have known that his journey through Spain would follow some of the route that Arthur Pascoe had travelled by motorcycle in June 1936. Nor would he realise, as he made the long climb over the Picos de Europa, that he would drive past the exact spot where Pascoe first encountered José. On this occasion, however, the mountain landscape was free from the perils of Pascoe's wartime trip, almost eighty years earlier.

On the other side of the Picos, Seymour joined the fast uncongested Spanish Autovia and the kilometres flew past. He bypassed Palencia and Valladolid and crossed the central plains of Castile and La Mancha towards Madrid. But he planned to avoid the urban sprawl and densely populated suburbs of the capital by driving around its perimeter on the Autovia Del Circunvalación ring road. However, while Pascoe's long diversion around the city in 1936 had taken a couple of weeks, Seymour's took less than an hour. South of Madrid he would branch off to complete the remaining forty kilometres to Aranjuez.

Twelve

*

He reached the City of Aranjuez late in the afternoon. Mateo Gomez had emailed directions to their home, and after crossing the River Tagus, Seymour arrived at the Vergal-Olivas Barrio, on the southern outskirts of the city. This part of his journey proved slowest, however, as it was difficult to negotiate through the many one way streets and several times he had to pull over and employ his faltering Spanish to ask directions.

Finally, he arrived at the house at the corner of Callé Talia. It was a smart stuccoed building with typical colour-washed walls, surrounded by a high decorative wrought iron fence, and overhung with fragrant lemon and fig trees. He rang the bell at the gate and both Gomez brothers ran out to greet him.

'Señor Seymour,' said one. 'I am Mateo and this is my brother Tomas.'

Tomas, who was the elder of the two, bade him enter the property. 'Welcome in Spain,' he said. 'We are very pleased to meet with you.'

They took his overnight bag and invited Seymour to join them beneath the shade of a large parasol in the back garden, where they offered him refreshments. Tomas and Mateo were perhaps in their late twenties, swarthy and tanned. Both were evidently well-educated professional people and spoke excellent English. Mateo, he learned, was a leading legal advocate in Aranjuez and Tomas had his own dental surgery in Madrid.

Once the formalities and introductions were completed, Seymour outlined the reason for his visit and the specific interest he had in their grandfather. Then he produced the Toledo photograph. Neither grandson had seen the image before.

'So you say the boy in the apron is our grandfather?' asked Tomas.

'Yes, I believe it is,' replied Seymour. 'It's the only picture we have been able to find of him from the Civil War period.'

'May we keep it?' Mateo asked.

'Yes, of course. I brought it as a gift for you. But I was hoping you had other photos of him.'

'Unfortunately, we have none of his childhood. This is the first we have ever seen of him as a boy,' said Mateo. 'I presume that the soldier standing behind is his Uncle Arthur? We have no pictures of him either.'

'I believe it is,' replied Seymour. 'He is a subject of particular interest to me and I am eager to more about him.'

'Grandfather spoke and wrote a great deal of Señor Pascoe. Though he always referred to him as uncle, it was a courtesy title – they were not really related. We understand he took grandfather under his wing and looked after him.'

'So, can you tell me how your grandfather came to know Pascoe?' Seymour continued. 'If you have no objection I'd like to record our conversation so that I may refer to it later.'

They began to recount the many stories that José had told of the Civil War, as well as of his many writings on the subject, including his journey with Pascoe through the Picos, La Mancha and Castille. They told how José had perched on the petrol tank all the way through Asturias, and spoke of the kindness of the long-suffering Manchego people. José had enthralled his grandsons with dramatised tales of the events he had witnessed in Toledo, animated as only an old man may do, so that they remembered much of it in scrupulous detail. It was more than an hour later that their epic narration ended.

'I can see that you loved your grandfather very much,' said Seymour.

'Of course,' said Mateo, 'but he was loved not only by us. He was a very important man and his name is still highly respected throughout Spain, for his personal courage and as a celebrated historian. It is a matter of great family pride that he was the youngest person ever to receive the Distinguished Service Award. President Franco himself made the presentation in recognition of grandfather's part in saving children from Toledo. He was similarly honoured by the United Nations, the International Red Cross and the Red Crescent, and was awarded the Order of Civil Merit for his academic work in 1973. He was particularly proud of that.'

'I had no idea that he'd accomplished so much,' said Seymour.

'I'll fetch his medal – it might interest you to see it,' said Tomas. He returned a few minutes later carrying two wooden picture frames. One contained the medal and the other a photograph that Seymour supposed to be of José. Tomas translated the commendation beneath the Order of Civic Merit medal into English.

"JOSÉ ANTONIO GOMEZ
Awarded in recognition of the civic virtue in the service which he rendered to the Nation, as well as extraordinary selflessness for the benefit of the people of Spain."

'You see, from humble beginnings this small peasant boy grew to be a man of some celebrity and substance,' Tomas concluded.

The framed photograph portrayed José in old age. The face was deeply lined and his hair grey and thinning. But the eyes immediately demanded attention. They exuded a level of intensity that Seymour had not anticipated. 'Your grandfather looked to be a very commanding personality,' he commented.

'Yes, he was, to the very end. He was often described as *fuerte* – in English I think you would say strong or powerful. But he retained all of his modesty nevertheless,' continued Mateo. 'He was entirely self-effacing and credited all of his success to the influence of Señor Pascoe. My grandfather maintained that his Uncle Pascoe had saved him from a wasted life and set him on a better path, and that he would have amounted to nothing, but for him. He maintained that he would not have survived the war without his intervention. Pascoe taught my grandfather that a man must do whatever small thing he can to make things better in the world around him.'

'So what became of your grandfather after Toledo?' asked Seymour.

'None of his family survived the civil war, we understand, and after Toledo our grandfather fled Spain. He crossed the Pyrenees on foot to France. From there he made it to Switzerland, where he lived throughout the Second World War. He was taken in as a war orphan and educated by the Sisters of the Resurrection at a convent in Lucerne. Afterwards, he graduated and gained his first doctorate from the University of Berne. He went on to acquire two others, one at the Sorbonne in Paris and the other in London. Over the years he became a successful academic and widely published author, as you may know.'

'I am sorry to admit that I knew very little of your grandfather's writing. It was only quite recently that I learned of his existence. But I shall make a point of looking into his work when I return to England.'

'You should,' Mateo continued. 'It will explain a great deal about his character. He became a distinguished linguist, fluent in five languages and able to read in several others. Grandfather lectured in three European universities and wrote books in Spanish, English, German and in Italian. He was also an acknowledged authority on the Civil War in Spain and his book on the Toledo siege has become a standard reference work. Yet, though he was educated and grew up abroad, he remained a true Spaniard at heart.

'Of course, he spent many years piecing together the events surrounding his Uncle Pascoe, but after Toledo

Twelve

the trail went completely cold. For a time grandfather assumed that Pascoe had died in the 1936 siege. Later, he had reservations.'

*

The three men talked well into the small hours, and Seymour gradually began to understand more of the relationship that had developed between Pascoe and José during the brief summer months of 1936. That night, as he lay in the guest room of the Gomez house, midway between sleep and waking, Seymour mulled over the stories that they had told him. The lasting impression Pascoe had made upon the young José in such a short acquaintance was little short of inspiring. But above all, the curious paradox of Arthur Pascoe plagued his thoughts. The two photographs he had seen of José - first, as a boy and then as an old man - were exactly what he might have expected. Unlike Pascoe. All the images he had ever seen of this elusive figure remained inexplicably youthful and curiously ageless.

*

After breakfast next morning, as Seymour was about to depart, Tomas presented him with a large bound notebook. Its loose pages were tied up with string.

'This was my grandfather's,' he said. 'We think it might help with your enquiries. My brother and I are both agreed that we would like you to take it.'

On the cover board was written in a fine cursive hand, the inscription:

"THE JOURNAL OF JOSÉ ANTONIO GOMEZ"

'But are you sure? This must be a family heirloom,' said Seymour.

'It is. But we think you should know of our grandfather's experiences. You will find some of his conclusions very illuminating,' said Tomas. 'We only offer it on loan, of course. We would like it returned, eventually.'

'Of course,' Seymour assured him. 'I shall take great care of it and return it back to you safely. I really am most grateful.'

'There is one more thing we must show to you before you leave,' said Mateo. 'If you will follow me, señor, I think you might find this equally interesting.'

Mateo led Seymour round to the front of the house and raised the garage door. The interior was stacked high with a profusion of packing crates, books and magazines. He picked his way through, moving boxes aside until he reached the far end. In the corner, a dark green dust sheet covered a large bulky object.

'This was his pride and joy,' said Mateo, as he pulled it back with a flourish evocative of a matador. Under the cover stood a vintage motorcycle – emblazoned on its black and polished chrome tank was a gold AJS logo. 'This is the machine on which Arthur Pascoe drove across Spain to Toledo.' He patted the tank several times and continued. 'And here is where my grandfather sat for some of that journey.'

Seymour ran his hand over the saddle and its smooth chromium tail pipes. 'May I sit on it?' he asked.

'But of course. My grandfather loved to do just that. Even in his advanced years he would occasionally take it out for a brief spin up and down the road outside.'

'It still works then?'

'Indeed it does,' said Mateo. 'As well as it ever did.'

Seymour sat astride it, twisting the throttle grip in his right hand. 'So how did he come across the bike? I would have thought it lost in the course of the war.'

'So he had also believed. It was only the internet that made finding it possible. Grandfather posted a photograph of the model in several online forums that

Twelve

specialised in veteran motorcycles. It had been his obsession, and his delight in finding it knew no bounds.'

'So where was it discovered?' asked Seymour.

'Still in Toledo, near the house where his uncle once lived. It had been abandoned, long forgotten, in a derelict out building. The present householder happened upon grandfather's posting and immediately contacted him. He purchased it and had it shipped back to Madrid. Of course, it was not as you see it now,' Mateo continued. 'Grandfather spent time taking it apart, renewing and sourcing parts from England, and over several years he painstakingly restored it to its present pristine condition. It was like a religious obligation for him. Tomas and I helped whenever we could. During those happy times he would entertain us with stories of Don Quixote and Sancho Panza. I remember at least two occasions on which he read the entire novel to us. The story seemed to have some special connotation for him, and it was particularly important that we understood its significance. We never really did, of course, but we assumed that because he had crossed La Mancha and slept under windmills with Pascoe, he felt some connection to the tale. Before he died he bequeathed the bike, along with his compass, to us both. It has remained with us ever since.'

'And did your grandfather discover the eventual fate of Arthur Pascoe?'

'Not much actual fact, but plenty of what he called compelling circumstantial evidence. His findings are all set out in the journal. Most of it is in Spanish, of course, but some passages, which he wrote while he was in London, are in English.'

'I'm grateful to you for allowing me access to it, Mateo,' replied Seymour. 'Are you sure it's okay to take it away with me?'

'*Absolutamente!*'

*

Seymour had already passed Madrid on his return journey northwards, when he stopped for a break and purchased several small tapas and a coffee at a service station on the Autovia. As he sat out on the patio in the early evening sunlight, he opened José's journal and began to read a few passages.

It was written in an immaculate hand, in simple clear language and with an easy to follow narrative. Periodically, when he came across more complicated Spanish sentences whose meanings eluded him, he skipped a few pages. Some of the more complex passages would need translation back home. There were research notes, reference for some of José's publications, and many pages of statistics. The enormity of the figures was daunting. He had recorded that more than half a million had died as a direct result of the Civil War, a quarter of these from disease or starvation. Fifteen thousand victims of the conflict were civilians who belonged to neither Nationalist nor Republican sides. More than eight thousand people had taken part in the Toledo siege.

But far more touching was José's account of the men he had seen die in that city. There were detailed accounts of Pascoe's work as a medical orderly and the extraordinary lengths he had taken to save lives. José recorded that, more than once, Pascoe had given his own blood to save severely wounded combatants. Recipients made inexplicably rapid recoveries, despite the seriousness of their wounds or the unlikely prognosis of survival, as if the blood itself held some magical properties. Pascoe had comforted dying men throughout the days and nights of the conflict. His treatment was fair, entirely without favour, and he had been equally respected by casualties of both sides. José wrote that he never once saw Pascoe shoot and kill a man:

"I began to realise that every time my adoptive uncle was forced to

Twelve

fight, he was habitually and intentionally shooting wide. It became clear to me, even as a young boy, that he was determined not to cause a single death or wounding. He hoped no-one would see this. But I did."

Seymour flipped a few more pages and read the account of the exodus from Toledo.

"We waded along the course of the river, keeping to the shallower side of the bank. Many children were small and the waters threatened to engulf them, so that the older stronger ones had to lift them onto their shoulders to keep them dry as they traversed deeper stretches. Others gave comfort to infants, who cried a great deal. Mostly, they whimpered for their mothers in the darkness, though tragically, many would never see either of their parents again. That was the way it was in those terrible days. And, although it was only a few kilometres until we could leave the river to make our way across dry land, progress was slow on account of the little ones. Often we had to rest from carrying them. Also, the waters were so cold that many of the smaller infants began to collapse and pass out; they were in the early stages of what I now know to have been hypothermia."

José's description was graphic and unembellished. Seymour read on.

"The two nursing mothers who accompanied us out of the city were as good as their word. I believe I would have become another casualty of war had it not been for their intercession on my behalf. The Nationalist soldiers were short on patience or sympathy, but the arguments of the women prevailed and I was spared. Troops gave blankets and prepared hot vegetable soup to help our recovery from the intense cold of the night.

"On one occasion a man thrust a lit cigarillo into my mouth, thinking I must have been much older, but I had never smoked tobacco before and burst out choking and coughing, much to the amusement of the seasoned soldiers around me. I remember this very clearly, because there were precious few opportunities for laughter

during those times."

Seymour became increasingly engrossed. This enormous resource had evidently taken years in compilation; certain sections had been added much later, typewritten and pasted over earlier entries. One page in particular attracted his attention. It was entitled in bold capital letters *"ARTHUR PASCOE"*, and read:

"I have tried for many years to discover whether Arthur Pascoe, my adopted uncle, survived the eventual taking of Toledo by Franco's Nationalist Army of Africa. I know that many Republican sympathisers were executed without trial and have no known graves. Therefore, I may never know unequivocally his fate, but there are circumstances which lead me to believe that he did indeed survive the blood-letting that followed."

Seymour skipped a few obscure paragraphs and read further.

"I have found reports of similar rescues of refugees in subsequent conflicts throughout Europe and North Africa since those hot days of the summer of 1936. I am of the opinion that Pascoe, in fact, played some part in the rescue of Jews from Poland within a year of the Toledo siege. There are several recorded accounts of a man whose description is remarkably similar to his, who, on numerous occasions led groups of Jewish men, women and children out of the Warsaw ghetto. He led them overland to Ukraine and from the port of Odessa under the protection and care of the Red Cross. Accounts that I have sourced in Tel-Aviv and Berlin describe the escape route that he established and the safe houses he set up on the way. Many of these refugees eventually made it safely, either to England or to Palestine. There is a great deal of evidence that he saved Jewish children during the German occupation of Sicily in early 1942.

"I have also been in contact with the Simon Wiesenthal Foundation in Los Angeles. During his life, Wiesenthal made it a personal mission to track down Nazi war criminals and his

Twelve

Foundation graciously granted me access to their extensive records. They offered information regarding a mysterious unnamed character who led so many German, Austrian, Italian and Polish Jews to safety. I am reminded of Percy Blakeney, the 'Scarlet Pimpernel', who rescued French aristocrats and saved them from the guillotine. Although that figure was entirely fictitious, this modern-day Pimpernel was quite real, and it is estimated that he was responsible for the survival of more than nineteen hundred people, perhaps many more. That person's identity remains unknown."

José's notes seemed to be leading to an inescapable conclusion. In his opinion, Pascoe was that man. He had identified possible links to war zones and conflicts over several years across Europe and Africa. Too many to read quickly, or to do them justice. Seymour turned a few more pages and came upon a heavily underlined passage:

"I am convinced that this elusive Pimpernel figure was Arthur Pascoe, my adopted uncle, and that our first meeting on the Picos de Europa had not been coincidental. I believe he came to Spain specifically to find me."

*

The return sea crossing from Santander afforded Seymour time to delve further into José's journal. Its pages led to an intractable and disturbing conclusion. It was staring Seymour in the face, though he found it difficult to accept. If the Arthur Pascoe whom he met in Grange-over-Sands was the same man who had been present at the siege of Toledo, then he would now be over a hundred years old.

*

The ferry had already passed the coast of Brittany and entered the English Channel, when Seymour's mobile rang. He recognised Katherine Chaplin's number.

'Charlie,' she began. 'I haven't heard a word from you since Covent Garden.'

Seymour hesitated.

'Are you there?' she persisted. 'Speak to me.'

'Yes, I'm still here,' he replied.

'Where on earth have you been?'

'Spain.'

'You haven't been in touch. Is everything all right?'

'Haven't you been listening to anything I've said, Katie? I thought I'd made myself pretty clear. This can't go on. People I love are being hurt. Please stop calling.'

Katherine remained silent as Seymour continued. 'I thought we'd agreed to sever all contact.'

'But why would you assume that?' she asked. 'We can remain friends, surely?'

'That's not going to work, Katie.'

'I don't see why not.'

'For one thing, Sarah knows everything. She'd begun to work it out anyway, and Golding sent her a text after seeing us together at Euston. That clinched it.'

'I knew that awful man had unnerved you,' said Katherine. 'But I tried to put it to the back of my mind.'

'I did too, but then there was your telephone call - the one that Sarah answered. That was the final straw,' he continued. 'You told me it was Fosse who had given you my whereabouts. Why did you lie?'

'I know I shouldn't have, and I'm sorry. It was foolish, but I didn't know what else to say. I hadn't expected your wife to answer and it was the first thing I could think of. I knew if I told you that I'd spoken to her you'd be furious.'

'I was!' he replied. 'I still am. The bottom line is this, Katie. I can't jeopardise everything that's important to me, just for a fling. You have to understand that. So we can't carry on ... not even just as friends. The break has to be absolute.'

'So has Sarah asked you to leave, then?'

Twelve

'No. I hope it won't come to that. I think she's agreed to talk things through when I get back. I don't know - it may already be too late, but I can only hope that something can be salvaged.'

'So I guess this really is goodbye?'

'Yes. I suppose it is.'

'I will miss you, Seymour,' she concluded. 'Maybe I'll see you around?'

He made no reply and hung up.

Chapter 23: Sarajevo

As the airplane made its landing approach into Sarajevo Airport, most passengers would have been awestruck by the natural beauty of the snow-covered mountains in winter. Charles Seymour, however, dared not look out of the cabin window. So palpable was his anxiety that his eyes fixed firmly on the seat in front. His flying phobia had deteriorated even further, if that were possible, and only necessity had persuaded him to travel by air at all.

The plane's descent was along a steep-sided valley where small pastures and tobacco plantations lay frozen in the sub-zero temperatures of early December. Few of those peering down on the landscape could imagine that this had been the setting for some of the bloodiest and most horrendous acts ever perpetrated by one human being upon another in living memory. In this seasonal topcoat, the picture postcard panorama was deceptively idyllic, but Seymour was otherwise preoccupied.

The steps down from the airplane were hard-frozen with packed ice, but he was glad of the scant security the handrail offered. To be on *terra firma* again, even on *terra hardly-firma-at-all*, and still in one piece, was a great relief. Even the long treacherous walk across the tarmac was welcome after the claustrophobia of the acclimatised aircraft interior, despite the shock of the wind chill that almost froze his breath in mid-air. Too cold to dawdle, he quickened his pace. As he entered the concourse, he was met with the distorted sound of Christmas carols booming out an early seasonal welcome over the public address system. At passport control he came face to face with an officious looking official.

'*Pasos, molim,*' said the man in Bosnian, Serbian, or Croat... He could not tell which.

Seymour presented his passport and police papers. The official immediately recognised the rank, and adopted a less assertive tone.

Twelve

'Can you come with me please sir?' he requested in broken English. Seymour had been expected. He followed the officer through a side door and was shown into a comfortable, if slightly dated lounge. 'Please to take a seat, sir, and I'll arrange for your baggage to be collected,' said the official politely.

As he waited for his contact, Seymour's mind turned again to José's journal. His notes had indicated that someone remarkably like Pascoe had been active during the Bosnian conflict in the 1990s, and Interpol records also placed Pascoe there at that time. What his role had been in the Balkans was unspecified, though it had attracted British and American security service attention. Seymour had his own concerns over the apparent discrepancies regarding Pascoe's age and José must have been similarly perplexed. These inconsistencies, combined with MI6 interest in Pascoe, had prompted the trip to Sarajevo.

Presently, the door at the end of the room opened and a man, whom Seymour supposed to be his contact, came in. He was a corpulent figure, perhaps in his late fifties, dressed in a thick sheepskin topcoat, a chequered homburg hat and a long woollen scarf that trailed almost down to his ankles. He was carrying a cane and walked with a defined limp. He came over and shook Seymour's hand firmly.

'Terzic,' he introduced himself. 'Sasa Terzic ... and you must be Detective Inspector Charles Seymour. Welcome to Sarajevo. I have a car waiting outside.'

Brief formalities dispensed with, he led Seymour out through the arrivals hall, walking at an alarming pace, despite his obvious impediment, purposefully bypassing all security checkpoints without obstruction. There was a certain authority about this fellow officer. Police and other officials stepped aside respectfully as he strode unchallenged out of the airport building. Clearly, his contact was well known and instantly recognised – a slightly intimidating figure, evidently of some power and importance.

Waiting outside was Terzic's car, an old Citroën Avant of late 1950s vintage. It had once been the preferred transport of the French police, but the old automobile had seen better days. Years of active service had furnished it with an array of scuff marks, and minor dents covered its entire bodywork. A porter was already loading Seymour's luggage into the back of the car.

'We shall first go to my apartment for a spot of lunch, if that is agreeable,' said Terzic. 'I expect you could use a decent meal after the junk you'll have eaten on the plane.'

Seymour realised that this was not so much a request as a statement of intent, but thanked him anyway.

*

The Terzic apartment was on the ninth floor of a high rise complex of post-war central European design, constructed of grey concrete, steel and glass. Little more could be said to its credit other than that it was solid and secure. In the lift Terzic maintained a constant soliloquy up through the various levels to the floor where his apartment was located.

'You must forgive my verbosity,' he said as they stepped out onto the landing. 'English is a language I have long admired and I get so few opportunities to speak it that I tend to get a little carried away when the chance arises. I am an unashamed Anglophile - and a loquacious one at that.'

'Think nothing of it,' replied Seymour. 'I'm very glad, because I don't speak a word of Bosnian.'

'The whole world speaks English these days,' said Terzic, as he opened the door and gestured Seymour to follow. 'Mostly American English, of course. I fancy *English* English will eventually be consigned to the status

Twelve

of a small regional dialect. I blame Microsoft!'

'Yeah, I know what you mean.' Seymour smiled.

'Our home is quite small and modest,' Terzic explained. 'But it's in a good neighbourhood and we are happy here.' He took Seymour's suitcase and placed it on the floor near the door, and his overcoat, which he threw unceremoniously across the hall table. Then he called out to his wife. 'Branka! I am home. Our guest has arrived, my little chicken.'

Mrs Terzic's head appeared from a doorway at the far end of the passage. She was a handsome woman, her jet black hair tied back into a ponytail with ribbon. She wore an apron and was holding a wooden spoon, evidently disturbed from cooking.

'This,' said Terzic, '...is my lovely wife, Branka.'

She dried her hands on her pinafore as she came over to welcome him. 'Very pleased to meet you, Detective Seymour,' she said in equally good English. 'I hope you'll eat a little dinner with us. I am preparing one of our local specialities. It's quite frugal but very nourishing and I've made enough for all three of us.'

Seymour said that he would be delighted to share dinner with them, but knowing nothing whatsoever of Bosnian food, he had reservations concerning what type of cuisine he should expect. He need not have worried. Branka's meal was unexpectedly delicious. A local delicacy of onions stuffed with minced meat, known as *Sogau-Dolina*. The accompanying selection of pickled vegetables would become one of Seymour's favourite dishes during his time in the Balkans - its sauce was particularly flavoursome. But he courteously declined the light Kameno wine that his hosts quaffed gustily throughout the meal. Instead, he maintained the pretence of enjoying the thick glass tumbler of water that he had requested.

Presently, Terzic brought out two cigars and offered one to him. They sat at the table, talking and smoking, while Branka busied herself working at the sink.

'To business,' said Terzic. 'So what have you got so far, and what can I do to facilitate your enquiries, detective?'

Seymour outlined details of the Pascoe investigation, before he handed over the case file, which he had brought with him. 'These are photocopies of all the relevant documents. You'll need some time to digest everything. As you can see, what interests us most is the role of Arthur Pascoe in Bosnia-Herzegovina, and what part he played in the events of the war, if any. If we could trace his whereabouts, and possibly any contacts he made here, we may be able to resolve the case.'

It had been a very long evening, and by the time Terzic had walked Seymour over to his lodgings, they had become well acquainted. The hotel room was modest, but the bed so large and soft that Seymour fell asleep almost immediately he had pulled the quilted eiderdown over himself. He had not bothered to open the light overnight case that his wife had packed for him, but slept fully clothed, as he often did when away from home.

*

'Good morning, detective.' It was Terzic on the telephone. 'I trust you slept well,' he said, cheerfully. Seymour looked at his watch. It was six-thirty. Terzic was far too buoyant for this hour of the morning.

'Very well, thank you,' replied Seymour, feigning equal liveliness.

'So shall we meet up – say around eleven o'clock then? The station is just behind the hotel where you are staying. You'll see it from your window.'

After a light breakfast of assorted breads, pastries and strong black tea, Seymour made his way over to the police station. Terzic was already waiting outside at the entrance, smoking another large cigar. He stubbed it out on the step and they went directly into his office.

Twelve

'I have gathered together all the relevant paperwork I can find,' said Terzic. 'But a lot of the documentary evidence for the mid-1990s was destroyed during the Serb withdrawal from Bosnia. They shredded or burned anything incriminating and only a few records survive in Sarajevo. But I have discovered that your man Pascoe ranked high on the VRS death list.'

'The VRS? What is that?' asked Seymour.

'Sorry, I take too much for granted. The *Vojska Republike Srpske* was the Bosnian Serb Army, commonly known as the VRS. A nasty bunch. Several of their top brass have been tried for war crimes. Many others have evaded capture and are still being actively sought after. The VRS had a list of people destined for execution, including teachers, intellectuals and so-called troublemakers. Pascoe came under the last heading.'

'What sort of troublemaking got Pascoe on their list?' Seymour asked.

'So far as I have been able to discover from what few records survive, he mounted stiff resistance to their ethnic cleansing campaign. The VRS carried out innumerable executions in Srebrenica and Zepa. Thousands of Bosnian men and boys, mostly Muslims, were rounded up and executed. The killings were followed by the expulsion of over thirty thousand civilians, women and children among them. We believe that Pascoe was instrumental in guiding hundreds of these refugees to safety in neighbouring countries. First into Montenegro and then, for a few, to Albania. The Serbs really wanted to catch him.

'Detailed information is a little sketchy and much of it is uncorroborated hearsay. But I have discovered the whereabouts of a surviving eyewitness from Srebrenica, who is still living here in Sarajevo. His name is Delic, and he is one of many men that Pascoe saved from the shootings. He has agreed to meet with us this afternoon. But I must warn you, he is suspicious of everybody nowadays, especially Serbs, foreigners and Christians, so how much he will be prepared to divulge is uncertain.'

*

Dusan Delic's house was severely damaged and had remained virtually derelict since the war had ended almost thirty years earlier. It had been repaired after a fashion, and was patched up piecemeal in a variety of materials. The former ochre rendering of its walls bore testament to the intensive and prolonged shelling that had taken place. Broken windowpanes were boarded over with wooden slats crudely nailed into the frame. The low-pitched roof was so badly damaged that little of the original remained intact; where once there had been a uniform expanse of terracotta pantiles, there now remained only a makeshift assortment of uncoordinated slates and corrugated iron sheet.

Terzic knocked at the door loudly. 'Delic is a little deaf,' he said, excusing his brusqueness. 'Two years of shelling took away most of his hearing. He is stubbornly determined to go on living here, even though his home is a wreck and barely habitable. Still, you have to give the old fellow credit. He has testicles, whatever else you may say.'

'Balls,' corrected Seymour.

'Pardon?'

'You mean "he has balls".'

'Ah yes – balls. English figures of speech are sometimes a little tricky.'

Terzic thumped on the door again. 'I doubt he'll have heard us. We'd better just go in.' He slipped the latch and they entered.

Delic sat facing the door, a drawn revolver quivering in his hand. Recognising Terzic, he relaxed and replaced the weapon in the table drawer beside his chair. The old man sat quite alone in the subdued light that filtered through the tattered curtain drapes and in the

Twelve

dimness of the interior, Seymour struggled to make out his features. As he relaxed, Delic placed both hands on the walking cane in front of him and Terzic introduced him in Bosnian. He spoke no English and Terzic simultaneously translated the introductions. Seymour handed over the photograph of Arthur Pascoe. Delic immediately recognised the face.

'What can he tell me about Pascoe?' Seymour asked. 'When did he arrive? Do you know where he came from? What did he do here and where did he go afterwards?'

Delic replied slowly in an almost unintelligible peasant drawl, but Terzic was well used to the local dialect and understood his words effortlessly. 'He says you ask too many questions, but he will try his best to remember.

'It must have been in late March of 1995,' Terzic explained. 'He remembers that the snow had begun to melt, though the mountains were still covered well down to the tree level. He says one day the man in the photograph just appeared from nowhere. He spoke like a native – like a man born in Srebrenica or Sarajevo. Except, no-one had ever seen him before. He says it was a small close community and a stranger stood out immediately. However, he didn't seem like a stranger. As Delic says, just like one of us.'

'Can he describe him?' asked Seymour.

'He reckons he was tall, had dark hair, wore spectacles and a neatly clipped moustache,' replied Terzic. 'Just like the photograph.'

'That's definitely Arthur Pascoe,' said Seymour.

Terzic continued his translation. 'Word of the advancing Serb army had reached the city, and Delic had already heard rumours of Muslim men being shot in villages to the north. At first, nobody gave credit to such stories. They'd lived through one World War and suffered under Nazi occupation; that was still clear in people's memories. Therefore, you can imagine, it was inconceivable that such atrocities could be carried out by our own compatriots. People just did not do such things nowadays. Or so it was believed. But Pascoe insisted that if they stayed behind they'd line us up against the wall.'

At this, Delic raised the walking stick and swung it in a staccato-like manner from side to side emulating a machine gun. '*Rat-a-tat, rat-a-tat, rat-a-tat!*'

'Many refused to accept the advice of a stranger and chose to remain in their homes. Unfortunately, most of those people were never seen again. It was only through DNA analysis after the war that we were able to identify the bodies and know their fate. Several were Delic's neighbours; many had been school friends. All massacred. He has not been able to face returning to Srebrenica since then.'

Delic took a cloth from his pocket and blew into it to clear his nose and wipe his eyes.

'This all seems to confirm what I know of Pascoe,' said Seymour.

Delic stared at him quizzically. 'He asks why you call this man 'Pascoe'. Was that the name he was known by?'

'We believe that was his real name, yes,' Seymour replied.

'That may be, but he knew him by another name. Around here he was known as the *Andeo Cuvar.*' Terzic struggled to translate the term. 'They had several names for him in Serbia, Croatia and Bosnia. The nearest translation would be something like *guardian angel.*'

'He has also been likened to the Scarlet Pimpernel by others,' said Seymour, 'because of his habit at rescuing refugees from war zones and other conflicts.'

'Delic says he remembers clearly. It was one night in early April,' continued Terzic. 'There had been a rapid thaw and one might walk unhindered at last. This Andeo Cuvar led him, along with about a hundred others, to a place of safety, bypassing the border checkpoint into

Twelve

Montenegro at Granicni Prelaz. They trekked a long way to Sitnica where they found temporary refuge for a few months. Then they moved on to Susanj, near the town of Bar. After that, according to Delic, he never saw him again. But he understood that this man took many others out. He made several return trips and others joined Delic's group later in Montenegro. Had it not been for him, he says they might never have known to leave Srebrenica and he wouldn't be here to tell the tale.'

*

When Seymour reported to the police station next day, he was met at the door by a stone-faced constable and shown into another office. He sat down, was offered coffee, and waited. Eventually, he was joined by the station chief.

'Detective Seymour,' the chief began. 'I have some bad news to convey to you.'

'I was expecting to meet with Inspector Terzic. What's happened?'

'He will not be meeting you today,' the chief continued. 'Regretfully, Inspector Terzic was gunned down outside his apartment around nine o'clock last evening.'

Seymour was stunned. The chief allowed a few moments for him to take in the gravity of the news.

'He must have been on his way back from my hotel,' said Seymour. 'We'd had a drink and I'd only just bid him a good night. Is he alive?'

'Yes, he survived the shooting. But we understand that his wounds are critical. Medics are still working on him and it is touch and go whether he will make it.'

'I must go to him right away.'

'You can do little at present anyway. He is still in surgery.'

'Have you any idea who did it?'

'We have our suspicions, but as yet no hard evidence. We are concentrating our resources on finding the perpetrator. We don't take lightly to the attempted killing of one of our own.'

'So do you have any leads?' asked Seymour.

'Ballistics has already identified the weapon. He was shot with two 18 millimetre bullets, most likely from a Polish P-83 semi-automatic pistol. They were standard issue side-arms to VRS officers. Of course, they should all have been decommissioned in the weapons amnesty after the war, but many were kept as trophies and never surrendered. We believe a Serbian ex-army or Albanian faction may have targeted Terzic.'

'But why him?'

'He had been asking a great many questions, which did not pass unnoticed. There had been threats as well as repeated attempts to block his enquiries. You see, he has accumulated a great deal of material concerning wanted fugitives, from his contact in Albania. Terzic is a good police officer and doggedly persistent, but despite warnings, he was too outspoken and has upset many people. People in high places, if you know what I mean. One needs to tread carefully in such matters and you should also watch your own step. There are many who want the recent past left undisturbed.'

'Have you spoken with his wife yet? Does she know?' asked Seymour.

'It was Mrs Terzic who raised the alarm. She heard the gunshots, looked out of the window, realised it was her husband who had been shot and immediately called the police.'

'I should go over and offer her my support.'

'I'm sure she would appreciate that,' he replied. 'She has spent all night at the hospital, but was sent home early this morning. There was nothing she could do except wait. She's probably sitting by the phone waiting for news as we speak.'

*

Twelve

Back at the Terzic apartment, a police officer checked Seymour's credentials before admitting him. The atmosphere was entirely different from his visit two evenings earlier. The delicious smell of the hearty meal still pervaded the room, but it was not a happy face that greeted him. Branka Terzic sat motionless, her face distraught and ashen.

'Thank you for coming, detective,' she said. 'I appreciate the thought.'

'Mrs Terzic,' said Seymour. 'I don't know what I can say. I fear I may be the reason that Sasa was targeted.'

'No. He was involved in this case long before you arrived, so you need not feel responsible. Sasa is very much his own man and when he is onto something, there's no stopping him. He is like one of your British bulldogs. I warned him to be careful. The war has been over for more than twenty-five years, but some grudges lie very deep. Despite reconciliation, the old Yugoslav states co-exist in a fragile state of xenophobia and ethnic divides still remain strong. They have rebuilt the bridge at Mostar, but it is more than a river that separates Christians from Muslims in Bosnia. Things are slowly getting better, though these are still troubled times and men of little conscience live amongst us. But this is all politics and not your concern.'

'Well, like it or not, I have become involved, so I intend to remain in Sarajevo for the time being. In the meantime, if there's anything I can do, or anything you need, you have only to ask.'

'You're very considerate,' she responded. 'I am afraid there's nothing anybody can do until we know if Sasa is going to make it.'

*

That evening both Branka and Seymour kept vigil beside the hospital bed. Terzic remained unconscious, one side of his head was bandaged and one leg suspended in an overhead harness. Two bullets had struck him – one had penetrated the cheek and exited behind the right ear, and a second struck his calf. Fortunately, the bullet missed the brain by a few millimetres and there had been no serious damage, though he had lost a great deal of blood and was very weak. The surgeon warned that when he did eventually regain consciousness they should not expect too much of him.

Finally, in the early morning, his eyes opened and Terzic looked around the room. 'The bastards finally got me, then,' he said in a faltering voice. 'God! I need a drink and a cigar.'

'Yes, finally they got you,' replied Branka. 'Don't try to speak. Rest.'

He looked at Seymour, disregarding her request. 'Glad you could hang around, old man,' he said. 'Sorry to drop this on you. Not what we had in mind, eh?'

'Not quite,' replied Seymour. 'But that is of no consequence. You must concentrate all your energies into getting better. The rest can wait.'

'Thank God the bloody Serbs were such lousy shots! For a while I thought I was a goner.'

'So did we,' said Branka. 'I am told that they emptied a whole magazine at you, and it was a miracle that only two hit their target. You've been very lucky.'

'Lucky? Shot in my bad leg again! That's twice now.'

'So you think it was Serbs?' asked Seymour.

'Or Albanian Mafia,' replied Terzic. 'It had all the hallmarks of one of their hits.'

'Never mind the Serbs and Albanians for now,' said Branka. 'The doctor said the bullet passed right through the calf muscle and missed the bone, so your leg should fully recover.'

'So when do they say I get out of here?' said Terzic. 'I'm dying for a smoke.'

'Don't be in too much of a hurry,' Branka continued. 'The doctors are still concerned about your head wound.

Twelve

You've had a very traumatic experience and it won't get better overnight. You'll be off work for a few weeks at least, maybe a couple of months. The investigation will have to be put on hold for the time being.'

Both men looked across and simultaneously read the other's mind.

'I don't suppose you'd be willing to take over my case as well as going it alone with your search for this guardian angel of yours, would you?' said Terzic.

'You must be psychic,' replied Seymour. 'But yes, I've come too far to give up now. I'll need access to your case notes, of course, but I'd be glad to continue your investigation along with my own.'

'Catch two birds with one rock, as you English say. It seems your guardian angel and my war criminals followed the same route out of Sarajevo.'

Seymour laughed. 'The expression is two birds with one stone! But yes, it seems they did.'

*

Back at the apartment, Branka brought out Terzic's notes from under the bed. 'These might help you,' she said. 'The files are very detailed. Sasa was never quite sure whom he could trust, even amongst his own work colleagues, so he kept these at home. He had already copied some out in English so that you could read them.'

Seymour took the two files and thanked her.

'As you can see from the dates, although you have only just begun your investigation, Sasa had been working on his for several years. His own father and brother were executed by the Serbs in Srebrenica and he was lucky to escape with a leg wound. Hence, the walking stick, and why this is all so personal for him. You must understand, Mister Seymour, that Sasa is on a mission. For him to trust a stranger like yourself is a rare honour; it was clear that he was delighted when you agreed to continue his work.

'Doctors say Sasa seems to be out of danger and his leg wound should fully recover, but it will be some time before he walks properly. The damage to his head is still a cause for concern, however, and will need ongoing treatment for some time. It's possible he might have lost the hearing on his right hand side. Only time will tell.'

*

Terzic's notes named men and women who had died; many were known to him personally, as well as some of those he suspected were responsible for assassinations, torture and other abuses during the ethnic cleansing. There were accounts of Serb police and militia regularly rounding up young women and systematically raping them. There were graphic details of exhumations and reburials in the Srebrenica cemetery, including photographs of the partially decomposed and skeletal remains that had been unearthed from mass graves.

Throughout the case notes, one particular name recurred – that of a VRS Colonel, Bogdani Skender. According to several corroborative eyewitness testimonies, Skender was identified as commander of local Bosnian Serb troops and had directly ordered the execution of Terzic's father and brother. Skender had presided over dozens of summary executions and beatings. His name was highlighted wherever it appeared in the files. Finding Skender's whereabouts had become Terzic's obsession. He had already identified the route Skender took out of Bosnia back to his native Albania after the war. There were also a few references to this so-called guardian angel who had apparently followed his trail into Albania. Seymour had little belief in coincidence, but his own and Terzic's investigations had now completely coincided.

*

Twelve

'I wonder if I may retain Sasa's notes for the time being, Mrs Terzic?'

'Of course. Sasa wrote them out specifically for you. I am so glad you have agreed to this,' she replied appreciatively. 'Having you continue his search alongside your own investigation is more than he could have hoped. But you will need transport. Therefore, we have agreed that you should use his car for as long as you need it.'

'That's a very kind offer,' said Seymour. 'But won't you use it yourself?'

'In the first place, I don't drive, so it would just be standing idle in the street, and in the second, you might live to regret accepting it. It's an idiosyncratic automobile, very unreliable and sometimes it refuses to start at all. I have urged Sasa to get rid of it many times over the years, but he loves his car. He always says it's like a comfortable old armchair.'

'In that case, I graciously accept,' Seymour replied.

*

Terzic's files related exclusively to events in the Balkans between 1991 and 1995, including the war as it affected Montenegro. They recounted how the overwhelming majority of Montenegrins voted in a referendum for federation with Serbia after the breakup of Yugoslavia, largely in order to maintain their long-standing affiliation with Russia. The remainder of the population, mostly Muslim and Catholic minorities, boycotted the vote, fearing their future under Serbian influence. Such fears were not altogether unfounded, as many Montenegrin police and military were known to have joined Serbian forces and some had taken part in the many gross violations of human rights. It was not until 2006 that Montenegro finally severed all political ties with Serbia and gained full independence. But bad memories are a long time in passing.

During that dark period, Bosnian refugees were often rounded up in Montenegro and transported back to internment camps in Serbia. It was Bogdani Skender who had instigated arrests and supervised transportation to Foca, and there were many eyewitness statements attesting to his criminal abuse of captives. Several dozen such atrocities were carried out upon Terzic's own neighbours and schoolmates, including Delic. Mass rapes were carried out against Muslims females – girls as young as 10, and women as old as 80 years of age. Mothers were frequently violated in front of their own children.

According to Terzic's account, hundreds of refugees had Pascoe to thank for their survival. It was recorded that he led war refugees out of Bosnia through Mostar and then on to Bar on the Adriatic Coast. Seymour would need to pursue the investigation into Albania.

*

Despite Branka's assertion to the contrary, Terzic's old Citroën started first time. There had been a heavy overnight frost, but after a liberal application of the manual choke, accompanied by clouds of spluttering grey smoke, the engine's worn pistons fired into action readily enough.

Roads were icy and treacherous, but Seymour soon settled into a steady cruising speed towards the Bosnia-Montenegro border at Granicni Prelaz. Only a single white line painted across the carriageway and a large welcoming poster in English and Cyrillic Script marked the crossing.

Light was fading as he drove through the eponymous black mountains, following road signs for Bar. Before long, the car rattled over the cobblestones of the town's congested historic centre. Soon he came to the modern quarter and sped quickly along its wide boulevards to the old port, where Terzic had recommended he find a cheap hotel.

Twelve

Seymour chose to stay overnight in small place near the harbour. It was a stark building of painted concrete, but boasted suites with balconies overlooking the beach. All the staff spoke Serbian; some also spoke Russian and a few, what passed for English. The place had no restaurant, so Seymour decided to treat himself to a meal at a local hostelry in the marina.

However, his plan to eat a juicy peppered sirloin steak that evening was soon dashed. Local cuisine seemed to be entirely comprised of seafood and pasta dishes and there simply wasn't any kind of meat dish. Therefore, he grudgingly opted for an indifferent black squid risotto followed by well-grilled sea bream. When the waiter brought the entrée, Seymour ordered a bottle of Boza from the wine list. This sweet powerful drink, made from maize, was popular throughout the Balkans in some variation or another. 'When in Rome,' he mumbled to himself, with a guilty smile.

*

Seymour awoke next morning to the familiarity of a dry arid mouth, a sickening sense of dehydration and the thick coated tongue that resulted from the two bottles of wine he had consumed that evening before he collapsed into bed. He had experienced such mornings following a binge drinking session many times before. But that didn't help.

'Shit,' he spat. A solemn promise broken and his self-loathing matched only by the inherent desire to drink again. He attempted to regain his better self with copious cups of sweet black coffee at breakfast.

On the outskirts of Bar he stopped to refuel the automobile and to purchase a road map of the Balkans. This done, he set off around the costal corniches to the city of Ulcinj, before turning east to Krute and on to the Montenegrin border with Albania.

Chapter 24: Podrega

A few kilometres inside Albania, Seymour stopped at a roadside rest area. Progress had been good, but he still felt the effects of alcohol and was already weary of driving. He decided to take a short nap in the back of the car.

Seymour settled as comfortably as he could in the hollow depression of the worn leather bench seat, but his mind was too active for sleeping. He opened Terzic's files and turned to the passages relating to Albania. Terzic had recommended he talk to an old friend and colleague by the name of Radic Pavli, who had once been a police officer. Pavli and Terzic had once worked together in Sarajevo and the material in the files was the result of their considerable collaboration. Seymour would pay Pavli a visit in Shkodra the next day, in passing. He draped his overcoat over his shoulders and had just begun to fall into a light slumber when he was abruptly woken by the vibration of the mobile in the coat pocket.

'Hello,' he said. 'Who is this?'

'It's Fosse,' the voice addressed him. 'Where are you?'

'I'm in Albania, Prof.'

'Albania? What on earth are you doing in Albania?'

Seymour told Fosse about the Terzic shooting and the events that had transpired in Sarajevo, as well as the reason for his trip into Albania.

'I've made a little progress myself,' said Fosse. 'I went back and resumed my observation of Pascoe's address. Someone has been there. The curtains have been drawn back since we last visited and last night a man came out of the house. That's why I called; I thought you should know. But I had no idea you were in Albania.'

'So was it Pascoe? Did you get a good look at him?'

'Well, it was dark, so I couldn't be one hundred percent certain, but on the basis of your description, I'm

Twelve

pretty sure it was him. I was able to follow him some way on foot, but he gave me the slip, so I can't say where he was going.'

'Keep watching the house then, if you have the time,' said Seymour. 'You never know, he may return. As for me, I am following the route Pascoe seems to have taken into Albania. This Inspector Terzic was also mapping out the same route in pursuit of a suspected Albanian war criminal, so I have now effectively taken on both investigations. Fortunately, either might help move the other forward.'

'Excellent. Look, I must ring off now. Keep in touch, Charlie. Call me when you have news,' said Fosse. 'Oh – one more thing, Charlie.'

'Yes Prof.'

'Don't call me Prof!'

*

Seymour phoned early next morning. 'Hello, is that Radic Pavli?'

'*Hallo, Pavli. Jeni anglisht?*' the voice responded. 'Are you English?'

'Yes, I am English. Sorry I don't speak Albanian.'

'I thought I recognised the accent. No problem, I speak English, a little, if you talk slowly. But to whom am I speaking?'

'I am a policeman from England. A friend of Inspector Sasa Terzic. We were collaborating on the Skender case. My name is Charles Seymour.'

'Ah yes,' replied Pavli. 'How is my old friend Sasa?'

'I'm afraid to say that he has been badly wounded in a shooting!' Silence ensued. 'Hello, are you still there?'

'Yes, I am still here. I was just a little shocked at the news. But you say he's wounded. So he's still alive?'

'Very much so. I am on my way to Shkodra, and wondered if I may call in to see you? Sasa said I should look you up. I can explain everything when I see you.'

'You are most welcome. Any friend of Sasa's is a friend of mine. Do you have my address?'

'I do. Thanks. He has given me all of his file notes and contacts, including yourself. It may be later today or early tomorrow. I am now just a few kilometres inside the Albanian border from Montenegro.'

'You should easily make it here by this evening. I look forward to our meeting. You can bring me up to date with how the case is progressing.'

*

Shkodra, known as Scutari before the First World War, is a large expansive city, nestling beneath the high mountains that border Lake Shkoder. It has been a major centre for Arabic and Islamic studies for centuries and in recent times, home to a large population of Muslim refugees from the Bosnian War.

Radic Pavli lived alone in a small house in the city and welcomed Seymour warmly at the door. The pungent aroma of roasting lamb permeated the whole ground floor. In the Baltic, it seemed, Seymour had been met with the delicious aroma of cooking everywhere he went. Pavli continued working at the stove while Seymour explained the dual purpose of his mission to Albania. He told him of the attempted murder of Terzic, of the investigation in which they had both become involved and the background to the elusive Arthur Pascoe.

'So how long have you and Terzic worked together?' asked Seymour.

'Terzic and I served together as police officers in Bosnia for many years before the conflict,' answered Pavli. 'I was born and lived in Sarajevo where we both trained as police cadets. Unfortunately, the war broke up a good many friendships.'

On the living room wall hung photographs of

Twelve

Pavli and Terzic in police uniform, next to a couple of impressive looking certificates that Seymour was unable to decipher. But it was obvious both men had been close friends, professionally, as well as personally.

'And I was also born a Muslim,' Pavli continued. 'Not exactly the best thing to be in Bosnia at that time. I am not a religious man, but practising or not, the Serbs and Bosnian Christians made no distinction. Culturally, we were all Muslims, and that was that. We were to be rounded up and either expelled or exterminated. Fortunately I was able to escape in time, led out like many others, by this man you call Pascoe. I am completely integrated into Albanian society now, of course, but sadly I can never return to the country of my birth. There are too many bad memories and I am too old to undertake such an upheaval.'

'But you have managed to retain a friendship with Terzic despite everything?'

'I have, distantly. Though I have not seen him in a few years. We keep in contact by letters and telephone. More recently by email. In our day we were very good companions.'

Pavli served dinner at the table, where the entire surface was covered in white wall lining paper. It was copiously covered with notes, scrawled in Croatian or Albanian. Seymour thought it quite odd, but said nothing – he felt it would have been impertinent to enquire over dinner. The meal of baked lamb and yoghurt, called *Tave Kosi*, and the spinach pie were excellent. This was followed by an Albanian walnut cake drizzled with a sticky lemon glaze. Although he lived alone, Pavli was an accomplished domestic cook.

On this occasion Seymour threw caution to the wind and accepted a small shot of a powerful alcohol, a mulberry Rakia. Thereafter he declined to accept more in favour of his customary tumbler of water. Secretly he felt proud in his untypical stand against the addiction, but worried that declining further might have seemed discourteous in the face of his host's importunate generosity.

'This man you seek, the man you know as Pascoe. He was known here as *'Sigurno Skrbnik'* I think,' said Pavli. 'He has become a figure of myth and legend in the Balkans.'

Presently, as the meal drew to an end and Seymour felt able to ask the purpose of the table top notes. Pavli explained that his memory was not what it used to be and he had found it helpful to write things down immediately they occurred, so as not to forget. The table top was convenient.

'These scribbled notes are the results of my most recent research,' he said. 'I admit that it all looks a bit excessive, but Sasa and I have painful memories of those times – many ghosts that need exorcism.' He moved plates and cutlery aside to reveal his writing more clearly, explaining their relevance as he did so. Just as in Terzic's files, the name of Skender appeared in several places around the table.

'Tell me what you know about this Colonel Bogdani Skender,' asked Seymour.

'Skender was a monster! I suppose he still is. Leopards don't change their spots,' replied Pavli. He brought out a photo of Skender from a sheaf of papers beside the table. 'This is an old photo of him – it must be thirty years old by now. He's the one that got away. But Sasa and I are both determined to use what time we have left and whatever resources are available to us to find him. We were committed to tracking him down and bringing him to justice. But with Sasa out of the picture, I'm not sure how I'll manage.'

'Well,' said Seymour. 'Now I'm on the case too.'

Pavli stood up abruptly, leaned across and shook Seymour's hands so heartily it seemed it might never stop. 'I'm so glad to hear you say that,' he said. 'I am getting too

Twelve

old for such adventures and was beginning to despair of finding anybody who could continue the investigation. Sasa was my best hope, but he lives hundreds of miles away. When you told me of the shooting I thought that nothing more would come of our efforts. I was summoning up the courage to go looking for Skender myself.'

'I have already promised Sasa's wife that I will continue to pursue his case along with my own,' replied Seymour. 'The files which Sasa gave me together with your latest material might bring us closer to a result.'

'Let's hope so,' said Pavli.

'So you have any idea where Skender is now?'

'He was last reported to be somewhere in the Dajti National Park region north of Tirana. It's a very big area where a man could disappear for years. A perfect place to hide.'

'You think finding him will be a big task, then?' asked Seymour.

'It will. But you should begin your search around Mount Dajti. There is a hotel near the cable car terminus at the summit. That would be a good place to start. It's very popular with tourists, so you'd need to make a reservation if you wish to stay there. I can do that for you by telephone if you like. But be very much on your guard. Trust nobody. Especially the local police – I wouldn't trust them any further than I can spit; a few have become very corrupt in recent times. However, I do still have one old friend in the force and the very latest information he has provided indicates that Skender may have been seen in the village of Podrega. It's about fifteen kilometres from Tirana.'

Pavli took out his old police service revolver and a carton of cartridges from a sideboard drawer. 'Take this,' he said. 'It might come in handy.'

'I don't think so,' replied Seymour.

'You should realise that Skender is unlikely to be

cooperative. He won't come quietly and his past record demonstrates that he places little value on human life. He wouldn't hesitate to kill you if necessary, or even just for the fun of it.'

'I thank you for your concern,' said Seymour. 'But I must decline. I intend to use whatever legal means I can, and despite what you say, I shall attempt to obtain the collaboration of the local police.'

'I wish you luck then. Remember my warnings and keep in touch.'

*

As Seymour drove up towards the mountains, the road became less well maintained and *"Fusha e Dajtit"* signposts indicated that it led to the Plain of Dajti. It was the route Pavli had advised. From a distance he could see the high peak, topped by its several radio transmitters. A few kilometres from the summit he picked up signs for the Dajti Bellorum Hotel, where a room had been reserved for him.

Seymour thought the severe geometry of the hotel intruded in the otherwise sylvan landscape, and was quite out of keeping with natural forest and surrounding mountain scenery. Alongside the main building was the gondola lift that carried less keen walkers to the top of the peak, from whence, reputedly, there were panoramic views of Tirana.

*

He was awoken from an afternoon nap when his phone rang. It was Fosse again.

'Seymour,' he began. 'Pascoe's been to the house again. A taxi arrived late last night and he left, carrying a large suitcase. This time I followed him ... to the airport.'

'Where was he was flying?'

Twelve

'I'm afraid I don't know. By the time I'd parked up I'd lost track of him. So I've no idea. I paced the length of the airport concourse, back and forth several times, but to no avail. He simply gave me the slip again.'

'Do you think he saw you following him?' asked Seymour.

'I doubt it. Fortunately, I did manage to get the name of the taxi company. They might know what plane he was catching.'

'Let's hope so. Do what you can and I'll take over when I return.'

'Any idea how long you'll be away?'

'No, I can't say. This trek just seems to go on forever. I'm currently up a mountain just outside Tirana, following a lead that a local retired cop has given me. I don't know where this is going yet. I think they call it flying by the seat of your pants.'

'Well, take care. I'll be in touch when I have something more.'

*

After a light breakfast, Seymour spent the morning looking around. Away from the hotel complex, the views were dramatic. The snow-capped peak of Mount Dajti towered behind and the lower reaches of the mountain proliferated with beech and oak. Higher still, swathes of Balkan pines filled the air with a heady perfume. Signs warned against confronting local wildlife, as areas of the park abounded with wild boar, bears and wolves. Ramblers were urged to give their territories a wide berth and motorists were advised to stay inside their vehicles.

After his brief reconnoitre, Seymour went back into the hotel, where he had seen a wall map of the National Park. He located the village of Podrega. It lay about six kilometres distant from the hotel. Pavli said this was where Skender was last seen, and Seymour decided to pay it a speculative visit.

*

The only road into Podrega was across a small approach bridge that led directly into the main square. The village occupied a superb defensive position, overlooked by the ruins of a castle that stood on a high rocky outcrop. There was evidence of a nearby quarry, as several huge blocks of stone lay around the edge of the square, awaiting transportation to the mason's yard. Albanian granite had been famous since antiquity and was highly valued by the ancient Greeks and Romans.

Around the square were several cafés and bars. Seymour chose the most central, the Café Milan, where workmen sat outside on the terrace, drinking coffee and smoking. The ingrained stone dust in their hair and on their steel-capped work boots identified them as quarrymen. As he passed by their table he nodded an acknowledgement, which they ignored.

Once inside, Seymour walked up to the counter, drew out a bar stool and sat down. A few heads turned and looked at him apprehensively. Presently, the barman came over and flicked his eyebrows upwards in a universal 'what can I get you?' expression.

Seymour answered, *'Coeffe ju lutem'* – 'Coffee please', in what little Albanian he had gained in the past twenty-four hours.

'Zezë os te Bardhë?' – Black or white?' the barman asked.

Seymour said that he'd like black: *'E zezë.'*

The barman returned moments later with a small tumbler of aromatic coffee and placed it on a paper coaster on the bar counter. Seymour took a sip and addressed him again in the best Albanian he could muster, *'Yo a flisni anglisht?'*

'Yes,' replied the barman. 'I am speaking the

Twelve

English ... a little.'

Seymour produced two photographs from his coat pocket. 'Have you seen either of these men?' he asked.

The man glanced impassively at the photo of Pascoe, without recognition. However, the other, that of Skender, made an immediate impression and a barely discernible muscle twitched in his cheek.

'No,' he replied without a moment's hesitation. 'I never seen either.'

Seymour knew it was a lie. The man clearly recognised Skender. Bogdani Skender was probably well known in such a small remote community. Pavli's information had proved correct. As for Pascoe, so far, nothing looked very promising.

*

After dinner that evening, Seymour relaxed in the hotel lounge. As he drank coffee and channel-hopped idly through the selection of Albanian and Italian television programmes, his attention was drawn behind to the bar counter, where three men sat talking and laughing raucously. He looked round and could hardly believe his eyes. One of the three was Bogdani Skender himself ... older, balder and fatter, but unmistakably, it *was* Skender.

He turned back swiftly, not knowing quite what to do next. Completely unprepared, his mind raced as he stared vacantly at the television screen. It was several minutes before he felt able to risk a second glance. When he turned back, all three men were shaking hands cordially. Then two of them left the hotel, while Skender remained behind and lit a cigarette, before walking over to the lift and going in. It ascended several levels before the panel indicated it had stopped at the third floor. A few moments later it began the descent back down to the reception. Skender was staying on the third floor.

Seymour walked back to the counter and

addressed the receptionist. 'Can you tell me who that gentleman who just took the lift was? He's staying on the third floor. He was drinking at the bar a few moments ago with two friends.'

The hotel receptionist was reticent. However, when Seymour placed a large denomination Albanian Lek note on the counter top and slid it towards him, his attitude softened.

'I'd prefer US Dollars or Euros,' the man whispered.

Seymour took back the banknote and replaced it with a crisp twenty Euro note. The receptionist covered it quickly with his hand before discreetly placing it in his waistcoat pocket. Then he wrote on a slip of paper, folded it and handed it to Seymour. He had written the words:

"HOXAH DARDAN, ROOM 302"

*

Back in his room Seymour immediately made two phone calls – the first to Caroline Massey in London and the other to Radic Pavli in Shkodra.

'Hello, Massey,' she responded.

'It's Seymour.'

'I was wondering what you were up to, Seymour. Can I assume you have something to tell me about Pascoe?'

'I am presently in Albania, having followed the trail from Bosnia through Montenegro, as suggested by Inspector Terzic. I'm currently staying at a mountain hotel above Tirana and I've spoken with several people who knew him or knew of him. But none recognised him by the name Pascoe. However, he seems to be regarded as a local hero in the Balkans – some kind of guardian angel.'

'Well that's something. Is there anything you need out there?'

Twelve

'Could you look into a man going by the name of Hoxah Dardan or Bogdani Skender and send me any information you have on him.'

'Is that him? Or them?' she queried.

'Well, I believe they are one and the same person. But he's probably calling himself Hoxah Dardan as an alias.'

'How does this relate to the Pascoe investigation?'

'I'm not exactly certain, yet. But what I have discovered points to there being one. It all stems from the information Terzic gave me. Pascoe may have been following Skender here from Bosnia. It's just a hunch at the moment, but I'd like to follow it.'

'Are you sure this is the best use of your time?' she asked. 'I went out on a limb for you, Seymour. There were others in the department who were against bringing in an outsider. I hope they were wrong and I haven't made a mistake. You're also operating naked out there ... we have no available support network or backup in Albania. You're entirely on your own.'

'I realise that. But with respect, ma'am, you enlisted me for my detection skills and this is the way I work. You have to give me the latitude or I'm completely hamstrung.' Seymour never felt more of a throwaway than he did at that precise moment.

'Very well,' she replied after a few moments consideration. 'Keep checking your email. I'll send what we can find. But do get some results for your efforts. My personal judgement, as well as your own professional future, depend on this.'

'I realise that,' he concluded. 'Trust me.'

*

'Hello, Pavli. I think I've found Skender.' This was his second phone call.

'That's great news. Where did you find him?'

'You sent me to the right place, as it happened. He was in the bar at the Dajti Bellorum Hotel with two other men. I don't know who they were, but it was all very pally and one of them was definitely Skender. He's older, but there's no doubt of it. He may be using another name. I'm expecting to receive more background information from London, possibly tomorrow.'

'So is there anything I can do in the meantime?'

'Yes, there is. You could let Terzic know what I've discovered. He'll be wondering how the search is going in his absence. I have no official jurisdiction in Albania, so you might look into how we are going to deal with getting Skender into custody.'

'I'll get right on it. There is a long-standing European arrest warrant out for him, anyway, so I'm sure Interpol will be interested, as will the Bosnian War Crimes Commission. This is excellent progress Detective Seymour. I knew you were the right man for the task.'

*

Next morning, Seymour accessed his mail on the computer in the lobby. Several messages had already arrived from Caroline Massey. They confirmed pretty much what he knew, that Hoxah Dardan and Bogdani Skender were the same person. However, while as Skender, he had effectively disappeared off the radar, a great deal of information existed on Dardan, much of it in the public domain, had anybody known to look for it.

It emerged that Dardan had enlisted as a foreign mercenary under the name of Bogdani Skender. He had risen rapidly through the ranks and by the end of the conflict, held the rank of colonel in the Serbian army. As such, he had overseen sections in several prison camps, including Foca. Radic Pavli had written about the many atrocities he witnessed at Foca. Its camp commandant had already been indicted for crimes against humanity and was

Twelve

currently serving a whole life prison sentence. But the whereabouts of his subordinate officer, Bogdani Skender, were unknown. Nothing had been heard of him since 1995.

All that was about to change.

Recorded information showed that Hoxah Dardan had purchased several properties around Podrega after the conflict ended. He was now chief executive of the local quarry, employed most of the men in the region, and had acquired the Café Milan bar in 1996. This purchase had been made outright, in cash, and though the source of his funding was under investigation by local authorities, so far, nothing positive had been proven, and nobody seemed in a great hurry to resolve the case. Under this identity, he had also become high-ranking in local politics. He was chairperson of the local branch of the Tirana Forest Department, so that he had effective control of the day-to-day administration of the whole area. As Hoxah Dardan, he had become a powerful man.

*

'Hello, Seymour.' It was Fosse on the phone again.

'Hi Max, how are things going?'

'Good progress,' Fosse continued. 'I got to see the local property register in the town hall planning department. It confirms that Pascoe does own the house. I also checked airlines. You know, destinations and routine schedules. At the time he arrived at the airport check-in, all things being equal, and stretching things a little, he would have had to have flown either to Frankfurt, Florence or Tirana. They were the only outbound flights remaining that day.'

'Tirana!' said Seymour.

'Another coincidence?' said Fosse.

'I don't think so.'

'Too unlikely?'

'You said it, Max. Maybe I will take a trip down to Tirana tomorrow see what I can find out. If Arthur Pascoe is here, then I'll be very interested to discover why he's in Albania now. Anyway, tonight I intend to visit the local stone quarry.'

'Anything I should know about?'

'Just a hunch, maybe nothing, but I'll let you know if anything useful materialises.'

*

Seymour followed the road signs to the Podreg-Tirane Corporation stone quarry, with only the dim light of the headlamps to guide him, and it took a while to find the turn-off that led down to the quarry compound.

He reached the bottom of the cutting after descending the rough stony track for half a kilometre. There were only a few buildings. One still had lights on – there were people about. He switched off the headlamps and pulled in behind a column of granite blocks where it would not be seen. Then, making his way slowly across the yard on foot, he concealed himself among the heavy plant machinery and excavators that were stationed alongside the nearest building. One of its windows was boarded up, but there were sufficient spaces between the slats for him to peer inside.

As far as he could make out, five men sat at a table, beneath a single electric lamp, drinking and playing cards. He recognised Skender immediately. Two others were his acquaintances from the hotel. Another was the barman from the Café Milan. A fifth man sat with his back to the window. As he leaned forward to pick up a card, a glint of shoulder insignia shone in the light. He was a policeman.

Suddenly, out of darkness, two strong hands roughly gripped Seymour by the shoulders.

'*Cfarë po bën këtu?*' a voice boomed in Albanian, 'What

Twelve

are you doing here?' Seymour was forcibly turned around and confronted by three uniformed policemen, two had handguns drawn.

'Nothing,' Seymour replied. His tone was defiant, but pointless.

'*Ejani na wit* – Come with us,' said one, coarsely. Then he forced Seymour's arm painfully up his back and frog-marched him into the building. The seated police officer stood up immediately and turned, looked him directly in the eyes and asked who he was.

'*Kush jeni ju?*' he demanded.

'I don't speak Albanian,' replied Seymour. 'I'm English.'

'So, you are English,' the officer repeated. Seymour guessed his rank was that of a Chief Inspector. 'What are you doing here?'

'My car has broken down,' said Seymour lamely. 'I was looking for assistance.'

For a few moments the Chief consulted one of the officers – they spoke together in a low voice. Then he addressed Seymour again.

'Apparently your car was perfectly serviceable when my men saw you drive in,' said the Chief. 'You have some identification?'

Seymour handed over his papers.

'You are a policeman,' said the chief. He contemplated the implication for a time, and glanced over to Skender, who shrugged his shoulders and stared back non-committedly. 'You have no entry visa and no jurisdiction in Albania,' the Chief continued. 'I ask again. Why are you here?'

'As I said, I'm just a tourist. I'm on holiday,' Seymour replied. 'I only came here to ask directions. I lost my way. If you release me I'm sure we can resolve this little misunderstanding.'

'There is no misunderstanding. You give two conflicting explanations of your presence here on private property. These are not the actions of a tourist. Your passport shows you have travelled from Bosnia without a visa. What sort of holiday is this?'

'I am touring the Balkans and the Dalmatian Riviera, that's all.'

The barman, who had hitherto remained silent throughout, came forward and whispered in the policeman's ear. Skender joined them and all three entered into an intense discussion in Albanian. Things were not looking good for Seymour.

'It seems you have been asking a lot of questions around the village,' the Chief said at length. 'There are serious issues that need to be explained, and I'm afraid we need to detain you while we make enquiries. Your actions seem very suspicious to us – not those of a legitimate tourist. Meantime your passport and warrant card will be confiscated.'

*

Seymour was held in a storeroom lock-up at the quarry, not in a police cell as he might have expected. Plainly, his confinement was unofficial. Alone, and in a foreign country, his rank seemed to offer little or no protection. All of his clothes were taken away. 'Naked' was the term Caroline Massey had used. Ironically, now he knew exactly what that meant.

Over the next two days he was questioned continually and roughly. Interrogation was carried out by what he assumed to be plain-clothes policemen and the process was forceful. He was frequently slapped or cuffed about the head when his responses did not satisfy. These prolonged interrogations stopped short of actual beatings, though periodically he was pinned to the floor or spat upon by his captors, which was more humiliating than painful. Much of the questioning was observed by Skender and the senior police officer, who stood silently at the back

Twelve

of the room, watching, but taking no active part in the inquisition.

'Why are you really here?' they repeatedly demanded. 'What is your interest in this place? For whom are you working? Who are you reporting to? You are a spy – things will go better for you if you will admit it.' The same questions continued interminably hour upon hour. He was constantly awoken and deprived of sleep. Such food as he was offered was sparse, unidentifiable and almost inedible – not at all the rich tasty dishes he had come to expect of Balkan cuisine.

But on the morning of the third day, the interrogation ceased, without explanation. A complete change of attitude came into play and he was left to sleep peacefully at last. When he awoke, he was allowed to bathe in one of the quarry shower rooms, his clothes were returned to him and he was given a decent breakfast of eggs, bread and coffee. After the meal, he was driven to the police station in Podrega, where a local physician gave him an unusually thorough examination and he was declared fit and well. A shaving bowl of hot water, an open razor and soap were provided. When he was done, a police sergeant returned his papers and Seymour was told that he was free to go. No charges were being made and no apology was given.

He walked down the steps from the station and saw the old Citröen parked at the kerbside, its keys in the ignition. He got in, started the engine and drove out of Podrega without looking back.

Chapter 25: Tirana

Seymour's nerve had been badly shaken by his ordeal in Podrega and he realised that it was unwise to remain in the mountain retreat. Once back at the hotel, he packed as quickly as he could, checked out and drove down the mountain towards Tirana where he might feel safer.

He stopped at a lay-by, a few kilometres clear of the Datji Bellorum, to check for accommodation in the tourist leaflets he had picked up from the hotel lobby. The Rogna Hotel on the Deshmoret Boulevard in the city centre looked most promising. It was large and he could get lost in its anonymity.

Immediately he had checked in, he phoned Pavli and related to him what had transpired at the Podrega quarry.

'I got caught,' he said, '... and they roughed me up a bit.'

'Are you all right?' said Pavli.

'Yeh, I'm fine,' Seymour replied. 'More shaken than hurt. But you were right about the police.'

'How did they get involved?'

'It turns out that a high ranking officer is one of Skender's mob. They were thick as thieves; he just stood by and watched my interrogation, apparently enjoying the whole thing.'

'Didn't they know you were a policeman?'

'Yes, absolutely they did. I handed over my papers, but that made little difference. They had little regard for me as a visiting copper and treated me like a criminal. Maybe I should have taken you up on your offer of a gun after all.'

'On reflection, it might have made matters far worse had they caught you with a weapon,' said Pavli. 'Do you think they knew the purpose of your trip to Albania?'

'I don't think so. I certainly didn't divulge anything, and I consistently maintained that I was just on

Twelve

holiday touring the Balkans. I think they are just suspicious of all strangers. And after all, I was snooping about the quarry, which didn't look good. It took a while, but I suppose they must have believed me in the end, as they released me without charge.'

'What charge could they have brought against you, anyway?'

'Trespassing at worst. I'm not sure if that's even a crime in Albania. I was a little naïve, I suppose. I'd assumed that if I were caught, I would just be asked to leave.'

'This is Albania,' replied Pavli, '... and the rules of cricket don't apply here. You should take extra care in future. Now they know of you, some of your initiative may have been lost.'

'Maybe they'll assume I've left the country and that'll be the end of it.'

'I wouldn't be so sure. They are policemen, and Albanian. It is in their nature to be suspicious – it's a hangover from the old Communist mind-set.'

'I'll take extra care from now on,' said Seymour.

'So have you any news of Pascoe?'

'Nothing first hand, but my colleague in England thinks he may already be in Tirana.'

'Coincidence?' asked Pavli.

'Against my better instincts,' Seymour concluded. 'But I can't think of any other explanation.'

*

During the next twenty-four hours, Seymour spent time trying to identify the senior police officer who had been present during his interrogation at the quarry. Eventually, he discovered a promising match online. It was either the man at the quarry, or someone who closely resembled him. There were three images, part of an online portfolio of a local photographic studio in the Rruga Musa Maci in

Tirana city centre, and the subject was named as Chief Inspector Lorenc Dishku. Seymour decided he would pay a visit to the studio the next morning.

Shortly after returning to his room, there was a loud and persistent knocking on the door. He opened it to be confronted by two uniformed policemen.

'What seems to be the trouble, officers?' he asked.

'Papers!' It was a demand. They stood outside in the hallway while Seymour quickly complied.

'You are English Detective Charles Seymour?' asked the first officer.

'I am.'

'What's the purpose of your visit to Tirana?'

'I am on holiday, touring by car.'

'How long do you intend to stay in Albania?' asked one officer.

'Possibly a few more days.'

'You are not welcome here, Mister Seymour. You will leave as soon as possible.' With that the policeman rudely thrust Seymour's papers back at him, turned smartly on his heel and both men left. It seemed that news of Seymour's foray into the quarry had already percolated down to the central Tiranan police.

Despite the warning, Seymour was determined to remain in town long enough to get a positive ID for Lorenc Dishku.

*

Foto Studio Blaku proved very accommodating. They were happy to identify the subject in the pictures and confirm that the face was that of Lorenc Dishku. He had commissioned several portraits to celebrate his promotion to the rank of Chief Inspector at the Podrega Police Station two years earlier. As a most prestigious client, they said, they were proud to display these high quality portraits as examples of their professional photography.

Twelve

Seymour had accomplished all he intended for the morning, and decided to take the tram back to his hotel. The short transit system was brand new; only the first inner city section had been completed and it had been operating for just a few weeks. The system was seen to herald the new forward-looking attitude in post-Soviet Albania, as it was preparing for its hoped-for membership to the European Union. It was a smooth ride and from the comfort of its plush seating, it offered excellent views of central Tirana through large tinted windows.

He was enjoying the passing city view, when suddenly he recognised the figure of Arthur Pascoe walking past on the pavement outside. Seymour craned his neck to look round and it took only a second to assure himself that he was not mistaken. Immediately, he jumped up, rang the bell to stop the tramcar, and quickly made his way along the compartment to the exit. As it drew to a halt, the doors opened, and Seymour jumped out. Immediately, he dashed back to where he had seen Pascoe, but the pavement was extremely congested and after five minutes fruitless searching he gave up looking. At least the information that Fosse had given was correct.

Pascoe was in Tirana.

*

It occurred to Seymour that if Skender had changed his name to avoid arrest, it was logical to assume Dishku had similarly adopted a new persona. Therefore, as soon as he got back to the hotel, he emailed Caroline Massey to inform her of the Pascoe sighting and requested any available information concerning Chief Inspector Lorenc Dishku.

Deeply ingrained habits and training quickly came into play and Seymour soon formulated a plan. He needed to observe and establish patterns of behaviour. So, equipped with an old pair of ex-Russian military binoculars bought at a street market, he decided to make another risky visit into Podrega. This time he needed to be more careful. He would leave the car off road, some way short of the village and circumnavigate his way on foot to take up a vantage point behind the castle walls overlooking the square. Before setting out, he sent an image of Dishku to Pavli and Terzic. Maybe he was already known to them.

*

The Citröen was well hidden in the undergrowth as Seymour set off to walk into Podrega. He kept well clear of the road, but more than once he had to duck down behind bushes to avoid being seen by trucks carrying stone from the quarry. As he crouched down he remembered the notice at the Datji Bellorum Hotel, warning visitors against walking in the woods, where bears and wolves roamed freely. However, on this occasion he had far more to fear from men than from wild animals. Nevertheless, he walked warily.

From the cover of one of the huge stone blocks, he surveyed the square for some time and planned a way around the periphery of the village. The chosen route took him scrambling across several loose scree slopes and steep inclines before he came to the relative flatness of the castle terrace. Few of the ancient walls had survived intact, and much of its stonework had been pilfered to construct buildings in the village. But sufficient remained to provide good cover and he settled down with his binoculars to watch.

Surveillance was, as ever, interminably boring, and Seymour was about ready to give up when a large saloon car pulled up in the square and stopped in front of the Café Milan. Skender and Dishku got out, the latter still in uniform, and they went into the café. Seymour looked at his watch. It had just passed one o'clock.

It was an hour and a half later that both men

Twelve

emerged and drove off again. By now Seymour's fingers tingled with numbness and he struggled to note the time in his pocket book. It was a routine thing to do.

*

There were two email replies awaiting his return to the hotel. The first, from London. Nothing was known of Lorenc Dishku before July 1995. He appeared in Podrega during that year, apparently out of the blue, and joined the Tirana Police Service shortly afterwards. Over time he had risen to the rank of Chief Inspector and was given charge of the Podrega station. Though this information was in the public domain, it proved hard to decipher, given the vagaries and complexities of websites in both Albanian and Cyrillic languages.

The second was from Pavli. He identified the figure in the photograph as a guard who served under Skender at Foca. But Lorenc Dishku was not the name by which he was known at that time. Seymour's intuition as to the identity had been right. According to Pavli, his real name was Ardit Chani, and he had been complicit in the many of the widespread abuses that had taken place. Pavli's identification of the man in the photograph was positive and unequivocal. He had personally suffered under the lash that Chani carried. Subsequently, both Dardan and Chani had been charged with various war crimes in absentia by the International Criminal Court in The Hague. Their whereabouts remained unknown, but several international warrants for their arrest and extradition were outstanding.

Chani's re-emergence as Lorenc Dishku added to the evidence that was mounting in the case that Seymour had inherited. As for the Arthur Pascoe investigation, apart from one tantalising sighting of him in Tirana, he was getting nowhere. He was at a loss as to what to do next, short of telephoning every hotel in the city, he had no other option.

Terzic and Pavli's case would have to monopolise his time for the present. Therefore, he spent the next six days observing the village square in Podrega from behind the castle walls. A clear pattern was emerging – both men regularly ate lunch at the Café Milan at around one o'clock every day. Seymour had established a clear behaviour pattern for Skender and Dishku, and he knew exactly where and when to find them.

*

Seymour had been in Tirana for more than a week before he received a telephone call from Terzic.

'Hello old fellow,' greeted Terzic. 'It's been a while and I thought we should catch up. Pavli has updated me on what you have discovered in Tirana. Excellent work, Seymour. Most promising, I must say.'

'Yes, apart from one minor setback, it all went better than I expected,' replied Seymour. 'So you've been discharged from hospital?'

'Not exactly. I discharged myself. Can't lie around in bed forever. We've things to do.'

'We?' said Seymour. 'I can't believe you're ready to go back to work yet. How's your leg? And the ear?'

'The leg is stiff and I limp a little. But that's hardly new - I always did. The head injury is healing slowly, and apart from being deaf on the right hand side, they tell me I'm making good progress, though it might be a permanent loss of hearing. So, apart from more-or-less continuous headache and increased grumpiness, so Branka tells me, I'm ready to work again. I have already been in touch with Captain Didier LaRoche at Interpol and we've got the extradition process underway. When I receive the Authenticated Conviction Order, he and I will be joining you in Tirana.'

'Is that wise?' said Seymour. 'Do you think you're

Twelve

fit to travel?'

'Fit or not, there's no way I'm going to miss this! I have too much time invested not to be there for the pay-off,' continued Terzic. 'So have you any news of Arthur Pascoe?'

'I saw him, just once. He's here in Tirana, but I have no idea why or where.'

'Well, good luck with that. I'll let you know when to expect me.'

*

The extradition briefing in the Committee Room at the Rogna Hotel had been arranged for eleven-thirty in the morning. Terzic's head was still bandaged, but he insisted on being the official representative of the Bosnian Police. He would personally deliver the Conviction Order. Apart from him and Seymour, also in attendance were the Chief of the State Police with two police officers from outside Tirana, Didier LaRoche, and a Secretary of the Albanian Ministry for Foreign Jurisdictional Relations. Terzic presented the formal extradition request, as well as a statement of offences with a copy of evidence. When the paperwork was approved, and all the appropriate protocols completed, the party left to drive in convoy to Podrega.

They planned to arrive at the Café Milan around half past one in the afternoon, when, according to Seymour, both of the accused were likely to be dining.

At precisely one-twenty-seven, all three cars sped into the village square and screeched to a halt in front of the Café Milan. The two uniformed policemen immediately sprang out and rushed into the bar ahead of the others. Around a table sat Skender, Dishku and the two other cronies whom Seymour had seen at the Datji Bellorum Hotel. Surprised, they rose sharply to their feet. One immediately reached for the pistol that was in his belt, but froze when he saw that Terzic and both policemen already had weapons drawn. Outgunned and outnumbered, he sat down, threw his weapon on the table and raised his hands in a gesture of surrender.

'What is the meaning of this?' snarled Dishku, visually compromised and outraged.

The Chief of State Police ignored the outburst, stepped forward and addressed them formally. 'Bogdani Skender, otherwise known as Hoxah Dardan, and Lorenc Dishku, otherwise known as Ardit Chani,' he began, 'I am provisionally arresting you both under the terms of the European Convention of Extradition for crimes against humanity and genocide.'

Suddenly from beneath the counter, the barman drew a shotgun. Terzic shot him dead in the head and he fell where he stood. In the distraction, the two seated men seized the opportunity, drew their weapons and a fierce gunfight ensued. Terzic turned to face Skender, who had a pistol pointed directly at him. The gun discharged at the exact instant that Seymour leapt forward, interposing himself between Skender and Terzic. He heard the loud report, felt the heat of the flash on his cheek and the sharp excruciating pain that hit his chest point blank. Seymour fell to the floor in a pool of blood, unconscious.

Chapter 26: The Twelve

'At last. You are finally in the land of the living again.' It was Terzic. Seymour opened his eyes and looked around. He was lying in a sick bed, but it was not a hospital room. He tried to raise himself up on one elbow, but severe pain shot through his body and he fell back against the pillow, weak and exhausted.

'How long have I been out?' he asked.

'Five days,' replied Terzic. 'It was touch and go, but you're a hard man to kill, my friend.'

'Where am I?' said Seymour.

'You're in Italy. At Pascoe's villa in Capella da Campo.' It didn't quite register. All Seymour could remember was the events at the Café Milan.

'What happened? Did we get them?'

'Thanks to you. Yes, we did ... and I am still alive. You saved my life, Seymour,' Terzic continued. 'We got them all. Dishku, the bartender and the two other henchmen were shot dead.'

'And Skender?'

'After he shot you, I fired back at him, but he only sustained a slight flesh wound. My gun jammed, so I couldn't get off a second shot and I beat him to the ground with my walking cane. I confess that I quite enjoyed that! He was arrested. He has already been extradited to Bosnia.'

It finally dawned upon Seymour. 'Did you say this was Pascoe's villa?'

'I did. No doubt you'll be seeing him later,' said Terzic. 'It seems, my friend, that we both got our man – I got Skender and you got Pascoe.'

'But how did I end up here?'

'You have to thank Mister Pascoe for that. He arranged a private air ambulance from Tirana to Florence. He said that Albanian hospitals were basic and thought you'd do better in Italy. It was only yesterday that you were pronounced well enough to travel again and he personally flew us both up here to his villa by helicopter. It was a somewhat hair-raising ascent up the hillside, I have to admit, but he seems to be a most competent pilot, thank God!'

'So you've actually met him?'

'I have. A most charming fellow. He's bringing your family over from England tomorrow. For some reason you seem to be very much in his favour.'

Seymour, however, had already fallen back into oblivion.

*

'Ah, detective. You're awake.' Seymour had been drifting in and out of a light sleep all morning. 'I trust you are feeling a little better. The doctor says you're making excellent progress.'

It was Arthur Pascoe, in the flesh, standing at the foot of the bed.

'I've been better,' replied Seymour, still in a slight stupor.

'I imagine so.'

'This isn't exactly how I'd planned things.'

'No matter. At least we get to meet face to face, at last,' said Pascoe. 'You've come a long way since that railway station in Grange, and I have to admire your doggedness. You certainly gave me a merry chase.'

'Just doing my job,' replied Seymour, modestly.

'Hardly,' replied Pascoe. 'But you must have a great many questions.'

'There's a lot I can't get my head around.'

'I expect there is, and you deserve explanations. But I think you've already worked some of it out, anyway. There's plenty of time to unravel mysteries later. For now you should concentrate on getting well. Sleep.'

Twelve

*

Bright sunlight flooded into the room through the partially closed shutters, and even though it was still midwinter, birds could be heard singing outside. Reflected light from the overnight powdering of snow flooded through the window and lit up the ceiling with such intensity that Seymour's eyes took a while to grow accustomed to the brightness. Gradually, he became aware that Sarah was sitting at the bedside. She was holding his hand.

'You don't have to say anything,' she began. 'They've told me everything that happened in Albania. You're lucky to be alive. Just rest.'

'How long have you been here?' he asked.

'Daisy and I arrived yesterday. Mister Pascoe sent a car to pick us up at Pisa. Who is he? I don't remember you ever mentioning him.'

'I'll explain everything, in time. It's complicated.'

'Well thank God for Mister Pascoe, that's all I can say.'

'Yes, there's a lot to thank him for. Where is Daisy?'

'She's playing in the garden with your friend Terzic. They're getting on like a house on fire. He seems like a very nice man. But what on earth's wrong with his head?'

'The bandages? He's recovering from a head wound. He was my police contact in Sarajevo, and he shouldn't be out of bed either.'

'The doctor says you'll be well enough to get up and walk around with a little help tomorrow. Mister Pascoe is laying on a special meal to celebrate your recovery.'

*

Assunta had prepared a veritable feast. Daisy and Terzic sat beside each other at the table, happy in their newly forged friendship. Seymour and Sarah faced each other from either side, and Arthur Pascoe presided at the head of the table, carving the roast wild boar with great ceremony. The deep red Sangiovese flowed freely, but Seymour settled for a jug of *frizz ante* with ice and lemon.

Conversation around the table had been light and rated no better than polite small talk, entirely avoiding the events that had transpired in Albania. But after coffee, Pascoe invited Seymour to walk with him a little, where they could talk more freely, out of earshot of the others. He led him into the corridor of portraits.

'Here we are, then,' he began. 'When Sandro told me that we'd had a visitor, I had an inkling it was you. I soon realised that the contact details you left were entirely fictitious, of course. And, I knew that once you'd seen the portraits, especially the Toledo photograph, you'd begin to put two and two together. It was only a matter of time till our paths coincided.'

'It is you in the photo, isn't it?' said Seymour.

'Yes, it is,' Pascoe replied. 'In fact, all the portraits are of me. It's a little narcissistic, I suppose, but we all deserve at least one weakness.'

'What were you doing in Tirana?'

'I came for you. To bring you back after the shooting in Podrega,' replied Pascoe.

'How could you have known that was going to happen?'

'You were my special assignment,' continued Pascoe. 'I knew what was going to be played out in Podrega, and of the events surrounding Skender's arrest. I knew the when and the where, but you were the catalyst.'

'I still don't understand.'

'You will. One thing at a time,' said Pascoe.

'I'm also having difficulty grasping how you could have been in Toledo during the Spanish Civil War in 1936. I know José Gomez was only a small boy back then, and lived well into his eighties. Yet here you are – not aged at all. So exactly how old are you?'

Twelve

'Perhaps you had better sit down,' said Pascoe. 'What I am about to tell you will be rather difficult for you to accept. I had planned on explaining everything once you'd made a full recovery, but perhaps now is as good a time as any.'

Seymour sat down in curious anticipation.

'Unlikely as it may seem, everything I am about to tell you is absolutely true. But before I begin, you must promise that it will remain a secret. You must solemnly swear it will remain between us.'

'I don't really understand,' replied Seymour. 'But okay, I give you my word.'

'So be it.' Pascoe paused to consider his words carefully, before he began.

'First, I have to tell you that I was born on the second day of July in the year 2241, on the Saint's Day of Mary Magdalene.'

Seymour's jaw gaped and he stared at Pascoe transfixed.

'I first came back in 1766,' Pascoe continued. 'I am 372 years old. The portraits, as you had already concluded, are all originals. They are not forgeries, pastiches or facsimiles. I sat for every one.'

Seymour remained in a stunned silence. Although he had long pondered the uncertainty and confusion surrounding Pascoe's age, this was far more than he could have imagined.

'You say you came back. You can't be talking about time travel? It's not possible.'

'It is perfectly possible, and yes, I am. Such things will be possible, just not yet. Science hasn't got everything exactly right yet – some of it, but not the whole picture.'

'But what kind of man are you?'

Pascoe smiled. 'I'm an ordinary man like you. It's just that I happen to be from the future. But I have no special powers. I'm not an alien or a superman. I assure you I'm quite normal ... for the twenty-third century, that is.'

'But over three hundred years old? I wouldn't call that normal. I'd have put you in your late forties or early fifties. You have none of the signs of old age.'

'I said it would be difficult,' replied Pascoe, 'but if you can suspend your scepticism for a while, I'll try to put things into a context that I think you'll understand.

'When I first came back in the mid-eighteenth century, average life expectancy was around thirty years. It was a very different world then. Life was hard, and very short. Many ordinary folk died prematurely – in childbirth, of the common cold, of simple things like infected cuts and grazes, of cholera, or the plague.

'Now move forward to the present. People born in the twenty-first century stand a very good chance of living well into their nineties or even to reach a hundred. And, as I speak, somewhere in the world, a child has already been born who will live to be one hundred and fifty years old. Great progress in medicine and scientific research will take place over the next two centuries. It's already begun – it's been going on for some time, but you haven't noticed. Think about it. Smallpox and other deadly diseases like polio and diphtheria have already been virtually eradicated. Heart conditions and diabetes are being controlled by new medications. Surgeons can already transplant hearts, kidneys, livers and lungs. Hips and knees are being routinely replaced. Regenerative medical procedures are already underway to re-grow and fully restore amputated limbs and to reconnect broken nerve endings. Advances in genetics are accelerating at little short of lightening speed.

'There's so much more yet to come. By the twenty-second century we will have eradicated life-threatening conditions like AIDS, cancer, dementia, multiple sclerosis and cerebral palsy. These will all be consigned to the pages of history, and unlike your generation, mine will be completely free of such scourges. In the future, we will have a considerably extended life expectancy, be healthier, and without the worst effects of advancing decrepitude.

Twelve

'There's so much more I could tell you – this isn't the end. It isn't going to stop. The future has already arrived - in fact, there is no future - just the past steadily accumulating.'

*

After breakfast next morning, Seymour ventured outdoors with Sarah for the first time since his arrival in Capella da Campo. He had not slept well. He was still in some discomfort, so that he became quickly fatigued and needed to take periodic rests. Coming to terms with Pascoe's dramatic revelations had also completely blown his mind, though he had said nothing of this to his wife.

'This is such a lovely place,' she said as they surveyed the mountains, during one of their rest breaks. 'Mister Pascoe is a very fortunate man. But you still haven't told me who he is.'

'He was helping with the enquiry into the Blackrod accident.'

'The missing rib case?'

'Yes, that was it.'

Just then Pascoe joined them from across the lawn where he had been clearing snow from the helicopter canopy. 'I see you've been admiring the estate,' he said. 'I forget how beautiful it is, even in winter. One has a tendency to take all this for granted, and sometimes it needs the eyes of others to see it afresh.'

'I could happily spend all my days here Mister Pascoe,' Sarah replied. 'No matter what the season. In the snow it is very picturesque and I can only imagine how beautiful it all looks in summer. The views are quite breathtaking.'

'Indeed they are.'

'However,' she concluded. 'I'm getting a little cold and you two men are obviously itching to talk again, so I'll leave you to it. Don't stay out too long, Charlie.'

She walked back into the house and they continued their conversation of the day before.

'I have thought a great deal about the things you told me yesterday,' said Seymour. 'But what exactly was your relationship with Patrick Cameron?'

'Cameron and I often worked together, and we planned to meet up in the Lake District. It was our custom to travel separately so as not to draw any attention to ourselves. But the drowning in Morecambe Bay was a tragic missed opportunity. Cameron was specifically tasked with preventing Cruikshank from crossing the sands. I was to be his backup, but my train was delayed, so I was too late, and unfortunately he never made it.'

'It was Cameron who prevented the Lahore bombing too, wasn't it?'

'Yes, it was.'

'Is that what this is all about? You came back to change things?' asked Seymour.

'In a way,' Pascoe replied. 'Perhaps not exactly in the way you mean.'

'Another paradox,' said Seymour.

'Things are rarely that black and white.' Pascoe hesitated. 'Life is more complex,' he continued. 'Tell me, have you ever heard of the Twelve Peers?'

'No.'

'Then I'll explain. The story began way back in the eighth century, when the Emperor Charlemagne commissioned a small group of knights. They became known as the Paladin, or sometimes as the Twelve Peers. Their mission was very simple – to protect the weak, fight injustice and to stand against evil. The medieval concept of chivalry almost certainly dates from that time. But the facts were overwritten by romantic tales and myths through succeeding centuries, spread throughout Europe by minstrels and troubadours. However, while their stories were fiction, the Peers were quite real. And, though they are almost forgotten now, their ideals survive.'

Twelve

Pascoe rolled up his shirt sleeve to reveal a tattoo.

'I've seen one of those before,' said Seymour.

'Yes,' replied Pascoe, 'Cameron had one.'

'So, you are one of these so-called Twelve Peers.'

'No.' Pascoe smiled. 'They disappeared into the mists of time, centuries ago.'

'So why the chess piece?'

'Our group of twelve embraced the aspirations of the Paladin knights years ago. I suppose you could say that, as we had taken up their cause, the chess piece tattoo was an appropriate emblem for us. The difference is, that unlike the original knights, we have no weapons other than information. We are warriors of sorts – not in the medieval sense, of course. There are no longer windmills to tilt at, but in our way, we still fight dragons. Grand titles like Twelve Peers or Paladin were thought to be a little too medieval for the twenty-third century. So, we simply called ourselves *The Twelve*.'

'So that explains why you are here,' said Seymour. 'But why now?'

'Because these are particularly dangerous times,' said Pascoe. 'The unprecedented technological developments you've made over the last three centuries are quite breathtaking. What you did with them, however, was little short of catastrophic – global warming, exploitation of the planet's resources, two world wars, and the threat of nuclear destruction. In the twentieth century alone, close on fifty million people died through industrialised warfare and genocide. And that's just the beginning. Death, Famine, War and Conquest – all of the four old Apocalyptic Horsemen seemed to have turned up at once. So we felt we were needed.'

'But twelve of you couldn't hope to prevent all that,' said Seymour.

'No, we couldn't. All we could do was to be very selective, and concentrate on saving a few people who could make a difference. Inspirational men and women who would be a major influence for good. Small fry who would do big things.'

'If you are from the future, as you say, you must have been aware that Cameron wouldn't make it to Grange. You knew Cruikshank would die in Morecambe Bay.'

'Ah, you have hit upon one of our intentionally inbuilt blindspots. You see, we cannot know our own destinies, or of the events surrounding our own lives. Such information is withheld from us, and perhaps with good reason. Cruikshank was important, of course – his work is well documented and he will be well known and celebrated as a ground-breaking scientist of the early twenty-first century. But none of us knew Cameron's fate. Apart from that, we were able to access all other recorded data. Before we were sent back we were armed with all the relevant information we would need to carry out our designated tasks - from recorded history, social media, news broadcasts, books and newspapers. We knew where and when Cruikshank might die, unless we could prevent it, and intervening to save him would have been of great benefit to all humanity. Sadly, as it turned out, we missed the chance.'

'So you did come back to change history then?'

'I can see why you would say that,' Pascoe responded. 'In one very limited respect, I suppose you have a point. But the future isn't set in stone, and it would be an over-simplification to say that we change history. After all, how is it possible to alter an event that hasn't yet happened? It's the age-old paradox – the mystery of Time. Then there's also the element of Chance – perhaps an even greater paradox. The choices we make may be very simple, but their consequences are often far reaching. Imagine, for example, if Cameron's flight into Manchester had been just a few minutes earlier. Or what if his plane had a strong tailwind and made better time than scheduled, so that it arrived fifteen minutes early at Manchester. Or what if he'd driven the rental car a few miles an hour faster? Then he'd have missed the tragic road accident and Doctor

Twelve

Cruikshank might not have died. Cameron would have been unaware of the outcome which the course of events he set in motion had caused. His small intervention would have had a much wider effect, purely by chance.

'You see, altering events presupposes they were already fixed in the first place, or that life follows a script and that can't be diverted from. There is no predestination. What happens over time isn't ordained. No. Changing history was never our primary purpose. Interventions were only to be made when absolutely necessary.

'Let me give you a couple of examples, and maybe you'll see what I mean. Cameron made an intervention a few years ago to save a Somali girl. She was from an obscure background and completely unknown. Her name was Samiila Mosi. She was just a young girl then, but in a few years time, she is destined to become Secretary General of the United Nations. Her work, and that of her husband Yusuf for UNICEF, will have a profound effect on the lives of children for the better, not just on the African continent, but throughout the world. Because of these two people, children will learn to read and have a chance to escape from squalor and deprivation. That small intervention has a potentially big outcome.

'I collaborated with Cameron, in fact, just a couple of days before he died. We helped rescue another young woman in Saudi Arabia. Aisha Halabi will be a leading spokesperson for womens' liberation in her country over the next few years. She will be the nation's first female government minister. It was important for her to survive.'

'So that explains the two unaccounted for days you spent in Saudi Arabia,' said Seymour.

'Yes, that was why we stopped over in Jeddah.'

'I saw the security camera footage when you flew in and met with Cameron at Manchester Airport.'

'You saw that?'

'Yes. You were profiled as terrorists. MI6 recruited me to trace you.'

'Yes, I knew about that,' said Pascoe.

'Tell me about Toledo,' said Seymour.

'Toledo was a very important intervention. I travelled to Spain in 1936 to ensure that José Gomez would survive the conflict. José was a leading authority on the Spanish Civil War and received many decorations and innumerable accolades for the work he did over the succeeding years. He was a philosopher, as well as an award-winning writer and teacher.'

'Yes, I know more about José than you might realise,' said Seymour. 'I have already met his grandchildren. They gave me his journal. He wrote a great deal about you and spent many years trying to discover what had become of you.'

'I regretted having to leave José. I was very fond of him, and though I miss his passing, it was necessary. You have to understand that for our work to continue, we have to maintain absolute anonymity. It was important that the world knew about José – not about me, so I needed to disappear. I was at his funeral, though, in the background.'

'I got to see the motorcycle you rode through Spain,' said Seymour.

'So the old AJS survived? I thought it would have been lost and forgotten.'

'It might have been, had not José spent years undertaking a painstaking restoration. It's now being ridden by his grandsons. I actually sat on it myself.'

'Ah, that's so good to hear. Well there you are, then. Little interventions that change lives, will eventually change the world. There are many more that I could tell you about. Over three hundred years one tends to cover a lot of territory!'

'That's a hell of an understatement. But you haven't exactly seen the world at its best. I don't think I could handle so much war and conflict. I'd want to get back to my own time as soon as possible.'

Twelve

'Unfortunately, we volunteered for a one-way trip. That's another drawback. You see, your century just doesn't yet have the technology to send us back. It will take almost another two hundred years, before you - before we - get the hang of it. We always knew we'd be marooned back here. Hence the physical enhancements that made us resilient to your nasty diseases. But, as Cameron's fate demonstrated, despite considerable customisation, we are not immortal. In time, I will die, just as you will.'

'So now that Cameron has gone, how many of you are left?'

'Originally there were six women and six men. At present, only eleven of the original twelve remain, including myself. You may have already seen Valeriya.'

'I've seen security footage of a woman. Only briefly. She was recorded visiting Cameron in hospital and later helping remove his body from university premises. But it was the briefest glimpse and I wouldn't recognise her again if she passed me in the street.'

'Good, that's the way it should be,' Pascoe concluded.

*

'Well, my friend, the time has come to take my leave of you,' said Terzic. 'Mister Pascoe's manservant is waiting to take me down to the railway station by tractor – that'll be a new experience. I've certainly had some unusual transport on this trip. It's been memorable. I'd like to say it's been a pleasure, but that would only be partially true. I've enjoyed your company, of course, but next time can you arrange that nobody tries to blow my head off, please? It would also be good if you didn't get shot either!'

'I'll see what I can do.' Seymour smiled. 'Does Daisy know you're leaving?'

'She does, yes. I have already said my goodbyes to her and to your wife.'

Terzic turned to Pascoe and shook his hand. 'Thank you very much for your hospitality, Mister Pascoe. I'm proud to have finally met you. It's been interesting, to say the least. Please look after my friend here. He has a habit of getting into trouble.'

'I'll do my very best.' Pascoe smiled. 'Have a safe journey.'

Terzic climbed aboard the tractor and it drove away up the narrow lane, chased by the wolf-dog.

*

'One thing you haven't explained yet,' Seymour continued, 'is the missing rib.'

'I was wondering when you'd get round to that,' replied Pascoe. 'That was all part of the enhancement procedure. It required stem cell and bone marrow extraction - one of several regenerative treatments performed at a molecular level to protect us from disease and to increase our longevity. The utmost care had to be taken that we were appropriately equipped to survive here. We needed to have strong resistance to all the diseases of your time, to which we had no natural immunity, to be so resilient so that you didn't compromise us in any way. It was also important that we didn't contaminate you. Hence the universal blood group we all carry – I have to admit, that's a pretty amazing concoction, even for our time. I realise this all sounds like so much science fiction, but I assure you it will become science fact much sooner than you think, and most of it before this century is over.'

'I'm curious to know how your wearing spectacles fits in with this physical enhancement regime you say you have,' said Seymour.

'I do age, like you, but at a very retarded rate. As I've already said, I'm a normal man, and, as I'm fast approaching four hundred years, I'm beginning to show signs of wear and tear. For me it's the eyes, and I've

Twelve

needed spectacles for some time. Other parts will begin to fail eventually. Nobody's perfect. Nobody lives forever.'

'After the post-mortem, we thought Cameron might have undergone some form of cloning procedure,' said Seymour. 'We also thought you might be brothers.'

'Hmm. It's a common misconception.' Pascoe sighed. 'No, we were not related. Like myself, he was technically a hybrid, not a clone as you understand the term. Had we been clones, we would have been carbon copies of the same person. But we were both separate and unique individuals, even though we shared many common genetic characteristics. It's not exactly a new concept. Every gardener and dog breeder knows how to do it. So Cameron's parents were able to choose what colour skin he would have. They preferred a darker tone, while my own chose a pale skin for me, so I'm viewed as European and he is often erroneously thought to be Asian.'

'Yes, at first we believed Cameron was from somewhere in the Middle East.'

'I can understand that. I suppose we are what you would call designer babies. By the twenty-second century, it will be commonplace practice and a matter of personal choice. You will be able to pre-select the gender of your baby or what colour eyes, skin or hair they have.'

'I'm not sure I like that. That sounds more like interference than intervention. Doesn't it remove all of life's pleasant surprises?'

'Maybe. But many of the unpleasant ones, too. In the future, babies will be born without tragic congenital defects. Interventions are made at a molecular level to correct bad genetic traits. Call it interfering if you like, but we think it's a price worth paying.'

'You must find the twenty-first century very barbaric, compared to your own time,' said Seymour.

'I have been here for most of my life,' Pascoe replied. 'In every sense this *is* my time, and I love it. The fact is that the future has lost much of the raw primitiveness that you still have – things that remind us we are human. Life in the future will be almost without risk, or challenge. We will have gained much but lost a great deal, and I wonder, after all, if this isn't the best time to be alive, despite everything the future has to offer.'

*

Christmas came and went, and the New Year brought with it several days of heavy snowfall. Almost four weeks had elapsed since Seymour arrived at Capella da Campo and it was time to return to England. During those weeks, he and Pascoe talked about many things, and Seymour had almost fully recovered from his injuries.

'Before you leave,' said Pascoe. 'I have a small gift for you.' He presented him with a brown paper package. 'Maybe this will remind you of our time together.'

'What is it?' asked Seymour.

'It's the Toledo photo.'

'What can I say? It's very generous of you. Thank you.'

'One more thing. I must remind you, again, that my anonymity is essential. You must never breathe a word of what you know to a living soul. Not that anyone is likely to believe you, of course.'

'Your secret will go with me to my grave,' replied Seymour.

'Then we are agreed, said Pascoe finally. 'So how will you explain things in your report when you get back to England?'

'I'll think of something.'

*

The next day, in view of the snowbound roads, Pascoe insisted on flying the family to the airport in Pisa for their journey back to Manchester.

Twelve

'We may just be able to make it to the airport before the blizzard sets in,' he said. 'It will be drifting badly by dusk, I think, so I can't hang around too long. I'll just drop you off, say a quick goodbye and leave promptly. I expect the villa will be completely snowed in until April.'

Seymour climbed aboard Pascoe's helicopter with considerable trepidation. He gazed down in silent terror when the craft lifted off through a flurry of swirling snow, and they ascended up the mountain side. From the doorway to the villa below, Assunta and Sandro stood looking upward and waving, accompanied by a barking wolf dog, whose tail continued its perpetual wagging.

As the helicopter rose vertically to clear the peak, the villa gradually diminished beneath and was soon obscured by clouds. Higher still, on the other side of the range, they caught a brief glimpse of the white scar of the Cararra marble quarries, before the helicopter banked sharply and headed east towards Florence.

*

A week after his arrival back in England, still officially recuperating at home, Seymour received a personal telephone call from Caroline Massey.

'I trust you're recovering well,' she began. 'Congratulations on the Skender apprehension, by the way. Job well done, Seymour. I confess that I wasn't at all certain your line of enquiry was relevant to the case, but as things turned out, it has brought great credit to the department. The Chief of Joint Staff is very pleased. So, if you are agreeable, we would like to extend your secondment indefinitely, with a view to a more permanent arrangement. Meantime, when you feel up to it, I look forward to receiving your report. You should take whatever time you need to recover. There's no immediate hurry. You've earned a rest.

'However,' she continued. 'While we're on the subject, I have just received a report from Italy that might interest you. It seems related to the Pascoe case and may be relevant in formulating your final report. GCHQ has picked up a news item from Reuters and the Associated Press agencies. If it concerns Pascoe, as seems likely, it brings closure to the case, and any further investigation is superfluous. I'll email it over to you now.'

Seymour opened the email attachment to read:

"It is reported by the State Police in Florence, Italy, that at 0925 hours Central European Time yesterday morning, a private helicopter crashed in the Apuane Alps in northern Tuscany. Conditions were bad with heavy snowfall and visibility limited by an exceptionally low cloud base. It is understood that the helicopter became fouled in overhead power cables on the mountainside near the village of Capella da Campo. It was engulfed in a fireball and impact wreckage was strewn widely down the mountainside. The pilot, thought to be either a British or an American National, is believed to have died in the crash. There were no others on board. Investigations continue."

*

Two days later, Seymour received a second communication from London. He immediately took it round to see Fosse.

'Come in. It's good to see you, Charlie,' said Fosse. 'How are you feeling?'

'I'm doing well, Prof,' he replied. 'A few winces now and then when I try lifting anything, but apart from that, no problems.'

'I must say how glad I am that you survived the Albanian ordeal,' said Fosse. 'You must tell me all about it. But what's so urgent?'

Twelve

'There was a helicopter crash a few days ago in Tuscany. The pilot died.'

'Yes, I heard about it on the news. You think it was Arthur Pascoe?'

'Had to be him. Who else would be flying it? London has acquired details of the post-mortem and just forwarded it to me. I came right round - I thought you want to see it. It's pretty long and detailed, but the last bit is very interesting.'

Seymour read aloud the closing paragraph of the report.

> *"The body of the pilot is charred beyond recognition. It is not possible to identify him other than circumstantially, by reference to ownership of the helicopter and the location of the accident. The remains seemed, inexplicably, to be missing a rib, with no evident point of entry."*

'Might not be Pascoe,' said Fosse. 'Could just be a coincidence.'

'Bugger coincidence!' replied Seymour.

--- THE END ---

James Sherwood

Twelve

MARE NOSTRUM
The Second Book in the "Time Interventions" series
Anticipated to be available through Amazon in late 2015.

Several generations of women in Valeriya Luzin's family share the same name, fingerprints and a distinctive chess piece tattoo. When her body is found floating in the Mediterranean, ex-detective inspector Charles Seymour is persuaded out of premature retirement to investigate the case.
The trail leads him apparently across three generations to events in the Russian October Revolution and to a Soviet labour camp, to the Second World War Allied invasion of Sicily and to possible Sicilian Mafia involvement in drugs and human trafficking, as well as smuggling in the south of France.

Printed in Great Britain
by Amazon.co.uk, Ltd.,
Marston Gate.